Contents

Brothers in Blood
Book 7 in the
Norman Genesis Series
By
Griff Hosker

Brothers in Blood

Published by Sword Books Ltd 2017

Cover by Design for Writers
Thanks to Simon Walpole for the Artwork.

PART ONE
The Curse

Prologue

I am Hrolf the Horseman. I came to the land of the Franks and carved out a land for myself and my family. When I came, we were the Raven Wing Clan. Now we are the Clan of the Horse, for many of my warriors now ride to war. A dream and a visit to a witch called Skuld made this so. I was told that my blood would rule not only the land of the Franks but the land of the Angles too. I was getting old now and I was not certain that I would live to see it. Now that I had seen more than fifty summers we had a toe hold on the land the Franks called the Cotentin. I was amazed that I had lived for so long. Most of the Vikings I had fought alongside were now dead. Ulf Big Nose, Siggi White Hair, Sven the Helmsmen were all dead. Last year Harold Fast Sailing and Erik One Arm had died too. My old friends were falling fast and I had heard that Rurik One Ear was not in the best of health.

I still believed that the Weird Sisters had something planned for me that they had made me live so long. Of course, Mary, my Christian wife, did not believe such things. She put it down to the church we now had in the Haugr. In fact, all of our strongholds had a church and Christians rubbed shoulders with those of us they called heathens. We no longer felt Norse although we still sailed our dragon ships and still fought in a shield wall. We were the North Men as the Franks called us. We called ourselves the Clan of the Horse for horses were an important part of our life. We were the equal of any Frankish warrior. My son Ragnvald was superior to them all. He was a horseman who had no peer. He had been trained by Alain of Auxerre. He had been my leader of horse until he had fallen ill with the coughing sickness. It was seven years since he had died. I missed him. Hugo Strong Arm led them now.

Since we had taken Carentan we had not expanded our land. There had been no need to. The land we had was more than big enough and our men farmed and raided in equal measure. My son

1

was the head of the clan now. He lived in Benni's Ville on the west coast of the Cotentin. With his wife, Mathilde, he had two living sons. A third, conceived between Ragnvald and Rollo, had died. Many, me included, thought that was a curse from the gods for a priest, Æðelwald of Remisgat, had witnessed the birth of his eldest, Ragnvald. When Mathilde was carrying Rollo, I had paid a volva to put a spell on the unborn child and protect him from the curse. When Rollo was born both healthy and strong I knew that there had been a curse. This was the worst kind of curse. It was not from a witch or a lord. It was a curse from the Mother. Only the Allfather was more powerful. A man was not supposed to witness the ritual of birth and a priest had. I blamed the Christians. They did not understand the natural order.

I liked my two grandchildren. But, I must confess, that Rollo was my favourite. I told no one. It was in my heart that I felt it. I treated them equally. Both had the same gifts of swords and helmets. I took them both hunting too but it was Rollo who warmed me. I think that at the back of my mind was the thought that Ragnvald was cursed too. The spell must have worked for Rollo was already huge and had grown quicker than Ragnvald. I joked that he was Rollo the Giant. Mary did not like such words. "He is a little boy! Do not call him names!" She was a Frank and did not understand that nicknames were important to a Viking. A Viking might have many names. We liked word games and names were another such game.

I did not get to see either grandchild as often as I might have liked. They lived on the other coast. Mary, my wife and also a Christian, missed them too although now that our daughters were mothers and their children lived closer to us she occupied herself with them. They were girls. I had but two grandsons. These days I spent my time riding and breeding horses. My days of war were gone. We feared no man and with our strong defences, we were safe from attack.

Ragnvald Hrolfsson

Chapter 1

My new drekar was made ready not long before the feast of
Eostre. My wife and her family called the feast Easter and we
were able to share a common celebration. *'Stallion's Fire'* was
the largest drekar we had ever sailed. She had fifty oars. If we
double crewed her we could take a hundred warriors raiding. I
was keen to raid. The Franks were becoming richer. They had
mighty churches they called cathedrals. They filled them with
silver and gold. The Christians amongst us disapproved of our
raids yet they benefitted as much as we did. When my mother
visited us she and Mathilde would try to persuade us not to raid.
My father always supported me. We had not raided for more than
a year. We had gathered enough in that time to make us
comfortable. The gods had been kind to us. My warriors had
families and they had grown. We had more mouths to feed and to
clothe. We needed to raid.

Ragnvald Ragnvaldsson was now twelve summers old and he
was keen to come to sea with me. Little Rollo Ragnvaldsson was
only eight but he was also desperate to follow his father. I would
have to leave him at home. He was too young. His size suggested
that he was old enough. He was far bigger than his brother.
Ragnvald appeared not to have grown while Rollo just grew and
grew. It had caused some conflict between the two. Rollo was a
gentle giant. It did not do to have them in close proximity. We
needed every pair of hands we had to fit her out and so I had
Rollo on the deck helping me. He worked as hard as any and
harder than most. The rest of my warband adored both of my
sons but Rollo was the one who had the winning smile. He was
the crew's favourite. That did not sit well with Ragnvald. Rollo
was the one with the sparkling blue eyes. He looked more like a
Viking than either my father or me. We called him Little Rollo
for he had been born small. It was not true any longer. He had
filled out and would be the biggest warrior in the clan if he kept
on growing.

I was at the steering board with Harold Haroldsson, my
shipwright and we were adjusting the withy when I turned and

saw Ragnvald deliberately push Rollo off the side of the drekar and into the water. They were boys and they were always into mischief but what concerned me was that Ragnvald did not offer to help his little brother back on board. In fact, he stood and watched Rollo as he flailed in the water. I ran down to the prow and threw a rope, "Rollo grab the rope! Ragnvald help your brother!" Rollo could swim but he had his sealskin boots on and they might have taken him down. He grabbed the rope and I pulled him up the side. He had strong arms for someone so young and he walked up the side of the drekar. Ragnvald held a hand out to help him but Rollo glared at him and carried on walking. Ragnvald shrugged.

"Sit until you get your breath back."

"I am fine, father." He glowered at Ragnvald, "He pushed me!"

Ragnvald turned, "I did not!"

I reached over and smacked him on the back of the head, "Do not lie! A warrior is never foresworn. I saw you! Now get ashore. I will decide on your punishment later!"

His eyes filled with hatred and he bunched his fists. Then he thought better of it and turned to head to the gangplank and the shore. Rollo said, "I was not hurt, I can swim! I am not afraid of the water."

I nodded, "Notice how the rest of the crew are barefoot. It is safer that way. Take off your boots and then go and help Karl load the hold."

He nodded cheerfully, "Aye father."

Leif Sorenson was coiling a rope, "I would not worry, Jarl. My brothers and I fought the whole time we were growing up. It makes a warrior stronger."

I was grateful to Leif. I was finding fatherhood difficult, "I only had sisters. I know not how these things work."

"The elder will keep the younger in place until the younger works out that he can outwit the elder."

It was another worry for me. I had enough on my mind. I would be leading three other drekar on the raid to Sarnia. It had been some time since we had done so. Their sheep had just lambed and their cows had calved. It was a perfect time to raid. We had already scouted out a beach on the western side of the island. The whole island was only five miles across. Their stronghold was on the east coast and faced us. When we had taken their animals, we would return and then raid Saint Maclou which lay further south on the mainland. There was a monastery there. As far as I knew no one had raided it before. Our ships had seen that they were building a stone defence to the port. If we were going to raid then we had to do it quickly.

Jarl Finni Bennison and Jarl Einar Bear Killer were already heading around the coast to join us in the raid. Jarl Folki Kikisson had further to sail for he had an anchorage close by his home at Carentan. His stronghold was the furthest south. Surrounded by water and wetlands it was the hardest to take. His warriors were not horsemen but there were no finer warriors in the land. When they arrived then we would raid. The men I led were all older than I was but my father had passed the leadership of the clan to me. I was honoured. This was the first time I had led four drekar. It was also the first time my father had not been with us. Would we have the same luck he always brought us?

When the ship was ready we all trooped ashore. I decided how to punish Ragnvald when we neared my hall, "Rollo, what say we take our horses for a ride before we eat?"

Rollo, of course, did not have a horse. He had a pony. Now that he was much bigger I was going to risk him on a larger horse. He nodded eagerly. "Yes please! Can I wear my helmet? I feel like a warrior when I do."

I had had Bagsecg make him an open helmet. He would not need to wear it to war but he enjoyed having it on his head and it was good to get him used to something that, when he became a man, he would wear all the time.

"Of course. We will ride along the shore. Our mounts enjoy running in the sea and it seems to do them good."

I chose Dawn's Light. She was a lovely horse to ride. She was not one for war but she was clever and the most beautiful colour; chestnut with golden mane and tail. I shouted to Rolf, my servant, "Tell your mistress we will ride before we eat. She should not worry."

"Aye, Jarl."

I turned to Rollo, "Take Thor today."

"Truly? I can ride a full horse?"

"Your legs are long enough and your arms are stronger. Thor is a gentle horse but we will ride along the sand in case you cannot keep your saddle."

"I am the grandson of Hrolf the Horseman! I will not fall!"

With his helmet on his head, we hurried to the stable and saddled our horses. We had servants but I had taught both of my sons that it was better to saddle your horse yourself. Horse and man became as one. Saddled, we rode back towards the shore and cantered along the beach. I say cantered but Thor, Rollo's horse had to gallop to keep up with my horse. I had no fear of Rollo falling, he had wonderful balance but, as we were riding along the sand and the water, little harm would come to him if disaster struck.

When I thought we had ridden far enough I reined Dawn's Light in. Rollo had excitement in his eyes and his cheeks were flushed. We let the two beasts regain their breath. "Father, why do you raid when we could take horses and raid from the Franks?"

"That is a good question, my son. The Franks fear us and they have made stone buildings along the border to keep us at bay. If we tried to raid, using our horses, then we would have to reduce stone walls. By the time we had done so they would have taken their treasures and animals and hidden them. This way we strike wherever we choose. We use rivers and we use the night to help us."

He nodded and we turned our horses to walk back to the hall. "When can I sail with you?" He gave me a knowing look for one so young. "I know that I am too young yet but I would like to help the clan. I am bigger than some of the ship's boys you will take."

He was right but I was more worried about Ragnvald. I wanted no hostility between the two of them. "Three more summers and you can come. How would you like to spend time with your grandfather while we raid this time?"

His eyes lit up, "Grandfather! That would be almost as good as sailing with you!"

"Then tomorrow, before we leave, I will take you to the Haugr while my other drekar arrive. It will do my father good. He has been a little lost of late."

Rollo nodded, "I thought that he was sad when last he visited."

"He has lost friends. His beard and his hair are grey. He is still a mighty warrior but Odin gives a warrior less time on this earth than a farmer."

"Grandfather is the heart of the clan, isn't he?"

I looked at my young son. Sometimes he was so perceptive that I thought him many summers older than he actually was. "He made the clan. He was a slave and was saved by the Dragonheart.

He made the Raven Wing Clan the most powerful warriors and then formed us, the Clan of the Horse. We are lucky to have him as the head of our family."

We reached the hall before dark. After unsaddling and rubbing down our mounts we went to the sea and stripped off. We both swam naked to clean the sweat and smell of horses from us. My wife Mary did not like the smell. Rolf had seen us and he approached with drying blankets and clean clothes. He dried Rollo. My son was popular with the servants and slaves too.

"Rolf, I would have you prepare clothes for Rollo and yourself. We will ride to the Haugr tomorrow. He will stay with my father while we raid."

Rolf grinned. He had been one of my warriors until an unlucky blow had hamstrung his right leg. "Then I will get to drink Brigid's ale. Since her husband died the beer has been better than ever. I hear it is because she honours his memory. She calls her new brew Erik's Blood."

"It is good ale."

When we entered the hall, we were greeted by Ragnvald's scowl. I had forgotten his misbehaviour. Mary cocked her head to one side. I would tell her later, "Now Ragnvald you know that you did wrong today. Firstly, you endangered your brother. He will be a warrior one day and we can forgive that... once." He looked defiantly at me. "What is harder to forgive is the lie you told me." I saw his eyes and they were filled with anger. "Perhaps I should not take you in this raid. I know that your mother does not wish you to go. I would be pleasing her and punishing you." I sat down and took the horn of ale Mary handed me.

His face changed in an instant, "No, father! I beg! Let me come! I am sorry. You are right I should not have lied. I will not do so again."

I turned to Rollo, "Do you forgive your brother, Rollo?"

Rollo was so happy to be visiting with his grandfather that he beamed and said, "Of course! It was nothing!"

I nodded, "Then you shall come with us."

He smiled but Ragnvald's smile was hollow. It was not in his eyes which burned hatred. I was disappointed with my eldest son. I had thought that the fact I was taking him raiding would have made him act more like someone older. He was still a child at heart.

Folki Kikisson had arrived by the time we were saddled and ready to ride to the Haugr. I waved as I headed north and east with Rolf and Rollo. The road we took was not Roman. It had been worn by our horses over the past years. It twisted and turned between farms. Families were working in the fields. Crops had to be sown and animals tended. Had we raided in high summer then we could have taken twice as many boats. The drekar I would lead were crewed with the real warriors; the ones my father had led on raids.

I spied my father before we even reached the Haugr. He was out riding. When he saw us, he put his heels to his horse and galloped over to us. He was still a fine horseman despite his advancing years. His tanned face broke into a smile when he saw Rollo. There was a special bond between the two of them.

"This is an unexpected pleasure! What brings you here?"

"I go raiding." My father nodded. "Rollo is too young. We thought he might spend some days with you and his grandmother."

"He can spend as long as he likes in my hall." He put his hand on that of Rollo. "You raid soon? The drekar left yesterday."

I nodded, "We will sail at sunset. It will take half a night to reach Sarnia then we have to cross the island to be there by dawn."

"Then you had best leave now. May the Allfather watch over you. Fear not for Rollo. When he is with me he is safe."

"I know. Take care, my son and obey your grandfather."

"He always does. He is a good boy."

Even as I turned I found myself missing Rollo. He was growing all the time. Perhaps I would be able to take him raiding sooner than I had taken Ragnvald.

The other drekar captains were waiting for me at the quay. The warriors who would be raiding were drinking and speaking of oar brothers who were now in Valhalla. Over the next couple of months, we would almost live together and then not see each other until the following year. We all lived in different parts of the land of the Clan of the Horse and we were all different. My warband was like my father's; we were horsemen. The men who followed Folki, Einar and Finni could all ride but they were not the equal of mine. They were old fashioned Viking warriors.

They greeted me warmly. Folki was now a greybeard and he had a greater girth now. He almost picked me up when he saw me. "When I saw you ride away I feared you were not leading us!"

"I was taking Rollo to my father. He wanted to raid."

Finni said, "Why not bring him? My son Erik sailed when he had seen but six summers."

I nodded, "You are not married to a Frank and a Christian! My wife worries about my sons. I think it is because she lost a child."

They looked at each other and clutched their amulets. They would not speak of it but all thought that the gods had punished me for allowing a man to be at the birth of Ragnvald. I had made certain that there were no men present at the birth of Rollo.

"So, Jarl Ragnvald, we raid Sarnia first and then Saint Maclou?"

"Aye, Einar. With the way the winds are that will be the easiest way to do so. I doubt that the Franks on Sarnia will be expecting us. It is some years since my father raided Angia. They may think we have forgotten them."

Folki shook his head, "Not so, Jarl Ragnvald. When we raided further south last year we saw, as we passed Angia, that they had put wooden palisades around their homes."

Einar laughed, "I have yet to see a wooden palisade that can withstand a blow from my axe!" The conversation was filled with past battles and raids against enemies we had subdued and defeated. We had been lucky. Few had tasted defeat. Victory was infectious.

We began to load our crews in the late afternoon. Ragnvald was excited and the sulkiness of the previous night was gone. He and the other ship's boys chattered like magpies as they scurried about the drekar. It would be an easier voyage north for them as the mast would be stepped. We would be almost invisible. Mathilde came to the quay with our two daughters. One, Brigid, was still suckling. Mathilde smiled, "Take care, my husband. I never worry about you when you are on the back of a horse but a ship is a different matter. You sail with our son. Bring him home."

I kissed Agnathia, then Brigid the baby and finally Mathilde, "We will both return and the voyage will help our son to grow. He will soon cease to be a child and he needs to act more like a man."

She shook her head. She did not understand the Viking way.

As the sun began to set we pushed off and headed due west. My drekar led and my men sang as they rowed. They sang the song of my father. We believed it brought us good fortune. Every single warrior knew how much they owed him. The ship's boys, although not rowing sang as they went about their tasks. I was pleased that Ragnvald joined in. He would be leading the ship's boys when they became men.

The horseman came through darkest night
He rode towards the dawning light
With fiery steed and thrusting spear
Hrolf the Horseman brought great fear

Slaughtering all he breached their line
Of warriors slain there were nine
Hrolf the Horseman with gleaming blade
Hrolf the Horseman all enemies slayed

With mighty axe Black Teeth stood
Angry and filled with hot blood
Hrolf the Horseman with gleaming blade
Hrolf the Horseman all enemies slayed
Ice cold Hrolf with Heart of Ice
Swung his arm and made it slice
Hrolf the Horseman with gleaming blade
Hrolf the Horseman all enemies slayed

In two strokes the Jarl was felled
Hrolf's sword he nobly held
Hrolf the Horseman with gleaming blade
Hrolf the Horseman all enemies slayed

We stopped singing when we turned to head north and east towards the shadow that was Sarnia. Sounds carried across the empty ocean. I still had some of my father's old crew with me but most of the men I led were mine. They had taken an oath to me. I had four warriors who would lead my men with me. It was not my father's way but I had found that it was easier to have a fifth of the crew following one man. I trusted Snorri Snorrison, Harold Strong Arm, Haaken the Bold and Leif Sorenson. They thought as I did. My tactic worked just as well when we fought on land. We had more manoeuvrability.

It was Ragnvald who came racing down the centre of the drekar to tell me that he had sighted the island. I was pleased that he had remembered his orders. He had not shouted. "Jarl, I have seen the bay." He pointed four points off the steerboard side of the bow.

"Good now go and prepare to leap into the water when we are close!"

"Aye jarl!"

He was keen to make up for his lie and impress me. Once we were in the shallows then he and the other ship's boys would take ropes and tie us to a rock, a tree, or anything which was handy, while the warriors leapt ashore. I had done it. I had not enjoyed it but it had helped make me a better sailor. I was pleased that Ragnvald was throwing himself into life as a ship's boy. It would make him a better warrior.

We slowed down our oars so that we crept inshore. The ship's boys stood by the figurehead. When they waved it would be time to back the oars and prevent us from tearing the keel from our drekar. Although we were landing at a sandy beach we knew that there were rocks. I saw Arne wave and he and Ragnvald disappeared over the side even as I shouted, "Back oars!"

I heard the splash as they landed and then there was the sound of the keel on the sand. We had been lucky. When high tide came we would be refloated but the grounding made it easier for the ship's boys. Rolf usually manned the tiller and commanded the boys when we were ashore but he was in the Haugr with Rollo. It was Leif Left Hand who would command. He had lost the use of his right hand in a raid. He still wished to be part of the crew and he had learned to fight left-handed. He could still steer with one hand and a stump.

I donned my helmet and grabbed my shield from the side of the ship. I did not use a spear. The helmet was the one I used on horseback. It had a simple nasal and was comfortable. I walked to the prow and jumped into the water. I saw that Ragnvald and Arne had driven in a stake and tied the drekar to it. "Well done Ragnvald, Arne; that was well done!" They both grinned.

I slid the shield around my back. I did not like the shields we used when we raided from the sea. I preferred the smaller oval one I used when on horseback. With luck, we would not need to use our shields. Some of my men still used cochineal and other colours for their eyes and faces. I know that my father had never done so but he had told me that Dragonheart used to do that. The other three drekar slid up on to the beach. I waved away Beorn

Tryggsson who led four scouts. It was not to find our prey it was so that we were not surprised by them.

By the time we were all ashore the sun was rising above our homeland. I raised my sword and we headed east into the rising sun. We had scouted the land before we raided. You could see much from the sea. I knew that there was a wooded valley which seemed to divide the island into two. Finni took his men to the north to gather animals and take cereal and slaves. Folki went south leaving Einar Bear Killer and my band to head to the main settlement in the west. They had a stronghold on an island just opposite the port. It was there to stop our raids. With a hundred warriors, we would surprise them by attacking from the landward side. I sent small groups of men to silence any farmers on our way to the woods. Once we had reached its cover then I would not worry about being seen. By then we would have just a couple of miles to go and we could run that far if we had to.

Our scouts met us at the eastern end of the woods.

"Jarl we have found the port. There are many farms to the north and the south of this track."

"Did any see you?"

"There was one man with a horse heading along the road. He is dead. We tethered his horse."

"Then we can collect that on our way back. Horses are always useful."

He shook his head, "It is a packhorse at best, jarl!"

I could see tendrils of smoke rising in the bright sky ahead. That was the port. We knew that they had a low palisade around their port and a shallow ditch. It would not be an obstacle. "Einar, take your men to the north of the port. I will lead mine to the south."

"Aye jarl." He led his men off at a lope.

I turned to my men. I pointed with my sword, "You know what to do."

"Aye jarl."

My four warriors raised their right arms and began to run to the south of the port with their nine men. The ten I led had the hardest and most dangerous job. We would run and take the gate. We would be seen and it would be barred. I wanted every warrior within the stronghold drawn to me for that meant my other ninety would have no opposition when they scaled the wall. We swung our shields around and we ran chanting as we did so. The chanting kept the rhythm and stopped us running too quickly.

Clan of the Horseman
Warriors strong
Clan of the Horseman
Our reach is long
Clan of the Horseman
Fight as one
Clan of the Horseman
Death will come

When we were just half a mile from the gates we were seen. I was surprised it was not before and then I realised they kept no watch in the gate. It was for night time only. I saw men running to close the gate. A bell tolled urgently. I knew there were forty men to the south of me but I could not see them. They were using the cover of the fields, trees and farms as they advanced. Any who tried to alert the defenders would pay with their lives. I saw heads appear above the wall. It did not have a fighting platform, it was too low. It had a step.

When we were fifty paces from the walls arrows came at us. I was at the front and I was flanked by Siggi Einarsson and Sven Big Chest. Our shields came up and we peered over the top. It would take a lucky arrow to hit us. The Franks did not use a plunging trajectory. They sent their arrows flat. Two thudded into my shield. It was big and it was heavy but I was grateful for its size for it stopped the arrows easily.

I held up my sword and we stopped. I began banging my shield and chanting. My men joined in.

Clan of the Horseman
Warriors strong
Clan of the Horseman
Our reach is long
Clan of the Horseman
Fight as one
Clan of the Horseman
Death will come

When we reached the last line we all stepped forward on our right leg and began to run at the gate. I felt a shield in the middle of my back. We did not slow down when we reached the bridge over the ditch. We kept running. I lowered my head and put my weight behind my shield. Eleven mailed Vikings with massive shields are like a human battering ram. We struck the gate. Although it did not burst asunder it creaked and cracked. One of the planks they had used fell. I could see the locking bar. Sven Big Chest shouted, "Watch behind!" He swung his axe one handed and brought it down to shatter the already weakened bar. A spear darted through the gap aimed at Sven. I brought my sword down and chopped it in two.

"Clan of the Horse!" We charged the gate and this time the two halves swung open. The Franks who met us outnumbered us but none had mail. They must have thought that we were mad to attack with just eleven men but soon they would feel the full force of our attack when the rest poured over the walls. Once inside I swung my sword in a wide arc and shouted, "Shield wall!"

Ulf Broad Chest stepped next to Sven and the next four put their shields over our heads. The last three placed their shields in their backs. We stepped forward on our right legs with our swords and axes held above the shields. The Franks hurled themselves at us. Swords, spears, axes and hatchets chopped, slashed and smashed into our shields. Had they been calmer they might have hacked at our legs. They were not covered by mail. The pressure from the Franks meant that we stopped. I was face to face with two of them. I slid my sword forward. The press was so great that the Franks could not get out of the way. My sword slid into the cheek of one of them. I angled it up and pushed. He screamed and tried to throw himself backwards. An axe came overhead and struck Guthrum's shield.

Then I heard a shout from my right, "Clan of the Horse!"

At almost the same time I heard Einar Bear Killer shout, "Clan of the Bear!"

Our distraction had worked. We were surrounded by the Franks who were, in turn, surrounded by my men. The man I had wounded had dropped to his knees and was whimpering as he tried to hold the cheek in place. Behind him, the Franks had tried to turn. They were stopped by the men who had scaled the walls.

"Break wall!"

My men pushed and hacked at the Franks who remained. I slid my sword across the wounded Frank's throat. He had a warrior's death. I saw the Franks fleeing before us. The boats in the harbour were already being filled as women, children, old and young boarded them to sail the short way across the harbour to the stronghold. Their warriors tried to hold us up. They delayed us but it was at a great cost. I watched the last, overcrowded boat push off and leave the now empty quay. Thirty Franks lay dead.

Others had thrown off helmets and discarded swords as they swam to their stronghold.

My men needed no orders. Bodies were searched. Any weapon, helmet or mail that was useful was taken. Einar led his men to the church. That would be where the real treasure was. Snorri Snorrison and Harold Strong Arm took their men to search the houses. I led the last ones to the halls and warehouses by the quay. As we did I saw the boats reach the stronghold. They feared being enslaved by Vikings. They had avoided that but lost all else. Haaken the Bold took his men to find carts and wagons. We found their winter barley. It had been harvested and stored in sacks. There were a few sacks of wheat. Leif Sorenson found a barrel of wine. It looked to have arrived only recently.

Once the wagons were loaded and Einar and his men had joined Snorri and Harold I shouted, "Quickly, back across the island." We headed back to our drekar. I was the last to leave. I wanted to see how much we had collected. It was one of the largest hauls I could remember. We would not be able to repeat it. They would build a higher wall. They would watch the western beach. That did not matter. There would be other places we could raid.

After we had passed through the wood I saw more of my men coming across the fields. They drove animals and captives. They carried sacks. They too had been successful.

The ships' boys were already loading the first of the sacks and the treasure. That would be placed below the deck. The animals and captives would be kept at the prow and it would be the ships' boys' job to guard them. They had raised the masts of the drekar. The crews would not have to row.

It was late afternoon as we pushed off. The animals complained and the women keened. The wind filled our sails and we headed south to my hall. This time Ragnvald had to work harder. He and the other ship's boys were kept busy the whole way home. We had lost warriors. That was inevitable. The men who had fought with me in the shield wall had wounds but none would stop them on the next raid. The ship was full of talk of what we had achieved and what we were going to do. A Viking never looked back with regret; he always looked forward with anticipation.

Harold Strong Arm spoke with me as we neared our home. "The island is now ruled by the Bretons, jarl. Many of the people who live there are Franks. Their lords are Breton. The Duke of Brittany has taken the island."

"I did not hear of a war."

He shook his head. One of the captives told me. The King of the Franks gave Angia and Sarnia to the Duke to prevent war."

"Will it?"

Harold laughed, "The Duke is ambitious. The King of the Franks is weak. There will be war."

I nodded, "And we will profit."

It was dark when we docked. I had left orders for lights to be kept burning at both ends of the quay to make landing easier. There were pens ready for the animals and the captives and my wife had ensured that there was plenty of food for the two hundred warriors who had returned successfully. I saw her watching for Ragnvald to make sure that he was not hurt. She was relieved when he and Arne strode off the drekar together, arm in arm. They were laughing and both flushed with the excitement of their first raid.

Chapter 2

We rose early and cleaned the ships. Animals and captives had both fouled themselves. The whole crew helped to clean it. Our chests were landed and then the decks swilled with seawater. When it was clean the chests were replaced. Our voyage to Saint Maclou would not take long. It was less than fifty miles and with the wind from our quarter, we could make the voyage in a few hours. We had also scouted out the town and the monastery. We knew of a good place to land. It was a beach to the east of the town. The Bretons who lived there had begun to build a stone wall and a stone stronghold. It was incomplete and now would be a good time to raid. There was a lord there. He was a Breton. They had once been the ones who had raided the land where we lived. My wife's family had lived in fear of them. This would be the first time we would raid them. It would be a message to them.

As our men cleaned the drekar I sat with the other jarls. Finni was eager to be on the raid. "My men are keen, jarl, to do as you did and fight warriors. Slaughtering farmers and herding animals, neither is warrior work."

Folki counselled caution, "When my brother, Fótr and I first fought the Franks we did not heed the advice of Jarl Hrolf. These Bretons have walls. They have mail and they have good swords. They can also use bows. The walls may not yet be complete but they will not fall over when we charge them. We will have to fight to gain access."

"And that is why we sail at dusk. I intend to scale those walls in dark of night. Einar Bear Killer you and your men can take the monastery. Three crews should be enough to capture the port. There will be ships in the harbour and this time we will not give them the chance to flee. I will send some of my men to capture them." We spent some time going over the details and the signals we would use. While we talked most of the crew took the opportunity, once the ships were cleaned to lie in the sun and catch up with their sleep. Ragnvald and Arne were too excited. When the other captains left they both came to me as I checked the new withies we had fitted. Sometimes, after the first voyage, they needed tightening.

"Father, when do we get to fight?"

I laughed, "One voyage and you would draw sword?"

Ragnvald had a short sword. He took it from its scabbard. "I have cleaned it and sharpened it. I have never yet drawn blood."

Arne took out his. It was not as good a blade and was little more than a long dagger. "And I, too jarl, have a sword I wish to use to kill our foes."

I shook my head, "It is harder to sink a blade into a man's flesh than you think. More than that, it is hard to be able to do so. Your foe will not simply let you stick a blade into him. He will try to kill you. It is not as easy to sink your blade into flesh as you might think. The first time I was in a battle I stood behind your grandfather and his oathsworn. Had I been in the fore I would have been in the way. Learn how to be a ship's boy and when the time is right you will come to war. Perhaps we will ride to war. However, you learn, it will be behind those who have greater skill."

"We are not afraid."

I smiled, "I can see that, Ragnvald but I am." They both gave me a quizzical look. "I am afraid that you might fight too early and pay with your lives. This next raid will be harder for you. Try to get some rest for when we raid you will have to watch the drekar with Leif Left Handed. Then, when we return, you will have your share of treasure from two raids!"

That replaced the disappointment of not fighting with the anticipation of riches.

We left the anchorage and, with sails full and billowing we set off to make the short journey to the land of the Bretons. The sea was not as smooth as it had been when we had sailed to Sarnia. That was because the weather was changing. At this time of year, a sudden squall and violent wind could spring up at any time. It was another reason that I had decided on two short raids which would yield great profit and yet not risk our ships. When we sent our knarr to trade it would not be across open water. It would be around the coast where there was always shelter.

The beach we were using to land was a long one. There were few rocks and our beaching would be easier. Our sails would make us easier to see and so, when we landed we would take down our masts and the men would row back. That was also the reason we were landing four miles from the monastery and the

18

port. It was a secluded part of the coast. The wind freshened on the voyage. That made it quicker but it also made it a more difficult landing. The ships' boys of all four drekar had to work quickly to make certain that the ships would not broach. Once we were stable they returned to take down the sail and then we stepped the mast. Safe on its mast fish we left the drekar.

"Leif, keep a good watch. This part of the coast is quiet but there are still more warriors here than in Sarnia."

"Worry not, jarl. These lads have sharp eyes and they will keep a good watch. We have bows and they have blades."

Even as we left I saw the pleading in Ragnvald and Arne's eyes. They were desperate to come with us. I would not risk them. With the scouts loping along the beach ahead of us we set off. We marched in silence and our helmets hung from the pommels of our swords. Those who lived in this land were good warriors. They fought us and they fought the Franks. My father had tried to use that to make them allies of us but the Bretons had spurned the offer saying that we were pagans and heathens. Marching on sand sapped energy from legs. The dunes, however, to our left hid us from prying eyes. I wanted surprise. The wind was from the sea. We would not be able to smell the town. We had to rely on the skill of our scouts.

Beorn Tryggsson and his scouts returned. They ghosted over the sand dunes. The sound of the surf surging on the beach would hide our voices. "Jarl we have found them. The walls are now taller than a man." He pointed to the south-west.

"Do they have sentries?"

"We spied men but we only counted six. Three of them guard the part which is still wooden."

"And the monastery?"

He pointed directly south. "It is just a mile that way. If the wind was in the right direction you would smell their candles."

"Einar, take your men. When you have the treasure then fetch it here and bring your men to aid us."

He nodded and took his men across the dunes. Beorn led us through the sand dunes. When we reached the top of the highest I saw, a mile or so away, the dark shadow that was Saint Maclou. I saw the tower on the church. We donned our helmets and began to move towards the walls. The port was to our right and I tapped Harold Strong Arm and Leif Sorenson on the shoulders and pointed. They took their men to capture as many of the boats as we could. If they were successful then they would take the ropes, sails and other valuable items and sail one or two of the ships to where our drekar were moored. It was why I had chosen the two warriors. Both were good sailors and both of them were able to make good decisions. They were not reckless.

When they slipped away, we moved towards the town. In places, they still had a wooden palisade. The stone wall had replaced it for most of its length. That explained why half of the guards were on the wooden section. They would see it as the most vulnerable. As we neared the wall I could see evidence of building. There were mortar pits and lime beds where they prepared the mortar for the walls. There were piles of stones ready to be lifted into place and there were small stones waiting to be used as infill. I saw a treadmill crane over what looked to be the gate to the port. We used the stones as cover as we skittered over the dark ground. When we reached the ditch, I saw that it too showed evidence of building work. There were still the broken remains of the palisade. The men of Saint Maclou wanted their walls erected as quickly as possible. They would clear the ditch when the wall was finished. It was a mistake. We could use their rubbish to enter the walls.

Nagli Olafsson was a good archer. He had a Saami bow. We had not needed it in Sarnia but here we would. He ghosted next to me and I pointed to the walls. He nodded. He unslung his powerful bow and nocked an arrow. He headed down the ditch looking for a sentry. With his sharp eyes and skilful bow ready, we could cross the ditch and begin our ascent of the walls. The walls were already taller than me. They had yet to be completed and that told me they would be much higher. Our task would be almost impossible then.

We picked our way through the ditch. The bank was easy to climb as there were lumps of hardened mortar, stones and parts of the palisade. We reached the wall. Sigurd and Snorri took a shield and held it for me. I stepped on it and put my hands on the wall for balance. They lifted me up. My head appeared over the top. There was no fighting platform. There was a single course of stones with a gap between. The inner section was the length of my arm away. I glanced down and saw that half of it had the infill of smaller stones already. I saw a sentry. He was forty paces from me. All along the wall men were doing as I was but they were watching me. I was the jarl and I would initiate the attack. I waited. Suddenly the sentry I could see doubled over and grabbed his middle. Nagli's arrow had struck him. He fell into the ditch.

There was a crack as his falling body hit and broke some of the discarded palisade. Even as another sentry shouted something I pulled myself on to the wall. I stepped on to the inner wall and then began to lower myself down. I dropped the last pace and a half and landed on more stones.

Whipping my sword out and sliding my shield around I turned to look for enemies as I heard a loud shout of alarm. We were seen. The cry was ended by Nagli's second arrow. The port had many houses and buildings. There were streets and paths both broad and narrow. It was perfect for us. My men appeared next to me as I heard the sound of orders being shouted. That was not my men. We were silent. When I saw that I had Siggi and Sven next to me I headed down the widest of the streets. From the top of the wall, I had spied what looked like a large building close to the church. That would be where the lord lived.

There were screams and shouts and I heard the word 'Vikings!' screamed out. Our name was one of our most effective weapons. The Bretons in Saint Maclou had thought themselves safe behind their wall. They had been abed and secure. Now they were under attack from the Clan of the Horse from the north. They ran and, in doing so, prevented the warriors and men of the town from getting to us. One man ran from his home wielding a wood axe. He swung it at Sven who took it on his shield. Sven's sword tore into his chest and he fell dead. I heard his wife scream. She was ignored. We wanted to kill the men. The women would be safe. The darkness was also our friend. They could not see our approach. My men swarmed through along every path, road and track in the small port. It had grown over the last years as the port had prospered. They had built wherever they could.

There were just women, children and old before us. They were racing towards the hall. We did not kill them. They would have become an obstacle in our way. I heard the orders given. The Bretons were making a stand before their hall. I glanced around and saw that there were just eight warriors with me. I stopped thirty paces from the line of Breton warriors. The women and the children; the priests and the old, all were cramming themselves into the hall. To my right, I heard the clash of metal on metal as Folki and his men clashed with more warriors. I turned as Finni and his warband arrived. His sword was bloody and he was grinning.

"Form a wedge!"

"Aye Jarl Ragnvald. Give me the honour of being the point!"

21

He was still aggrieved at having missed out on honour and glory when we had raided Sarnia. "Aye, your warband can have the honour. Sven, make a second wedge with our men. We will attack on our shield side."

I just had twenty-five men with me. Finni had more than forty. The Bretons were in a two-deep line which bristled with spears. The men had had time to don mail. Finni would be attacking their lord. He was encased in mail with a high domed helmet. I hoped that Finni was not overconfident. The Bretons could outfight the Franks. The jarl had yet to fight them.

My men formed up on me. It took us less time to form our wedge as there were fewer of us. As soon as we were ready we advanced. It would help Finni for we would weaken the right side of the Breton line. When Folki and his men reached us, they could attack the left side of the Bretons. Although I had counted forty shields in the Breton front line I knew they would have more packed behind the first forty. The front rank would be their best warriors. I levelled my sword over my shield. We were at a slight disadvantage for the Bretons had spears and we had none. They would strike us first.

Clan of the Horseman
Warriors strong
Clan of the Horseman
Our reach is long
Clan of the Horseman
Fight as one
Clan of the Horseman
Death will come
Clan of the Horseman
Warriors strong
Clan of the Horseman
Our reach is long
Clan of the Horseman
Fight as one
Clan of the Horseman
Death will come

We sang as we stepped. It must have sounded like the knell of a bell which heralded their doom. I had my eyes peering over the rim of my shield. I saw the man I would kill. I was the point of my wedge. I would be the one who struck the first blow. I would be the one to receive the first spear. The Breton shields were slightly smaller than ours. I saw that the Breton had his shield held high to protect his face. I dropped my sword so that it was level with my shield. With no warrior next to me, it was easy. There were four spears which would come towards me. Any one of them could slide over the top of my shield and take out an eye. It was a risk but my father had told me of a warrior, Haaken One Eye, who fought with the Dragonheart. A warrior could fight with one eye.

The Bretons began to shout at us as we neared them. Their words were lost in our chant. They were cursing us. They were trying to give themselves courage for the sight of a Viking warband marching towards you was a terrifying one. I heard their priests chanting prayers to the White Christ to save them. They would have been better off wielding a weapon. My men were used to fighting behind me. They had practised for long periods. We had been getting faster as we neared the Bretons. By the time we were four paces away we were almost running. At three paces I dropped my head beneath my shield for I saw that every spear was aimed at my head. We stopped singing as we struck their line. We roared instead. We sounded like a metal covered wild beast. I had the weight of twenty-five men behind me. As we hit them they reeled and I brought up my sword, blindly into the morass of men before me. It tore up into the mail and then through into the flesh of the warrior I had faced. I twisted as I struck and he screamed. I pulled back my sword.

The gap I had created allowed Siggi and Sven to slash and stab at the men whose spears had been aimed at me. I lowered my shield and saw a spear come directly for my head. I flicked my head to the side and the spearhead scored a line along the helmet. Once again, I thrust. This time there was no mail and I felt my sword scrape along the bone. These were not the best warriors we faced. I looked up and saw just two ranks remained and none had spears. Now was the time to bring all twenty-five of my men into action. "Break wedge!"

I stepped on to my shield leg and punched at the man on my left. I raised my sword, ready to strike at the one to my right. Suddenly my head rang as a stone from a sling hit it. The man to my right took advantage and lunged at me. I was lucky that I wore mail made by Bagsecg. The links were tightly made and riveted. The tip of the sword caught in them. As the Breton pushed and the tip touched my padded kyrtle, I brought my sword down and cracked into his blade. It forced it down. The man I had punched with my shield lay on the ground beneath me. I stepped onto his face as I swung the shield sideways at the man who had tried to stab me. My shield had a metal rim. The man beneath me screamed as my seal skin boot broke his nose and jaw. My shield hit the Breton under the chin. As his head was knocked backwards his arms flailed to help him keep his balance. I swept my sword across his middle. It ripped through his kyrtle. I saw what he had eaten last!

I saw that there were no more men before me. Sven and Siggi had slain the others. Sven reached down and slit the throat of the man with the broken nose. There were one or two men to my left still fighting but the main battle was around Finni. "Reform on me!"

"Are you hurt, jarl?"

"No Sven. I am lucky. The gods have been kind this day."

As our men gathered behind the three of us Sven said, "Not so Jarl Finni!"

I saw what he meant. His wedge had Bretons lapping around the side. He was in danger of being defeated. He had overestimated his men. There was no time to wait, "Clan of the Horse, Charge!"

We threw ourselves into the flanks of the Bretons. We took them by surprise. The first three were slain by us before they even knew we were there. Tearing their bodies from our fore we punched with shield and sword into the backs of Bretons who had no mail. I heard, from the other side, the clash of wood on wood as Folki and his men hit the other flank. We had them beaten but Finni was still in trouble. As I stabbed a Breton in the side I saw a Breton weapon rise and strike the helmet of Jarl Finni Bennison. His helmet disappeared.

I fought even harder. My arms were already aching from the battle thus far but one of our oar brothers was in trouble. I was lucky to have two such strong warriors next to me. They stopped any blows from striking me as we gouged our way through the Bretons. They had now turned to face us and that, alone helped the oathsworn of Finni Bennison to protect their jarl.

A mailed warrior who was next to the Breton lord faced me. He had, not a sword, but a mace. They were a deadly weapon. Although they had no edge they had spikes of metal and could break bones and shatter skulls even those protected by helmets. I was aware of that as I faced him. My helmet had been scored by

24

the sword and struck by stone already. I held my shield higher. The Breton would have to swing the weapon. I would have an idea of the direction. He used a direct approach. He smashed the mace against my shield and my arm shivered. He was a powerful man and I felt the blow. I feinted with my sword at his head and when his shield flicked up I changed the move to a thrust to his thigh. I hit his leg just above the knee where there was no mail. As it sank into flesh and grated off the knee cap I twisted. I did not take my eyes from his face. His face contorted and he swung again at my head. He had quick hands. As I pulled out my sword I took the blow from his mace on my shield. I was driven back. I saw his mouth widen in a grin as he saw his chance. He made the mistake of trying to thrust off his left leg. It would not support him. He sank to his knees. Off-balance myself, I managed to lunge forward and my sword went through his throat. As I tore it out blood sprayed in every direction.

I was about to attack the Breton lord when Karl Pederson brought his axe over to hack through the arm and into the chest of the lord. He fell to the ground his lifeblood pumping away. The death of the lord and his oathsworn was the signal for the end of the battle. Those that fought on had no heart and many surrendered. I turned and knelt next to Jarl Finni Bennison. I saw that he had been struck by the mace of the man I had killed. The helmet had broken and the side of his skull was broken. He had lost his right eye too, yet still he breathed.

"Karl, go into the hall. Find priests and healers. The jarl might yet be saved."

"Aye jarl. Thank you for coming to our aid." He disappeared into the hall. My men had already broken down the door and I could hear screams from inside. My men were not harming the women, children, old and the priests. They were making sure that none had weapons. You do not harm your own goods.

Folki came with a bloody and scored arm. "They fought hard, jarl!"

"They did. Sort out the ones worth selling as slaves and have the men collect all the treasure."

"Aye Jarl. Will Finni live?"

"That is in the hands of the Allfather." He turned to begin giving orders. "Sven and Siggi, go to the port and see if we have ships. If we do then we can begin to load them. Find a small fast vessel. We may have to send Jarl Finni back to our home."

"Aye Jarl."

I took off my helmet. It would need work. The scoring could be buffed away but the dent from the stone would make it weaker. I had a spare but I liked this one.

Karl appeared with two priests. They were shaking. I spoke to them. "Save this warrior. If you do then I will allow all of the priests to go free."

One nodded but the other said, "Viking, his skull is crushed."

The first priest was already cleaning the wound, "Brother Peter he breathes and the skull is just cracked. If we bind the bone together and stitch the head he might live." He looked up at me. "You will keep your word, Northman?"

"I am never foresworn."

He nodded and the two of them bent over Finni.

"Can we trust them, Jarl Ragnvald?"

"I believe so but we have little choice, do we?"

"We could give him a warrior's death."

"If they fail then we can do so but let us help him cling to life eh?"

Dawn had broken even as we had fought and the Breton lord had died. One of my men found some fermented apple juice and I used that to quench my thirst.

A warrior from the Clan of the Bears ran towards me, "Jarl Ragnvald, my jarl says he has taken the monastery. When he has taken the treasure to the beach, he will join you."

I shook my head, "The battle is done. Tell him to guard the treasure on the beach. We will come to you." At the time it seemed the right thing to do. They say that when you look back you always have perfect vision. When you look forward it is as though through a fog. The Weird Sisters were spinning and threads were being cut.

The priests had finished by the time Sven and Siggi returned. I looked at the priest who had worked on Finni, "Well?"

"It is in God's hand now. We have put the bones back into place and we have stitched the skin. We washed the wound with vinegar and we have bound it. That is all that we can do."

"What about moving him?"

"I would say no but I know that you will not leave him here. If he is jolted then he will likely die."

That made perfect sense to me. "And if we carry him on a litter and put him on a ship what then?"

"He might live."

"But we need someone to watch over him."

Brother Peter said, "You promised us our freedom."

The other priest smiled, "Peace, brother." He turned to me. "Viking if I come with you do you swear that I will be returned here unharmed?"

"I will so swear."

He pointed to the horse amulet around my neck. "On that?"

"You are a clever priest. What is your name?"

"Brother Paul."

I lifted the horse amulet and, after kissing it said, "I swear that Brother Paul will be returned unharmed after we have delivered the jarl home."

He nodded, satisfied.

"Karl, have your men make a bier. Sven, free the priests. Tell them that they may go."

"Aye Jarl Ragnvald."

"Siggi, is there a small boat?"

"There is, jarl."

Karl had returned, "Then Karl, take your jarl back to Benni's Ville. My men can take the other ships when they are loaded. I want the priest bringing back here. Is that clear?"

"Aye jarl but what if Jarl Finni dies?"

"Then the Allfather wants another warrior at his table. No matter what happens Brother Paul will be returned here. I have given my word."

"Aye jarl."

As Brother Paul gathered his things he said, "You are a strange Viking. Are you the one they call the Horseman?"

"No, that is my father."

He nodded and left with Finni's oathsworn. It was noon by the time we had loaded the ships and sorted the slaves. With the crews for the ships we had taken, we would have fewer men to row home. That could not be helped. We had had a good raid. The wounded and the dead were taken aboard the ships. They would be home first. I led the men and we trudged back to the beach to meet Einar. Before we left we fired the hall. That proved to be a mistake but then we were looking ahead and not back.

Einar Bear Killer was waiting for us on the beach with his men. They had some priests as captives and a great quantity of treasure. There was a holy book, some metal platters, linens, candles and their candlesticks. They also had sacks of provisions and wine.

27

Einar Bear Killer looked pleased with himself. He pointed to a chest, "We also found a chest of coins!" He looked around and saw that Finni was missing. "Where is Finni?"

"He was wounded. He had his skull broken. We sent him back to our home by boat."

"Then let us hurry. This treasure will aid his recovery."

We could see our ships. They were a mile away along the open and deserted beach. We did not have far to go. Suddenly we saw movement on the ships. Then we heard a horn and saw horsemen heading across the dunes. The fire had been seen from Cancale. Horsemen had come to see what was amiss in Saint Maclou. Our ships' boys would be slaughtered.

"Folki, guard the treasure. The rest of you, let us run as though the Allfather had given us wings."

I dropped my shield, helmet and cloak. I could run faster without them. I heard shouts and screams coming down the beach. Leif should have cut their ropes and drifted out to sea. We could have recovered the ships. Our ships' boys would be slain and our ships destroyed. All the treasure and captives we had would avail us nothing. My main concern was that my son would be safe. I remembered the curse of his birth. I still did not know why I had listened to others and allowed the priest to be there at his birth. The Mother would continue to punish me until the end of time!

The younger warriors were racing ahead of me but I would still be amongst the first to reach the ships. I saw *'Stallion's Fire'*. There were a group of ship's boys fighting at the steering board. They were still alive! I hoped that Ragnvald was one. There were forty horsemen and they saw us. I hoped it would make them flee but they must have seen that we were spread out. Perhaps they did not know that we were horsemen too for they suddenly left the drekar, mounted their horses and galloped towards us. Armed with spears and shields, they would have slaughtered any Viking warband caught in the open; any warband but mine. We fought from the backs of horses and knew the pitfalls. I held my sword in two hands and ran towards the leading warrior.

I saw him pull his arm back and lunge at Benni Siggison. The spear caught Benni in the shoulder and he spun around. The Breton saw me and wheeled his horse towards me. I ran towards his spear side. He must have thought me mad. He pulled his arm back for a killing blow. I spun around to my right and brought my sword around in a sweep. It hacked through the tendons in the back of the horse's hind leg. The rider was thrown as the horse slewed and fell to the side. Sven took the rider's head with his axe.

The next rider saw what I had done and he slowed slightly. He was watching for my move. Still holding Sun's Vengeance in two hands I allowed him to lunge at me. I swept the head away with my sword and, spinning the blade around brought it down across his thigh. His horse veered into me and I was knocked to the ground. The rider fell from his horse and I quickly rose as a third Breton rode at me to try to pin me to the sand. I was on my feet as his spear came down. It hit my sealskin boots and I lunged up with the sword held in two hands. He wore no mail and my sword tore up through his rib cage. My men were now arriving in numbers. Sven, Siggi and Einar had also helped to break the back of their charge. Twelve horsemen lay dead or dying. They had slain five warriors and wounded another four but they had had enough and they turned to flee.

Nagli had his Saami bow. He had quick hands and a horse and rider is a large target. Two riders fell before they had gone more than a hundred paces. He hit two more and two horses before they were beyond his range. I would congratulate him and my other men later. First, I had to find my son. I sheathed my sword and I ran. I saw, as I neared my drekar, that both he and Ragnvald had survived. I clambered up the rope and walked up the hull. I saw that there had been a battle aboard my ship. Leif Left Handed lay dead but five Bretons lay dead around him. Peder, one of the ship's boys was dead but Guthrum, as well as Arne and Ragnvald, had survived. I saw that their swords were bloody.

"Are you hurt?"

They were all in a state of shock and they shook their heads. I looked at Leif's body. He had been cut many times. He had died hard. I was not sad for him. He had died well. To have killed five men with just one hand was worthy of a saga.

I knelt and closed his eyes. "Well done, Leif Left Handed, you have killed five enemies. You have died a hero and we will drink to you in Valhalla!"

Guthrum said, "No, Jarl Ragnvald, Leif slew three. Your son and Arne slew the other two. I just stood and watched."

I could see that Guthrum, the youngest of the ships' boys was upset at his lack of action. "Never fear Guthrum your time will come. Go to the other drekar and find out how many of their crews survived the attack."

Eager for something to do he said, "Aye jarl," and scurried off.

I could see that both Arne and my son were still in shock. Their hands shook and they still held their weapons. I took the weapons from them and laid them on the bloodied deck, "You both did well. Men will speak of your courage. You have done what Dragonheart and Haaken One Eye did when they defended Old Ragnar. You remember the tale your grandfather told?"

Ragnvald nodded. "I did not know what to do, father. Leif told us to run but we could not leave the ship. When they slew Peder it was as though a dam had burst. I jumped on one and slit his throat. His blood was hot. Why is that?"

"We will talk of this later. Go and fetch pails of seawater. We will swill the deck. I will rid the deck of the Bretons." I wanted them busy. That would drive what had happened from their minds.

They went to fetch pails. I took the weapons and anything of value from the five men before dumping their bodies over the side. The tide was on the turn and already the first body was drifting out to sea. We had missed the tide. It would be harder to leave but we had so much to do. My plans had been to leave before dark.

Arne and Ragnvald brought the water and began to wash the blood and the entrails from the drekar. It ran from the scuppers. Guthrum came back. "Jarl, we three are the only ones to survive."

I was angry. I was angry with myself for leaving the ships so far from us and not leaving a guard. I was angry because we had fired the town. Had we not done so then twelve ship's boys and four warriors might still be alive. I looked at Ragnvald as he and Arne brought bucket after bucket of water. It was as though they were trying to wipe away the memory. When they were home, in the safety of our hall they might enjoy the tale that would be told but at that moment it was too close. My son was closer to becoming a man and I was happy I had not brought Rollo. He might be where Peder was.

Chapter 3

We left in the middle of the night. It took that long for us to load the captives and the treasure we had taken. Had we been able I would have taken the horses, if only to punish the Bretons. We took our dead. They would be buried with honour. I confess that some of the men were harsh with the captives. The other jarls and I had to exercise control over them. The boys who had died had been popular. It was a hard row back. We had fewer crew and the deaths were still fresh. We had few ships' boys. We had lost warriors and others would be sailing home. They would be wondering what had happened to us.

With no Leif Left-Handed to steer I had that responsibility. It forced me to concentrate and to think about sailing and not dwell on either the curse or the Norns. Karl and the others must have reached home long before dark. There were fires burning on the quay to light us in and a crowd of people awaited us. We were many hours late and we came in silently. There was no song. There was no joy. That would warn them of our mood.

Mathilde stood wrapped against the cold. My daughters were not with her. She stared at the steering board. I pointed to Ragnvald who lithely leapt ashore to tie us up. I saw the relief on her face. Others were looking for husbands, brothers, fathers and sons. Some would be disappointed. I saw Brother Paul. He was standing with my priest, Æðelwald of Remisgat. I had the bodies carried off first. That way the families would know the worst straight away. Then the wounded were taken off. Finally, the captives and the animals left the four drekar. The captives were subdued.

I raised my sword, "I swear that the Clan of the Horse shall have vengeance for our dead shipmates."

Every warrior took his sword and began banging the deck. The chant rang across the seas. The men of Cancale would learn to fear us. Mathilde wrapped her arm around Ragnvald and hurried off with him. I would explain all later. As I stepped ashore I spoke with the priest. "How is the jarl?"

"He opened his eyes and asked for ale."

"Good. I fear it is too late to take you home."

31

Æðelwald of Remisgat said, "He can stay with me, jarl. I have explained to him that you are not the barbarians most men think you are."

I laughed, "I think we are quite barbaric but then so are the Bretons. Each tribe does what it must to survive."

Ragnvald was asleep when I entered my hall. Mathilde said, "He told me he killed a man. He slit his throat. Is this true?"

"If he had not done so he would be dead. Which would you rather, a whole Breton or a dead Ragnvald?"

"He will not go to sea again!"

"We do not sail again this season but he will do what he will. Today he has earned the right to have a voice. I am proud of him."

She was unhappy. She did what all women do at such times. She refused to speak to me. My father had told me that my mother did the same. I would endure the silence and the hateful looks. They would pass. All of the crews and jarls had stayed at my hall. When I rose, we gathered all the treasure to share it out. Three of the swords I had taken from the Bretons I had kept for the ship's boys. The families of the dead boys would also be paid weregeld for their loss.

When all was given out I stood and said, loudly so that all could hear, "Is this good? Is there one who objects?"

This was the time for anyone who was unhappy to speak. My father had introduced the idea after Raven Wing Island. There had been a dispute with some members of the clan. They were newcomers and did not like the way Siggi White Hair had run it. This prevented any bad feelings festering. I knew I had been fair and no one objected.

Einar Bear Killer stood, "There is one thing we must speak of."

I knew what it was but Brother Paul had not yet left. I held up my hand. "I know of what you speak. First, let us send the priest who saved Finni Bennison back to his home. We are all grateful to him."

Æðelwald of Remisgat brought the priest and I walked with them to the small ship. Three of Finni's crew would take him and drop him at the beach where we had battled.

The priest looked at me, "I spoke with Æðelwald of Remisgat last night. I would like to get to know your people a little more. I believe that I could convert you."

I laughed, "Æðelwald of Remisgat has failed but you are welcome to try. We will never be Christian so long as your God says to turn the other cheek. That is not the warrior's way."

"Then I will read the scriptures for an answer."

I watched him sail away. Æðelwald of Remisgat said, "He is a good man and a fine healer. Jarl Finni would be dead but for his ministrations. He was on his way to Lundenwic from Constantinople when you took him."

When we reached my hall the jarls and all the others were watching me expectantly. "Speak Einar Bear Killer."

"The men of Cancale killed boys. We want vengeance."

I said nothing. Others were present but only warriors were allowed to speak. Folki spoke up. "We had just raided their countrymen. I can understand why they fell upon us."

"Are you saying that we do not take revenge?"

Folki was older than Einar. He had lived in our land longer than almost any. He was slow to anger. Einar had implied that Folki was sympathetic to the Bretons. "No jarl. I think we take revenge but that is just because they are Bretons and I would like another rich haul such as the one we took today. I am saying that if we take revenge on everyone who fights against us then we have the whole world to fight."

Harold Strong Arm laughed, "I think, Jarl Folki, that most of the world is already against us."

Folki said, "I would hear Jarl Ragnvald's words. He is as wise as his father."

I shook my head, "I do not think that for an instant but I would like to visit our wrath upon the men of Cancale. What I do not want to do, is to do so yet. Jarl Finni is still wounded. I am certain he would like to come with us. We have men whom we have lost. Would you fight with small crews? My view is that we wait. Perhaps we will raid at Tvímánuður when they have their crops in and we can punish them twice over." I saw nods for it made sense. "There is something else. I would like to raid from the sea and the land."

This time I had surprised them. Einar Bear Killer said, "From the land?"

I nodded, "When we left the beach we left twenty horses. The Bretons have good horses. They are the equal of ours. We had to leave them. If we raid from two directions then we have more chance to defeat them and we might be able to capture many horses."

33

Einar shook his head, "My men are not horsemen."

Folki said, "Then you would sail. I think the jarl sees this as a bigger raid than just four ships."

"You are right. I would visit with my father and see if his horsemen and those of Lord Bertrand and Lords Gilles might join us."

"Even so you would have more than a hundred miles to travel. There are Franks and Bretons between us. For a drekar that is not a problem but for a horseman?"

"Then let us agree on this. At Tvímánuður we will raid Cancale. If I deem it possible then I will attack from the land with our horses and our ships will attack from the sea."

Men looked at each other and then began banging their shields. It was approved.

As the drekar and the knarr were loaded. Jarls and chiefs came to me to thank me for the invite to raid. Although I was now head of the clan I was both flattered and touched by their comments. Until now I had been the son of the Horseman. Now I was a leader in my own right. With my two sons, I could build for the future.

I had planned on travelling to the Haugr to bring back my son but my people had need of me. As jarl, they came to me with requests and they asked for favours. They brought me gifts. They sought my approval. This was especially true when we returned from a raid as everyone had benefitted. It was the middle of the afternoon before I had seen all those who wished to see me. I was heading to the stables to take one of my horses for a ride when I heard the clash of steel on steel. I found Arne, Guthrum and Ragnvald. They were practising but with the swords, I had given them. I was just grateful that my wife had not seen them.

"What are you doing?"

"We would be warriors father. We practise."

"Not with those swords."

They all looked surprised, "Why not, jarl?"

I took out Sun's Vengeance, "This is one of the finest swords in the land. It is my sword. It is part of me. The swords I gave you are good swords. They were warrior swords. I would not practise with my sword. I would practise with my second sword. My second sword is the same length and the same weight. It has the same balance. I made it so with the binding and lead weights. If I blunt my second sword it does not matter. If I damage my

34

second sword I will not be hurt in battle. Until you are more skilled use wooden ones. The swords you have could hurt you."

I pointed to my men who were also practising. They were using staves.

"See how Harold Strong Arm and Haaken the Bold use staves. It helps make you a better swordsman for you have to think of attack and defence. You can be hurt with a stave but you cannot be killed."

I saw understanding dawn.

"You are right, father. We will keep these sharp and oiled. We will make scabbards for them."

"Good."

"And when we get new ships' boys can we help to train them?"

I smiled. That made sense. Einar had been the eldest ship's boy and he had trained the others. Now, these three were the most senior. "Of course. I am pleased you are taking on the responsibility."

"Yes father, for one day I will lead this clan. I want to be the best jarl I can be."

That night I was weary. The raid had taken more from me than I cared to admit. I had seen more than thirty summers. A raid which saw me without sleep for two days would inevitably catch up with me. Ragnvald ate with us but scurried off as soon as he had filled himself. I suspected he wished to be with Arne and Guthrum. The wet nurse had taken my daughters off and I realised why when my wife ended her angry silence and spoke.

"Why do we need to raid our neighbours? We have all that we need. It is not Christian."

Perhaps my weariness made me shorter than I meant to be, "And we are not Christians. We are Vikings and we raid. But you are wrong we do not have enough. Our family does but our clan does not. There are farmers who have more children than they can feed. There are widows and there are orphans who need what I provide." I darted a hand to point, beyond the wall, at the church. "And I give money to a church I never visit. Perhaps I should stop raiding and use the money I give your priests to the poor."

She scowled at me. "That is our money!"

"And as I took it I decide how we spend it."

She stared down at the food she had picked at. Then she raised her head, "And Ragnvald now has a sword! He will hurt himself."

"I have spoken with him. He will not use it again."

"You will be going to your father's home for Rollo tomorrow. How do you know?"

I sighed, "Then I will delay my journey by a day so that I may watch over my son."

As I lay in bed that night I realised that the curse was very real. Since Ragnvald's birth, my wife and I had argued more. It seemed she had become more Christian and I had become more pagan.

When I rose, I decided to keep my son with me. "Come we will visit Jarl Finni."

He was in the warrior hall. He was sitting at the table when we entered. One side of his head was black and blue and the top of his head was encased in a bandage. He looked like an Arab. "Are you supposed to be up? You were almost in Valhalla. The priest barely saved your life."

He laughed but quieter than he normally did. "He said I should not leave the hall. He did not say I should stay in my bed. Thank you Jarl Ragnvald. It was your prompt action which saved my life. Had you not come to my aid then my oathsworn and I would be dead. I owe you more than a life."

"I was jarl. I led the raid. It was my duty."

"And I hear we raid them again."

"We have some months for you to heal."

"Aye, I will send to your Bagsecg for a new helmet. I would have one with longer sides." He suddenly seemed to see Ragnvald. "And here we have the hero, Ragnvald the Breton Slayer."

My son seemed to grow when the words were spoken. "Arne killed one too!"

"Then he should be Arne the Breton Slayer. You will be brothers in blood. There will be a bond between you. That will make you special. I can see the Allfather has picked you and Arne out. To have killed your enemies when you are so young is rare. Even the Dragonheart was older when he slew his foes."

"Do not give him ideas, Jarl Finni. Yesterday I had to tell him not to practise with the Breton sword I had given him."

"Your father is right, Ragnvald the Breton Slayer. Keep your weapon sheathed until you go to war. Then it will be sharp and

36

hungry for blood. Just as we row when we have to so we rest
when the gods send us a wind. Your sword should be the same."

We chatted for a while about the men we had lost and which
goods would be traded when the knarr sailed and then we left. "Is
that my name now, father?"

"Men will call you that but it is your choice. Your mother
will not be happy."

He was silent. "She wishes me to be Christian." He looked up
at me but I remained silent too. It was a hard question to answer.
Whatever advice I gave him would be wrong. A warrior had to
do what was in his heart. "I wish to follow the old ways and there
is something else."

"Yes."

"I prefer being on a ship rather than riding a horse. Does that
disappoint you?"

"No, for I think Rollo prefers the horse and the two of you
will lead the clan when I am gone. This is a good thing."

He stopped, "I am the eldest. It should be me who leads the
clan."

"Rollo is your brother and he will help you."

"Arne is my brother. He can help me."

"And when we need to raid where there is no river and no sea
then how will you do so? Rollo can lead our horsemen."

Ragnvald shrugged, "If it is not on a river or by the sea then I
care not."

Our conversation disturbed me. Was this the curse again?
Was there a division between the boys already? They were young
and they might change. I decided that I would speak with my
father. His advice was known to be sage. I waited until the knarr
had sailed and I was certain that Ragnvald had heeded my words.
Jarl Finni's naming of my son seemed to have been taken up by
the rest of the clan. He and Arne were the only ones who were
not yet warriors to have such a title and the younger boys flocked
to be with them. It was the start of Ragnvald's own oathsworn.
He and Arne became very close. I often heard people talking of a
new Dragonheart and Haaken One Eye. As I rode to the Haugr I
reflected that this was not necessarily a good thing.

I called at the hall of Rurik One Ear. I had not seen one of my
father's oldest friends for a long time. I also valued his advice.
His wife Agnathia met me at the stables when I dismounted,
"Ragnvald Hrolfsson it is good to see you but I must warn you

that my husband is not a well man. Do not be surprised at what he does or says."

"Why, what ails him?"

She smiled. My father had said that she was the best thing that had ever happened to him. She was both a kind woman and a firm one. Rurik needed both in equal measure. "He is old but he has the coughing sickness and he does not see as well as he used to. It is not that. It is that he does not remember as well as he did. We know it happens to all but there are warriors he does not remember. Do not be offended if he does not know you."

I smiled, "He is like an uncle to me. No matter what he says I will not be upset."

I regretted my promise when I was taken to his chamber. He lived in a stone building built by the Franks. He had a room with a window. When we entered a servant left. There were shutters to keep the warmth in during winter and, as we walked in, light shone on the bed. I was shocked. Rurik One Ear had been a big warrior. My father had teased him as he got old about his size. He had not gone to war for as long as I could remember. Now he looked like a skeleton.

His eyes opened as I passed before the light from the window. "Is that you Hrolf? It is good to see you."

I sat on the bed so that he could see me closer, "No, it is his son Ragnvald."

I saw him concentrate and try to remember, "Hrolf has a son? You look like him. Do you ride a horse too? He is Hrolf the Horsemen. The Franks fear him."

I looked up at Agnathia who had sat on the other side of him and was holding his hand. She nodded and smiled.

"Aye, I ride a horse. I have just raided the Bretons."

He looked at me sadly, "I will not raid again. I was a warrior once you know. Rurik One Ear. Your father and I lived..." he shook his head, "I cannot remember." Tears came into his eyes and he looked fearful. "Why can I not remember?"

"It was Raven Wing Island."

He smiled, "Aye you are right." He reached up and squeezed my hand. "Erik One Arm and your father were there and we saved the island for the clan. Then I was a warrior."

He began coughing and I saw blood on his lips. Agnathia said, "He is tired and he will sleep now. I have a draught for him."

I stood, "I will tell my father to visit with you."

Rurik's eyes were closed and he murmured, "That will be good."

Once outside she said, "Thank you for that. He remembered more than I thought he would."

"It is sad to see him thus." I hesitated. "You know to keep his sword by the bed?"

She nodded, "He is a warrior and he would go to his Valhalla. When I am not there a servant waits by his bed. We will give him his sword when his time is near. Tell your father to come soon or it will be too late."

"I will." As I rode north I realised that all of the warriors I had grown up admiring were getting old. How much longer would my father have? When I was young I had believed that my father would live forever. Now that I was older I realised that was not true. My father's remaining years would be counted on the fingers of my hands.

Rollo had seen me from a distance and he raced up to my horse, eager to tell me of his adventures with his grandfather. There would have been a time when I could have picked him up and hugged him. Now he was almost as tall as me. I had missed him and I embraced him. He began chattering away like a magpie and I watched my father walk towards me. I knew he was a little younger than Rurik but now he suddenly looked much younger. Rurik had given up his warrior ways. My father never had. He still rode each day and he still practised with his weapons. He could still send an arrow almost as far as I could.

"You have come too soon, my son. I hoped for half a year with this young one. He makes me feel young again."

"And I have missed him too, father. He lights my days. I will stay awhile for I have much to tell you and we need to speak."

He was not Rurik and nothing escaped his notice. "Rollo take your father's horse to the stable and then join us in my tower."

"Aye grandfather."

My father's home had a stone wall and two towers made of stone. He had a room with a window in the one which faced north-west. He told me that he liked to look that way. Many leagues and two oceans away lay the Land of the Wolf. That was where he had become a warrior and he had never forgotten it. As we walked to the tower he said, "What concerns you, my son?"

I quickly told him about Rurik. I would tell him of the raid when Rollo was there.

He shook his head. "I have put off visiting him and that is wrong. I will go tomorrow. Will you and Rollo come with me?"

"We will but I will not take Rollo in. I fear it would confuse old Rurik. He thought that I was you."

He smiled, "I take that as a compliment." We entered the small room. There were two chairs and a table. It was simple. The light made the room feel warm, even without a fire. The shutters could be closed when it was night time or there was a storm. It was cosy and I envied him his refuge. I wished that I had one.

I spoke of Mathilde and Benni's Ville until Rollo arrived, breathless. I told them both of our raid; Finni's wound and the attack of the Bretons. Rollo said, "I would have fought alongside my brother!"

"You are too young yet. Peder was just a little older than you and he died."

"But he was not your son. He was not the grandson of the Horseman! He was not as big as I am."

I looked at my father. There was pride in his eyes at my son's words. "But you prefer a horse to a ship."

"I do not mind ships."

My father said, "Rollo, do not say something just to impress your father. You told me that you would rather lead men from a horse than a drekar. That is what is in your heart. Do not deny what the Allfather has made."

"You wish to be a horseman?"

He nodded, "I like horses. I have enjoyed these days with my grandfather. He has taught me much about riding already."

I nodded my approval. My father said, "And now we had better see your mother or she will be unhappy. You are her only son and she does not see enough of you!"

Mother made a fuss of me. She had much in common with my wife. She too was a Christian who disapproved of our raids and so I did not bring that up. Instead, I stayed on safer ground and told her of my daughters and Rurik's ill health.

"I like Rurik. He is rough and he is bluff but there was never a more loyal supporter to the two of us on Raven Wing Island. With Erik gone as well as Sven and Harold, our past is fading. We should go and visit with him."

"I would make it sooner rather than later."

"Then on the morrow, we will go. But I feel rude leaving you here."

I smiled, "Rollo and I will amuse ourselves. I will enjoy drinking Brigid's ale. She is still a fine alewife?"

"Aye, she is."

"Good, then I will drink and see the land of my birth. It has been some time since I visited Bárekr's Haven and ridden this land.

My mother had been the daughter of a Frankish lord and she liked to do things properly. We did not just have a meal, that night, we had a feast. My father had been brought up a slave and he preferred simpler food but he smiled and endured the fuss. What was hard was keeping the subject of war from the table. Rollo was eager for news of the raid and I managed to evade his questions. When my father and I were alone we would be able to talk at greater length.

With a large candle to light us, we sat in his tower and drank ale warmed with a poker and infused with spices and butter. Four years since we had raided the lands of Al-Andalus and captured a shipment of spices. We had only sold half and the rest we enjoyed. I told my father of my worries about Ragnvald and the curse. He was silent.

"Speak father. There should be no secrets between us."

"I should have told you this secret five years since. I am sorry for not doing so."

"Five years ago?"

"After your wife lost the child in childbirth I feared it was because of the curse." I nodded. "When you visited us, I paid Old Seara to put a spell on your wife and your unborn child. Rollo was born healthy as were your daughters. She said she could do nothing about Ragnvald. It would take a more powerful witch than she. Now that she is dead..."

"But he may not be cursed. Look how he and Arne defeated and killed two warriors. Perhaps that means the curse is lifted."

"A curse of the Mother?" He shook his head. "There is but one who might do it and that is the Dragonheart's daughter, Kara."

"That is a long voyage."

"There is more. Since he has been with me your son has told me how Ragnvald hurts him. At night, when they are alone he tries to frighten him. Sometimes Rollo is awoken by his brother hitting him."

I remembered the incident on the drekar. "When I get home..."

"You will say nothing. From what you say Ragnvald is now a hero to the other boys. What kind of life will he have? Ragnvald may well be cursed. There may be something in him... I know not what. There could be a seed. The priest should not have witnessed the birth. We are being punished. All I know is that Rollo wept when he told me what his brother had done. They were tears of shame. Your son is unhappy."

I was a bad father. I had not noticed. "What do I do then?"

My father was wise and he sighed, "If you leave him with us for a while we can fulfil his dream of becoming a horseman. Gilles and Bertrand live close by. He could learn about horses. He could serve as a squire to Hugo Strong Arm. Other young boys serve. They groom horses and help my horsemen to keep their equipment in good order. It gives them discipline."

"What will his mother say?"

My father laughed, "The same thing as your mother! She would not approve. Do you want your son happy or unhappy?"

"You are right. I will speak to him in the morning. I can see why you had but the one son."

"That was not my choice. That was the Allfather's. I often wonder what might have happened had the priest not witnessed his birth. Would the Mother have sent you only daughters as she did with me?"

I felt a chill run down my neck. It was nothing to do with the evening. When I had allowed the priest to watch my son's birth I had thrown a stone in to a pool. The ripples were still rolling. The curse was not yet over.

My parents left early to visit with Rurik. Hugo and his men escorted them. I thought how fine they looked in their dark blue cloaks with the silvery-white cross on their shields. We mounted two horses and rode, first to Bárekr's Haven. I liked to visit the port. I thought it a better anchorage than the Haugr. For one thing, it was easier to navigate and, as it was closer to the headland it was easier to find a wind. After we had visited with the men I had known as boys and spoken of families and friends long dead we headed for Ċiriċeburh. Bertrand, who ruled there, was a Frank. He had never raided with us on a drekar but he led fifty warriors who were all mounted. They represented the largest single body of horsemen we possessed. If we were to raid Cancale by land then I needed him and his horsemen.

I turned to speak with Rollo. His face was filled with the joy of riding and, I believe, riding with his father. "Your grandfather told me of Ragnvald."

His face changed in an instant. He hung his head. "I did not want him to! I can handle this myself. I am bigger than Ragnvald now. He cannot bully me as he once did."

"No, you cannot. He has others who would join with him. I am disappointed that you did not tell me."

"It is not the way of a warrior."

"You are not a warrior. Your brother is much older than you are and he has allies." We rode in silence for a while. I waved at one of the farmers who was tending his apples on the hillside. "Your grandfather has offered you a place in his hall."

"Ragnvald will think I am afraid of him and I am not."

"He will not. You wish to be a horseman. Hugo can make you a better one than I ever could. He knows even more than Lord Bertrand and your grandfather. If you are to be a horseman then you should be the best that you can be."

"I would like that but I would miss you."

"Do not worry. If you are here then I will visit every month. I have not seen enough of my father of late. Do you wish me to ask Hugo?"

He was silent and then he nodded, "But I am not afraid of my brother."

"I know, my son. I never thought so for an instant."

At that moment we made a decision that would change the clan forever.

Chapter 4

We rode to Bertrand and he agreed to help me raid Cancale.
He had trained me. Now with grey hair and children, he was keen
to do all he could for me. "Ragnvald, why have you not advanced
our lands further south? It is rich farmland. Carentan might
become flood every year but south of it the land is fertile and the
ground has no rocks. The Franks do not have many strongholds
there."

"Could we take it?"

He poured me some wine. I saw Rollo taking in every word
we spoke.

"The land to the south and west of ours is Breton. We have
kept the peace with the Franks and, thus far, they have not
bothered us. It seems to me that by raiding the Bretons in Sarnia
and Saint Maclou you have begun to make war."

I sipped some of the wine.

"Surely you knew that when you raided?"

"It was a raid."

"I am no Viking but I know that your people did not raid their
close neighbours unless they wished to war and to take their land.
That is what your father told me happened in the Land of the
Horse and now half of that land is Norse."

"I raided because we needed food and supplies. The coin we
got will make our people safe."

"And that means your people need land. We can raid Cancale
by horses. It will be dangerous and it will cost men and horses
but we can do it."

"Then you say do not do it?"

He laughed and looked at Rollo. Bertrand's servants had
brought in the foreleg of a pig. He handed the platter to Rollo.
"Eat this Rollo."

"All of it?"

"Could you?"

My son considered and then, taking his knife out he cut a
piece. He began to eat it. He nodded appreciatively,
"Eventually!"

It was my turn to laugh. "A good illustration. We take it piece by piece. How far is it from Coutances to Cancale?"

"Seventy miles. The Bretons took Périers two years after we sacked it. They hold it but have not fortified it. That is halfway from Carentan to Coutances. You retake Périers and then Coutances."

"We do not have enough men to hold them."

"Then do not. All you are doing is making certain that when you travel to Cancale there are no enemies in your path."

What he said made perfect sense. We had not raided on horses for some years. We needed to do so gradually. I saw now the foolish nature of my initial idea. Bertrand had refined it for me. "That would mean beginning our move south in early summer."

"In less than a month."

"Would you be ready to accompany me?"

"We would. My men become rusty and my young men grow restless. If they cannot fight another then they will fight amongst themselves. Aye, we will come. You will need Folki and Einar too. From what you say Finni will be in no condition to help."

"Then I will see you at my hall in thirty days from now."

As we rode back to the Haugr I could tell that Rollo had been listening carefully. "You do not go to conquer these lands? You go to raid them and then punish the Bretons for the attack on our ships."

"You were listening, good."

"One day will we conquer them?"

"Perhaps. Let us take short steps. As Bertrand said, we must eat this piece by piece."

For the rest of the journey, I was not questioned, I was interrogated about how we would do this. I was secretly pleased for it showed that my son had a sharp mind and understood strategy.

When my parents returned it was not for two days. Rurik One Ear was dead. My father believed he had waited to say goodbye to his oldest friend first. The death of Rurik changed my father. When he returned he seemed determined to make more of what he had. We went to his tower with a flagon of wine and we drank it all. It was a Viking custom. "I put his sword in his hand. Agnathia held his other and I heard his last breath. He is now in Valhalla with Siggi White Hair and Ulf Big Nose. They will tease him about his girth and speak of our battles on Raven Wing Island. You and I, my son, will send him hence with this wine."

After had told me the tales of Rurik, most of which I already knew, he told me that he would make sure that my son was safe with him. Hugo was more than delighted, he was honoured to be given the task of training the grandson of Hrolf the Horseman. I told my father what Bertrand had said. "I can see the wisdom in that and I will send what horsemen I can. I know that Gilles' boys, Rollo son of Gilles and Erik son of Gilles would like to go to war and there are young men here. Hugo and the others I will retain. I will not be coming. That is not because I do not wish to but I do not want you to worry about me while I am with you and you would. Besides I have a task here. I am going to make a horseman of my grandson."

"Thank you, although the way he is growing we will need to breed bigger horses if we are to do so!"

"Aye, he may well be the biggest horseman ever! He has grown a hand span since he has been here. He will be a giant when he has finished growing."

"The volva cast a good spell!"

I called in at Gilles' horse farm on the way south. As I had expected his two sons were keen to take part in a campaign. They both had men who followed them. With the men promised by my father, as well as Bertrand and Gilles, now I had almost eighty horsemen to add to my thirty. One hundred and ten horsemen would be enough to challenge any Bretons.

When I broke the news of my son's training I could not have had a more contrasting response. Mathilde was appalled that she would not be seeing her son. She used the word abducted. She flew into a rage and told me that Ragnvald would not be leaving her any time soon. Ragnvald showed complete indifference to the news. It was as though he did not have a brother. It confirmed, if confirmation was needed, that Rollo had spoken truly. When Mathilde stormed off with my daughters and Ragnvald made to follow I stopped him.

"You have been tormenting and hurting your brother."

He did not deny it. "Has that milksop been blubbing to you? I was trying to make a Viking of him. He is soft."

I was sorely tempted to backhand him but one day Rollo would return. Hopefully, he would be able to handle himself. If I struck Ragnvald then it might be even worse between them. I nodded, "I do not think so and I am jarl but I am disappointed with you. My estimation of you had risen after the raid now I think less of you."

My words hit him harder than any slap I might have used. He coloured. "There are others in the clan who do not agree with you."

"Be careful, my son. If you surround yourself with flatterers and deceivers then you are laying yourself open to treachery."

"I know who is true and who can be trusted. When I am jarl I will reward those who support me."

"And I am not certain that you would make a good jarl. You are young. Perhaps you will change... for the better. I hope so."

He tried to outstare me but failed. He turned and left. He was angry. So was I but I was the warrior. I would have to forgive him and try to change him. I wanted him to be better than I was. The man who led the clan would need to be better if we were to fulfil the Norn's prophesy and rule Frankia. I put him from my mind as I prepared the assault on the Bretons.

The first thing I did was to visit Finni. I needed to tell him my plans and invite his assistance. I was pleased to see him walking about although I noticed that his men hovered close by for he looked unsteady on his feet. "Like a baby, eh Jarl? I am learning to walk again. And I get pains in my head. That priest of your wife says it is to be expected. Even ale does not numb them!"

"So long as you heal. I need a favour from you."

"I owe you a life."

I nodded, "I am going to take men to raid the land to the south of us. When it comes time to raid Cancale I want the Breton land to the south of us to be a wasteland. I need you and your men to guard my home for I will be taking my best men with me."

"Then we will guard your home and your ships."

I sent a message to Erik Green Eye and Einar Bear Killer. I asked if they had men who wished to raid over land into the heart of Brittany. If they said no they knew I would not be offended. I sent Leif Sorenson. He was a quietly spoken man and known to be of my hearth weru. I rode to speak with Folki myself. He had the largest warband. With Carentan's walls to guard he needed many men. I rode with my other three hearth-weru. Snorri Snorrison. Harold Strong Arm and Haaken the Bold were all competent riders. They were better warriors in a shield wall but they had skills as leaders which outweighed any deficiencies they might have had in the saddle. My younger warriors would be around me in battle. They would be behind ready to fill gaps with other warriors. Like me, they wore the helmet with the nasal and carried an oval shield which protected their upper left leg. Their byrnies were split to enable them to ride.

"You plan on taking Périers, Jarl Ragnvald?"

"Aye, Harold."

"It fell quickly enough last time."

"Perhaps we should have held on to it, eh?"

"At the time, Snorri, we did not have enough men. My father took the decision to hold on to Benni's Ville and Carentan. Since then we have grown. Coutances will be a more difficult prospect but I would like to take that one and hold it. It is close to the sea and there is fine farmland."

"I would prefer to fight on foot, jarl."

"I know Harold but we must move quickly. A horse is the fastest way to cover great distances. With luck, Jarl Folki and his men will give us the opportunity to do as we did last time and sweep around the flanks of the enemy. We fought Franks then, not Bretons."

"We beat the ones on the beach!"

"We were lucky, Haaken. Do you think they would have been so reckless against a Viking shield wall?"

I rode with a handful of men to Carentan. Folki had not changed the Frankish town. He had just moved in and used it the way he found it. It had been me who captured it but I had not wanted to rule there. Benni's Ville was close to Mathilde's parents' home and the Haugr. We had been spied from afar and Bergil Bjornson his lieutenant greeted me. "The Jarl is with his wife and sons in the hall. One of the men had composed a saga about our raid."

Nanna was Folki's wife. She was a lively woman and a wonderful mother. With flaming chestnut hair, now tinged by the first hints of grey, she threw her arms around me. "Jarl Ragnvald! Your wife is a lucky woman! You still look like a young man and yet my Folki looks like an ancient piece of rock." She shook her head, "A large rock!"

She liked to tease Folki and he always took it in good part. "Perhaps the jarl would look as old as me if he was married to you!"

She laughed, "I will have a chamber prepared for you."

Most of Folki's hearth weru were gathered in the hall. These were the ten men who guarded Jarl Folki in battle. He had more than I did. Part of that was to do with the battle which had cost his brother and most of their clan their lives. These heart weru were the last remnants of that clan. Others had joined them but these eleven had a special bond.

"What brings you here, jarl? I do not think it would be to enjoy our food."

"You know that we plan a raid at Tvímánuður?" He nodded. "I plan on beginning to pave the way for that by raiding Périers and then Coutances. I want to clear the land of Bretons. That way when we raid at Tvímánuður, we will not have to worry about our lines home being threatened."

His servants had brought ale. He drank some. "We lost few men on the last raid. I could bring forty men. Would that suffice?"

"I have over a hundred horsemen promised. We would seal off the two hamlets and you would assault them. It might be if the Bretons have not repaired the walls that we could take the towns with our horses."

"But you need a shield wall." He nodded.

"I hope to have more men. Erik Green Eye and Einar Bear Killer may join us. Their men will have sown their crops this would be a good time."

The jarl looked at his hearth weru. Bergil Bonecruncher grinned, "I speak for all of the men, jarl when I say we relish the chance of taking land and treasure from Christians! It is easier than taking eggs from hens!"

By the time we left the next morning all had been arranged. Folki had young warriors who would scout out the two hamlets and we meet up with them at Lessay. That had been Frankish too but after we had defeated them the inhabitants had fled. A couple of families farmed there.

Erik Green Eye himself awaited me. He was also a greybeard now. With him was his son, Rollo One Ear. His son was a hero who had been with my father when we had made our land safe from Frank and Dane alike. As soon as I saw him my spirits were lifted.

"Jarl Ragnvald, we received your message although your father had already mentioned it to me. I am too old for such things. My heart would be there with you but I fear that my arms do not have the strength they once did. My son would lead my men."

I turned to Rollo. "It would be an honour to have you fight alongside us. How many men could you bring?"

"I have fifty warriors who seek adventure, glory and, I hope, treasure."

"The adventure and the glory I can promise but I am unsure about the treasure."

"We will take our chances. You and your father are both known to be lucky warriors. When would you want us?"

"Twenty days hence at Lessay."

"We will be there."

"What of Einar Bear Killer?"

"He went to raid the Franks up the Issicauna. He said that he enjoyed the raid against the Bretons but he did not get to kill enough enemies."

I was disappointed but I had almost two hundred men. It would be enough.

Rather than repairing my old helmet Bagsecg Bagsecgson had made me a new one. I had approached him when I had visited my father. We had made enough coin for me to pay him well. He had used some of the candlesticks and melted down the brass to make a strengthening band around the helmet. It ran down the nasal and up to the crown. It added to the look of the helmet. He also repaired the mail. It was a time-consuming process to make a whole new byrnie. I chose the two horses I would take with me and I had more spears made. These were longer than the spear we used in the shield wall. We had learned that enemies could lie on the ground. We needed something to deter that. My horsemen did not use bows but Rollo One Ear and Folki would make sure that we had plenty of arrows. The Bretons used crossbows but they did not have many of them.

Ragnvald kept away from me. He worked with the other ships' boys. Our drekar needed maintaining and with new boys to train he would be busy. Nonetheless, it was obvious to me that he was shunning me. I had no time to worry about that. I worried more about Rollo for he was at the haugr and I missed watching him develop and grow. When this foray was over then I would visit him and my father again.

Folki came to visit with us. His scouts had returned. "Périers has no wall, jarl. They kept the ditch but they have yet to rebuild the wall. It will not cause us much of a problem. We saw men who were armed but most appeared to be farmers or men who work in the village. We saw smiths and potters as well as tanners.

There is no warrior hall. Coutances is a different matter. They
have a ditch and a wooden wall. They also have a watchtower
with a bell. They have learned from Carentan. They have cleared
the land around it so that we cannot sneak up, save at night."

"Then we take Périers quickly and isolate Coutances."

"Saint-Lô may be a problem. They have ramparts and they
have mailed men there. There is a Bishop and he has a cathedral."

"But we do not raid Saint-Lô."

"I know, jarl but the lord there is powerful. He has ridden up
to our walls on more than one occasion. We are too strong for
him but he is not afraid of us. Lord Saloman's family were given
the town by Charlemagne himself."

"What is his sign?"

"It is the sign of a hunting bird on a yellow background. He
likes to wear a yellow feather in his helmet. Those of his men
without mail wear a yellow kyrtle over their leather."

"Thank you for discovering that. We will have Rollo One Ear
with us."

"That should be enough warriors." He looked around.
"Where are your sons?"

"Rollo is with my father and Ragnvald is working on the
ship."

"Ragnvald the Breton Slayer already has songs sung about
him. My warriors were impressed with both him and Arne. You
are lucky to have such a son."

I wondered about that.

Bertrand and Gilles's sons were the first to arrive. They
wanted to rest the horses for a couple of days before pushing on
to the land of the Bretons. All three knew their horses and they
had brought spares.

"Our father stays at home. He was thrown by a wild horse
earlier this year. His leg has not recovered."

"You need not apologize, Erik Gillesson. I am just grateful
that you came. As you and your men do not wear mail I wanted
to use you as scouts. Your horses are fast and should be able to
outrun the Bretons. Lord Bertrand's men have mail vests. I want
the two of you to operate as our eyes and ears. The men from
Gilles' stad can find the enemy and Lord Bertrand's men will
shield us from their sight. I wish my men and those sent by my
father to remain hidden. Fifty mailed men should come as a real
surprise to our enemies."

"We can do that."

Over the next two days, Rollo One Ear and the men from the
Haugr arrived. They were a magnificent sight. All had mail
byrnies. Their helmets had all been made by Bagsecg. Each had a
shield which bore my father's sign, the horse. Rollo's banner was
a horse on a green background. It had been his father's. As soon
as they arrived I felt more confident. My own banner was a white
horse on a blue background with a sword in the corner. It fooled
our enemies for often they took the sword for a cross. It was not.

My wife complained about the number of horses. The
farmers, on the other hand, were happy for their fields were
fertilised. My wife's complaint was the smell. I did not say that I
preferred it to the smell of fish. That would have been one more
argument and I had had enough of late.

The arrival of so many warriors brought Ragnvald and Arne,
as well as the other boys, to admire the armour and weapons of
the warriors. They came and spoke to them. It was the closest my
son had been to me since I had returned from the Haugr. I saw
the envy on his face and the disappointment knowing he would
not be going to war with us. As with all boys they were
fascinated by wounds and they questioned Rollo One Ear about
his injury. I knew that he was proud of his wound for he had
helped to save the life of my father. I watched as Arne and
Ragnvald exchanged looks. They had tried to save Leif and
failed. It put their heroics into perspective.

We left early. My own goodbyes were cold. My men left to
cheers and hugs.

It was just fifteen miles to Lessay. With Gilles' men ahead of
us I was confident that we would reach the former Breton village
without incident. The Norse who farmed there had told us that the
Bretons rarely bothered them. They said that the Bretons feared
the wrath of the Northmen. Folki was already there. The village
had been burned but there had been a stone tower. Folki had built
the camp around that. He had put stakes in and fires were burning
for food when we arrived. It had taken half a day to reach the
village. We would use speed when we had to. That would be
when we had taken Périers.

Périers was just six miles from us. I sent Erik Gillesson and
four men to scout it out, while we held a council of war.

"Lord Bertrand I would have you take your men tomorrow
south of Périers. Cut them off from Coutances. I will lead my
horsemen to take the town. Folki you and Rollo One Ear follow
up with the men on foot. We should know, when Erik returns, the

size of the force we face. When we have taken Périers we scout out Coutances. I have no doubt that they will quickly hear of Périers and wish to do something about it."

"You would bring them to battle?"

"Yes, Bertrand. I do not want them to gather an army to attack us. I want them to come to try to rid the land of us. They will just see two warbands of horsemen. They will not see Folki or Rollo One Ear. We draw them on and eliminate them. My main intent is to destroy both places. I want them empty when we come south at Tvímánuður."

We had ale for the first night. After that, we would be reliant on taking from the Bretons. Erik and his men rode in when we had just begun to cook the food we had brought. It was late afternoon.

"Jarl they have some horsemen there."

I looked over to Folki. "They did not have them when we scouted ten days ago."

Was this a coincidence or a trap? "Any new defences?"

"They have just the ditch."

"Then my plan does not change. What did they have upon their shields?"

"We were too far away to see clearly, jarl, but they appeared to have some sort of bird on a yellow background."

Folki said, "Lord Salomon."

I drank sparingly and lay watching the sky above. I had not known the name of my enemy in Saint Maclou but I knew this one.

One of my young warriors had asked to carry my banner. Karl Bennisson was the son of Benni the Builder who had made my walls and my hall. He was young and that was why I allowed him the banner. His orders were to ride behind me and to signal the rest of my warriors. He would be more likely to survive that way. This was his first raid.

With five men left at Lessay to watch our spare horses and supplies, we set off before dawn had broken. We would not attack in the dark but when the people were half asleep would give us the greatest chance of success. Gilles' sons and Lord Bertrand led their men in a long loop south of the town. We left at the pace of Folki and his men. That would allow my other men to be in position before we attacked. We headed south-west. Although Périers was small it was important. The old Roman roads crossed at that point. The Franks who had lived there before the Bretons had realised the strategic significance of the site and built a small stronghold there. We had destroyed it. We needed it removed so that our attack on Cancale could succeed.

The land over which we travelled was flat and much of it had been cleared of trees. It was perfect for horses. As dawn broke in the east I spied the buildings which made up the village. I reined in just a mile from the first building. It looked to be a farm. I turned to Folki. We will begin our attack. Fetch your men behind us but do not exhaust them."

"Are we here just to be observers?"

I smiled at Folki, "When we reach Coutances you know that it is we who will be watching. This is horse work and that will be axe work." He nodded. I waved my spear to have us form into two lines. The experienced warriors from the Haugr and from my hall rode in the first line with me. We were not a long line. We were just twenty-five men long but that would be enough for Périers. I dug my heels and Dawn's Light responded. My mount began to canter. There was no avoiding the sound of our hooves on the ground. There had been rain and the ground was not bone hard but the vibration would travel to the village. The earth would feel as though it was shaking.

I heard shouts. As we neared I saw faces appear. Spears were shaken and orders were shouted. The screams and shouts grew and I saw the people begin to flee. We were drawing inexorably closer to them and yet we were still riding at an easy pace. There were even more horsemen waiting to catch them on the far side of the village. A dozen men armed with spears, shields and wearing helmets formed a line across the road. They were brave men and they were trying to slow us down to allow their families to escape.

I lowered my spear and pulled my shield a little tighter to me. The dozen men were clearer now. I saw a couple of greybeards and others without beards. Those without beards had never fought. Whoever had formed the line had not done so with any thought. Two of those without beards fled when we were just forty paces from them. They did not want to face death. They were not yet ready. That left gaps and, as the Bretons shuffled to fill them, we struck.

I lunged at the warriors in the centre. His spear came towards Dawn's Light's shoulder. The warrior had fought horsemen. I was taller than most men with a longer reach. Had I not been then his spear might have hurt my horse. As it was my spear struck him in the left shoulder and spun him around. We were tightly packed and our horses could not avoid the Bretons. Soren Asbjornson was next to me and his horse trampled over the warrior, crushing his skull. I did not pause. The two men who had fled were being caught by us. Soren urged his horse on. We did not need a single line now. The young warrior kept glancing over his shoulder. That was a mistake for it added to his fear and slowed him down. Soren had time to choose his spot. He speared the man on his left side just below his shoulder blades. The Breton gave a scream as he died.

I was now ahead of the others. They had spread out to cover as much of the village as they could. The other young man was almost within range of my spear. I thought of my sons. I would not want them to die in their first battle. I held my spear out horizontally and the haft smacked into the back of his helmet. He pitched forward and lay still. I passed no one else until I reached the southern edge of the village. I saw the villagers who had fled. They were surrounded by Lord Bertrand. I slowed my horse to a walk and headed towards them.

The women and the old held their families close together. I saw Bretons with their eyes closed and hands together as they prayed for forgiveness before they died. They were resigned to death. I saw that all of Lord Bertrand's horses had riders. None had been hurt. I took off my helmet and planted my spear into the ground.

"Who speaks for you?"

One older woman looked around and stood. "I am Bertha wife of Arles, the headman. You have killed him, speak to me, barbarian."

I heard Soren take an intake of breath.

"Peace Soren. She is a brave woman. I like that." I pointed towards the south-west. "That way lies the land of the Bretons. This is now the Land of the Horse. You have two choices, return to your own people or swear allegiance to me and mine."

She raised her head and jutted her jaw, "Obey the orders of a heathen who eats babies? Never. We will find our own people and they will come and retake this land from you."

"Perhaps but you would not have it had we not taken it from the Franks." I pointed behind me. "One of your young warriors is back there and wounded. If you wish him to live then go fetch him."

There were six young boys close to the woman. They looked to be twelve summers old. They had knives in their belts. The woman pointed and they began to move. Karl backed his horse away so that they had a clear passage.

I turned in the saddle, "Go and search the village. We will use this as our base."

My men turned and left. Lord Bertrand said, "Erik and Rollo, take your men. You know what to do."

The two young men whipped around their horses' heads and galloped off in the direction of Coutances. The boys carried the helmet, shield and spear of the young man. He was supported by two others. I saw that his head was bloodied but he was awake. As he passed me he glared up at me. I leaned down to speak to him, "You have been lucky today, Breton. I gave you your life. You do not deserve it for you deserted your shield brothers. Become a better warrior. You are the last man of your people now."

He thought about replying but did not and he joined the thirty villagers who began to trudge south to Coutances. I turned my horse and headed for the village. Folki and the others had arrived. "Karl ride back and bring our supplies and spare horses from Lessay."

"Aye, jarl. That was easy."

"The next battle will not be. There are horsemen at Coutances." He galloped off and I dismounted and led my horse to the water trough in the village. Dawn's Light drank deeply. The men who were on foot were already at work. The huts were being demolished to make barriers behind which they could defend our gains if we needed. When we had no further need of them they would be burned. They would not be able to rebuild before Tvímánuður.

Snorri Snorrison brought me a horn of cider. "It is not ale, jarl but it will quench the thirst." I nodded and began to drink. "There is little that we want from here, jarl."

"We have all that we need. We have the crossroads. When next we come we can be sixty miles inside the land of the Bretons before they even know it. When we attack Cancale it will come as a complete shock to them. After that, we may build here."

Lord Bertrand had dismounted next to me and he had heard my words, "I think this Lord Salomon of Saint-Lô will not let us build anything here."

56

"Then we raid Saint-Lô and destroy it."

Lord Bertrand laughed, "You seek more land than your father."

"I do as my father did. I seek security. We will not countenance reducing Saint-Lô until we have punished Cancale but this land is good horse country."

"You are right there and with a hall such as the Haugr then a few men on horses could control this whole land."

We found the village bread oven. We were able to save the bread before it was burned and my men use the prepared dough to bake more. The villagers had food and we took that too. While our horses drank, we ate.

"Send a rider back to Folki. Tell him that when he has eaten he can follow us to Coutances."

Snorri nodded, "Aye jarl."

Chapter 5

I turned to my men, "Come let us advance on Coutances." I was about to lead the men off again when Erik Gillesson and two of his men rode in.

"Jarl, there are horsemen coming from Coutances. We saw them five Roman miles from here. There are fifty of them. They are led by the six mailed riders from Saint-Lô. My brothers and the others are shadowing them. They will tell us if they deviate."

I smacked one hand onto the table. "They have taken the bait! Folki, prepare a shield wall. Riders, mount!"

As we left the village I retrieved my spear and I led my men down the road. Coutances was ten miles away and due south. They would be more tired than when we met them. They would have ridden hard. Rollo Gillesson and his men galloped towards us. Behind them, I could see the banners of the enemy. They were galloping and they were spread out. I had no time to give orders. This battle would be fought as we clashed. It would tell me if we had improved as horsemen. Rollo Gillesson and his men and his men rode around us to join at the rear. Our front rank was filled with mailed warriors.

"Stay behind me, Karl!"

"Aye, jarl!"

This was not the thunderclap of two lines of warriors meeting each other and clashing. There would be no cacophony noise with shattering spears on shields. This was a series of cracks, cries and bangs as we met piecemeal. We were travelling at speed. This was not like riding down a man on foot. The end of my spear wavered up and down. There was almost as much luck in a kill than skill. The six mailed men were Franks and they led the line. They were their best warriors. I aimed it at the chest of the Frank who hurtled towards me. I kept my shield held tightly to my chest. It was slightly bowed. If the Frank's spear caught the rear side it might well slide off. If it hit it on the front then I might be unhorsed.

My spear struck his shield and although he lurched backwards he held his seat and my spear was shattered. His spear smashed into my shield and splinters of wood flew in the air. I

was gripping Dawn's Light with my knees. Had I not been then I
would have been thrown. I drew my sword. Dawn's Light had
begun to swing to my right and I used that swing. Karl barely
managed to move out of my way. I galloped towards the Frank
who was drawing his sword. Already our two bands of horsemen
were intermingled. Our collision had not been cataclysmic. It
had, however, stopped us.

I saw the Frank pull back his sword to sweep it at one of Lord
Bertrand's men who just wore a mail vest. I dug my heels in and
my sword slashed at him and tore some of the mail on his back.
My blade came away bloody. He whirled around, for his horse
had almost stopped and he swung his sword at me. I blocked it
with my shield and lunged at his chest. He was not expecting it
and, as he lurched back, the wound came into contact with the
cantle at the rear of his saddle. His back arced. I swung my shield
around over my horse's head and it hit his sword arm. As Dawn's
Light was also stopped I stood in my stiraps and brought my
sword down on his helmet. He was unable to block the blow for
his shield was on the wrong side. I broke the metal of the helmet
and his eyes glazed over. He fell over the back of his saddle.

"Jarl, watch out!"

One of the Bretons who had followed the Franks lunged at
me with his spear. As I fended it off Karl rode at him and
punched him in the side of the head with the end of my standard.
He fell from his horse. Our superior numbers had won the day
and the horsemen were fleeing.

"Karl go and fetch Folki. Tell him we assault Coutances
now!" My men would have eaten and be following us. I needed
them to march quickly.

"Aye, jarl!"

"Clan of the Horse! Follow them!"

I turned Dawn's Light and followed the fleeing Franks and
Bretons. Two of the mailed Franks remained and over twenty
Bretons. They would be our passage into Coutances. I looked
around and saw that Erik Gillesson was with me still. His leather
jerkin was bespattered with blood. "Erik, keep with the Bretons
and see if you can gain entry to their walls. Do not engage them.
Just follow them into their walls. They will have to leave the
gates open. If they are still open when you reach them then hold
them and we will come to your aid."

"Aye, jarl!"

This would be a long chase. It would take Folki and his men almost two hours to catch up with us. I realised that my men would have to fight on foot if we managed to take the gate. I began to prepare my orders for my men. I looked around. There were still over eighty men with me. It was gone noon. By the time Folki and his men arrived, we would be approaching sunset. The Norns had been spinning. I had made plans and changed them. Now the Norns had changed them again. We had thrown the bones. I would have to see which way they fell.

I slowed down Dawn's Light. The lighter warriors could keep their spears in the backs of our foes. I saw two Bretons lying on the ground. They were testament to the skill of my men. Bertrand's lighter armed men were also outpacing us. Lord Bertrand joined me as we cantered along. "What is your plan, Ragnvald?"

"Try to take the gate while it is open."

"They would be fools to do so."

"There are still two Franks there with them. If the gates are closed then they will be killed."

"I do not understand."

I had only just worked it out. "Coutances is now Breton. There are Franks fighting with them. Lord Salomon has come to an arrangement. Breton and Frank are now joined against us." It was the old adage, *the enemy of my enemy is my friend*. They would be bedfellows until our threat was gone.

The enemy horsemen were tiring now. Gilles' sons had obeyed my orders. They were not engaging the enemy. We were now catching them. The Bretons, led by the Franks had almost exhausted their horses. Timing would be all. We just needed the gates open. Folki, Rollo One Ear and the rest had not fought. When they arrived, they would be eager for battle. Their legs would be tired but they would be ready for war. I hoped that the returning horsemen would sow confusion amongst the enemy ranks.

Suddenly I saw one of the Franks turn his horse and head east along the small track which joined the Roman Road. He was heading for Saint-Lô. Did I let him go or follow him? Coutances was the key. We had to take it and then face whatever Lord Salomon threw at us. I saw that the gates of Coutances were open. Men lined the walls. They had a couple of crossbows. I saw one of my men tumble from his horse as it was hit in the head by a bolt. Luckily, they did not have many of those hated weapons and they took a long time to load. A horseman is a harder target to hit than a slower moving warrior on foot.

Erik disobeyed my orders and I was glad. He did engage the Bretons but he waited until they were in the gate. He and his brother urged their horses on and they used their swords to slay one of the Bretons. He and his horse fell in the gateway. The defenders would have to shift his body before they could close them. Erik and Rollo were stuck in the middle of the Bretons and their men galloped to their aid. I dug my heels in Dawn's Light's flanks and my horse leapt forward. I barged into the rear of the Bretons who were trying to get into the blocked gate. Soren and Leif were with me as well as Karl. Our four horses knocked three riders into the ditch. I swung my sword and it split the spine of a Breton before me. Soren and I reached Erik and Rollo when they were about to be overwhelmed.

I leapt from my horse and handed my reins to Erik. "Take my horse and your men back. You have done enough."

Soren and four other men had dismounted and they ran, with me, up to the blocked gate. Erik and Rollo forced their way back to our advancing men and I ran at the Breton who was trying to close the gates. I swung and took the fingers from his right hand. Karl rammed the standard into the face of the man who was trying to pull the body clear. I put my head behind my shield and launched myself at the mass of men who were trying to bar our way and close the gates. I could leave Lord Bertrand to deal with the remaining horsemen.

"Clan of the Horse! With me!" I knew without looking that, unless they lay dead, Snorri Snorrison, Harold Strong Arm, Haaken the Bold and Leif Sorenson would be behind me. I had seen Soren and Karl dismount. Eight of us would have to hold the gate. "Shield wall!"

We could not form a true shield wall for we had oval shields but we could lock shields and make them try to shift us. I saw Leif Sorenson on one side and Haaken on the other. I held my sword over my shield. The Bretons charged. Half had stayed on the walls to send arrows and bolts at the men milling outside. The rest took any weapon they could find and they tried to butcher us. They hit us hard. One warrior was so keen to get at us that he ran straight into Soren's sword. The press of men had not helped. My sword clanked off a helmet while two spears shattered on my shield. I was forced back a pace. Suddenly I felt a shield in my back. A voice said, "Lord Bertrand sent us, jarl. Help is on its way."

I knew then that we would hold them. I lunged with my sword It was a blind stroke but there were so many faces before me that I hoped I would strike something. An axe hit my shield as I felt my sword strike the soft flesh of a cheek and then grind against a jawbone. I twisted and pulled it out sideways. Harold punched with the pommel of his sword into the face of the man nearest him. He kept punching until the man's eyes glazed over and he started to slip. He was held in place by the press of men.

Suddenly it felt as though we were being pushed from our feet. More men were behind us and, as I regained my balance, the Bretons before me started to slip and slide on the blood and the gore. When two slipped and fell we burst through the gate and into the town. I had quick reactions and I swept my sword backhand across the middle of the Breton warrior before me. My men poured through the gap.

I heard a shout, "Folki and Rollo One Ear are coming!" My men cheered and, in that instant, the resistance of the defenders ended. Their horsemen all lay dead. The Frankish warriors who had come to their aid were dead or fled and we were inside their walls. They poured south towards the other gate. There was no chance of us running after them. We had fought two battles and we wore mail. We turned and began to kill those who remained. I saw the warrior whose horse had been killed by a bolt race up the ladder to the fighting platform. The crossbowman tried to defend himself but horsemen love their horses and he hacked the crossbowman to pieces.

"Clear the gates for Folki and his men. Fetch in the horses."

I looked up and saw Lord Bertrand and his men. They were still mounted. I pointed at the Bretons fleeing for the south gate, "Keep your swords in their backs. Ride through the burgh and make sure they have fled. Kill any warriors that you can find. Close the other gate and make it secure. The Franks will be coming."

We had not escaped unscathed. Karl had a long cut along his cheek. Soren's arm was badly gashed and would need stitching. I saw damaged mail that would need repairing and spoke of wounds beneath. However, we had gained two Breton burghs in one day. That was unheard of. I sheathed my sword and hung my shield from the saddle of Dawn's Light which had just been brought inside the gate. I sling my helmet on the saddle.

"Harold, keep four men here and when the last of our men are inside then bar the gates."

"Aye jarl! A fine victory!"

"Do not tempt the Norns. When we are back in my hall then we will speak of victories and success. Snorri clear the enemy bodies, put them beyond the ditch. We will burn them when time allows."

"Aye jarl."

"Leif, search the houses. Make sure that no one is hiding and seek any treasure that you can."

"Aye jarl."

"Haaken get men to sort out some food. Our warriors have earned it." I waved Karl over, "Fetch the standard."

I hurried down through the town to the west gate. Lord Bertrand had taken it upon himself to secure that gate too. His men were just barring it as I arrived. I climbed up the ladder to the fighting platform. "Two of you stay here on guard until Folki and Rollo One Ear arrive. Karl. I want my standard to fly from this wall. When Lord Salomon comes I would have him know who owns this burgh now. Then find a healer and have your face seen to. It is a mark of honour but it needs cleaning up."

"Yes, jarl."

"And then see to our horses. Have them stabled."

I looked east. There were one or two refugees fleeing towards Saint- Lô. The Franks there would know that we had thwarted their plans and Lord Salomon would come. I turned and looked across the town. I saw that they had a stone church. Their hall would be close by. The Franks and the Bretons liked halls with windows and they made them places that they could defend. Any documents or treasure would be within.

I made my way to the tower. Men cheered me and called my name as I passed them. I waved my arm in acknowledgement. I had raided without my father but this was the first time I had fought two battles on the same day without him. The first he would know of my success would be when I spoke with him.

I found Leif and his men in the hall. He looked pleased with himself. "The lord must have just collected taxes. We have found a chest of coins. And he must have left without his mail for we found a fine suit of mail in one of the chambers."

"We will use this tonight for the jarls and their hearth weru. Is there a warrior hall?"

63

"There is, jarl, Eystein Tall Standing is there searching it."
He lowered his voice. "Will there be more fighting? The horses
suffered today."

"There will be but that is why we brought the spare horses.
One reason I wish the jarls to stay here this night is to discuss my
plan."

He laughed, "Then the Franks are in trouble. You and your
father both have minds which I cannot fathom. I am just a warrior
with a sword and shield but the two of you are something
different."

I heard the sound of Folki and Rollo One Ear as they led their
men over the bridge and through the gate. I left Leif to his work
and headed towards the north gate.

Folki shook his head, "I see there is nothing left for us to do!
Perhaps we can butcher the dead horses!"

"You can have your men stand a watch this night. I want the
jarls and the hearth weru in the lord's hall this night. We need to
plan for the morning."

"We shall do that. Did you lose many men? We saw their
dead."

"No, we lost few because we took them by surprise. If they
had not tried to come to the aid of Périers then it might have been
different. They thought us a raid by a small band of Vikings. The
next battle will be harder."

I sought Karl and our horses. I examined Dawn's Light. She
had suffered no wounds but I would ride Allfather's Gift on the
morrow. It was not the youngest horse and I rarely rode it but my
father had given it to me when we had defeated the Count of
Carentan. We would not have to ride far.

I noticed that Karl's face had been stitched. "It will itch when
it heals."

"I know jarl. It is a small price to pay. I am still alive and I
killed your enemies. Life is good."

"We sleep in the hall this night."

"Jarl I would sleep here, with the horses."

"Are you certain?"

"Yes, jarl. I am weary and I know that my horse saved me
twice today. He turned when I was too slow and the blade which
would have taken my head just gave me a scar. I would watch
over our mounts."

Our men used the bread from the town and whatever food
they could find to make a stew. For many years after men called

64

it Coutances stew. They found chickens and hams as well as freshly collected mushrooms. Added to the spring greens and cider they discovered it made a pleasant meal.

The hall was full. I sat with my jarls and leaders at one table. "We were lucky today. The Allfather was watching over us."

"He was that. We lost barely twenty men and yet we slew more than a hundred. There were also five Franks we slew."

I nodded, "Find five warriors who excelled themselves this day. If they have no mail then give them the byrnies. They are well made."

"You could sell them, jarl. This was your victory. You made the right decision at the perfect time."

"No, Folki, we are in this together. I need not the coin."

Rollo One Ear poured himself more cider. "I would have said that we were done, jarl but I can tell from your words that we have not."

"The Franks cannot let us stay here. They must have made some sort of pact with the Bretons. That is the only explanation for the presence of the six Franks. We have no prisoners else we would know for certain. Lord Salomon will come. However, it is my intention to make him come to us and to come here angry. I want every rider who has a fresh mount to ride with me tomorrow. We will raid to the south of Saint-Lô."

Folki threw a chicken bone to one of the dogs which had remained when the Bretons had fled. "You intend to draw them here."

"I do. I want caltrops making tomorrow and we will seed the ground by the east gate with them. We will burn the bodies. At this time of the year, the wind is from the west. The smell will spread to Saint-Lô. We will clear the ditches and embed stakes. We did not have to breach this wall and it is sound. It is not the Haugr but it will do. I want Lord Salomon to chase us back here. We will ride a path through the caltrops and into the town. His men and horses will fall foul of caltrops, arrows and ditches. We will hurt him. When we are rested we will sortie from another gate and attack him."

"Perhaps he will not come."

I looked at Erik Gillesson, "If he does not then that means he fears us and if he does then we shall take Saint-Lô. For now, I am happy that have cleared the enemies from our path at Tvímánuður. I am confident now that we can take a hundred horsemen through this Breton land and attack Cancale from the land and the sea. We have never done that yet. This might be the way we raid in the future."

I was tired and I slept well. Even so, I was awake before dawn and I walked the fighting platform and visited the sentries. "Any sign of the Franks?"

"None jarl. It has been quiet save for the carrion feasting on flesh."

I nodded and walked all around the fighting platform. I saw that they had built the wall hurriedly. The wood was not tightly bound. There were gaps and it was green wood. It would split. They had built in a hurry. I stopped at the east gate. The warriors on watch gave me space to stare towards a Saint-Lô I could not see. I had thought to raid to Cancale but perhaps the Norns had different plans for me. Taking Périers and Coutances had been far easier than we could have hoped. The vaunted Breton and Frankish horsemen were little better than we were and their foot warriors could not compete with mine. What would my father do? Then I realised that I was beyond my father. I was jarl and I made the decisions. My plan was still a good one. We would tempt the Franks from their walls.

I smelled bread. Someone had fired the bread oven and, even better, had made fresh bread. A man could fight all day with hot fresh bread and butter in his belly. I followed my nose to the smell. It was Rollo One Ear. "I did not know you could bake!"

"My mother taught me while my ear was healing. I find it helps me to knead the dough and I like the magic that happens."

"Is it ready?"

"It will not be long. I will fetch beer. That is the secret of good bread. Add beer to it." He poured me a horn.

"Where is Jarl Thorbolt these days? I did not see him when I visited the Haugr."

"He left last year. He and his men fell out with my father. I was not there and I know not the reason. The rumour is that he went to raid the men of Cent."

"He was a good warrior."

"Aye, he was."

He brought out the fresh loaves. There were ten of them. They were too hot to eat and would make me ill but I enjoyed smelling the bread. The anticipation of fresh bread made it taste even better. Others followed their noses and, when the bread was cool enough, I cut a large piece and smeared it with butter which melted almost immediately. I added cheese and ate a blissful breakfast.

Niels Eriksson came over. He was the son of Erik One Arm. Rollo One Ear had told me he was with the warband but I had not had the chance to speak with him yet. He was young and he looked more like his mother than his father. "I was sorry to hear that your father died, Niels."

He nodded, "Thank you, jarl. He was ill for some time. It was a mercy when he went. We put his sword in his good hand. I think he waited until I was a warrior. He gave me his sword and made me swear to follow Jarl Hrolf and his son."

"And I am glad that you do. Today or tomorrow there may be bloodwork. This will test you. You know that?"

"Aye, jarl. I will be ready."

I left the hall knowing that with men like this behind me I could do anything. Karl had saddled my horse and men were now preparing themselves for whatever the day brought. There was a happy feeling in the town. We had won two battles. We were well fed and we had walls behind which to fight. The weight of expectation was on my shoulders. I had to bring them to battle or this would be wasted. I led my men east and south. There were many farms around Quibou and Canisy. This was rich farmland. My plan was simple. We would slay every warrior and steal every animal until the Franks tired of it and came to send us home.

My scouts and lightly armoured men formed a screen before us. They spread out in a line half a mile wide. Soon, some of them returned driving animals before them. Their swords were bloody. I replaced the ones who headed back to Coutances with fresh men. I saw smoke appearing on the skyline as my men burned the farms they had taken. As the number of animals and bloody swords increased so we moved closer to our scouts. We had taken no strongholds but, as we passed Quibou, I saw the bodies of half a dozen warriors who had defended their farms. My men had had orders to drive women and children east. Lord Salomon would hear of us and he would do something!

The burning of the farms alerted those in Canisy and it was empty by the time we reached it. They had taken all of value and so we burned the town and turned to raid further south. Saint-Lô was just five miles away. This was as far as I wished us to travel. I had thirty warriors left with me. The rest were driving animals and taking sacks of supplies back to Coutances. I wished to scout

out the land which we had not seen before. This was land which was deep into Frankish held territory. We had never raided this far south. My father had once travelled this way but that was many years earlier.

We saw just isolated farms and no towns over the next mile or so. I wheeled my grey around and headed back to Coutances. We had been travelling along the small rural road for a short time when Karl said, "Jarl, there are horsemen to the south of us."

I turned and saw that he was correct. The ground rose and fell in small hills and hollows. They were at the top of one of the hills. They must have seen us at the same time as we saw them. It was not in our nature to run away and so I turned my men and we headed to meet them. We did not gallop. We were almost fourteen miles from safety. The last thing we needed was to be unhorsed in this land. Lord Salomon would punish us for such a mistake. The men who rode towards us numbered less than twenty. It was only after that I realised they thought that we were Lord Salomon's men. On horseback, we did not look like Vikings. They were less than two hundred paces from us when they realised their mistake. They had galloped hard to reach us and I saw that their horses were lathered. They turned and tried to run.

"After them!"

We could afford to chase them a short way. If we could capture one then we might discover more about the leaders of the men of this land. My father liked to know his enemy. Allfather's Gift was no longer a young horse. Others raced ahead of me. I saw Bergil Svensson lead the chase. He swung his blade and it bit into the back of a Frank who wore no mail. He tumbled from his horse. A second turned to see how close we were and in that moment of inattention, his horse found a rabbit hole and threw the rider.

"Hold. Save your horses." I had reached the warrior slain by Bergil. His shield was green with a red diagonal line across it. These were not the men of Lord Salomon. Karl appeared behind me. "Take his weapons and his horse." Karl dismounted to search him and I headed for the rider who had fallen.

Bergil had dismounted and he looked up, "Jarl, he is badly hurt. He will die. Should I give him the warrior's death?"

I dismounted. "He is a Christian. He may not wish that." I knelt and saw that this was a youth. He had barely begun to shave. He opened his eyes and stared fearfully at me. I took off my helmet and I smiled. "You are hurt, young Frank. I fear you are to die. Would you have us end your life?"

He winced as pain coursed through his body. "I cannot move."

I nodded, "Your back is broken. You may live for some time but death is coming."

"I cannot die without confession."

"I am no priest."

He tried to move his hands but could not. "Put my cross in my hand, I beg you."

I took the cross from around his neck. It was a well-carved wooden one. I placed it in his hand. He closed his eyes and mumbled a litany of some kind. I guessed he was confessing his sins. I slipped my seax into my left hand. He opened his eyes. "Do you wish your sword in your hand?"

He said, "No." he seemed to see me for the first time. "You are a Viking, a pagan!" His eyes widened. "We thought you were the men of Lord Salomon. We came to ask what you were doing in our lands."

"Our lands?"

"Count Louis rules the lands around Caen and west." He winced. "I beg you barbarian end my life now. I am ..."

I plunged my seax into the vein in his neck. Warm blood gushed and he died. "Go to your God young warrior. Today the Norns cut your thread. Today was your time."

We took the two horses and the two Frank's weapons back to Coutances. We did not see any other riders. I was silent as we rode. Harold asked, "What is bothering you, jarl?"

I smiled, "Nothing Harold. I am taking in what I learned from that young warrior. There is a lord who is greater than Lord Salomon; a Count Louis. I am guessing there must be some sort of dispute between them. They thought we were Lord Salomon's men. Perhaps, and here I am just guessing, Lord Salomon is trying to enlarge his own lands. Joining with the Bretons might not be just a way of defending against us. This is the first time in years that we have ventured south. The alliance may not be against us but against Count Louis."

There was much I did not know about my enemies. We had stayed behind our walls and used the sea to raid far and wide. King Charles the Bald ruled Frankia. That was all that I knew. Were there divisions in that land? If there was a rift then we might be able to exploit it.

We reached our new walls safely. Folki and Rollo One Ear were keen to discover what had happened. I told them that night as we ate. "We should have taken a prisoner. I know there is a Duke of the Bretons. He fights with the King of Frankia. This Lord Salomon, who is he?" I looked at Lord Bertrand.

"I have never heard the name. I know that there were lords who ruled this land from Caen. Count Louis sounds like a Frank. To be truthful, Ragnvald, this Salomon sounds like a Breton name."

"Yet he rules a Frankish town."

Bertrand shrugged. "Franks and Bretons are not like Vikings. The royal families marry their children to gain thrones. This Salomon may have a Breton father but he could have married someone who is of royal blood, Frank blood."

Harold was a simple warrior, "It does not affect us, jarl."

"It may do. We ride tomorrow but I intend to close with the walls of Saint-Lô. We have taken much already. Tomorrow we stay together and see if this Lord Salomon comes to fight us or not. Then we burn this town and head home."

Folki looked disappointed. "I have yet to wet my blade."

"We are not yet home."

I rode Dawn's Light as we headed towards Saint-Lô. Erik's scouts rode back, when we were just a mile from Coutances. "Jarl, an army comes. They have the bird on the yellow shield."

"Lord Salomon!" I looked around for any sign of somewhere we could use for an ambush. "Ride back to Jarl Folki and tell him that our enemy comes." I took out my sword and pointed up to a stand of trees on a small rise. "Up there."

We would be a hundred paces from the road but, more importantly, there would be dead ground behind the trees. We would be hidden. If this Frank was coming to retake his town then I had the choice of attacking him now or letting him close with our men and catching him between our walls and us. We reached the woods and I dismounted and, with Lord Bertrand, crept back to the woods where we could watch Lord Salomon.

I saw the army. It was made up largely of men on foot. There were a few mailed horsemen but also many other mounted men who appeared to be armed with throwing javelins. There were too many for us to attack. The horsemen flanked the marching men on foot. I decided to watch and to wait. There was no baggage. The rear was guarded by another twenty mailed horsemen. They bore the sign of Lord Salomon. When they had gone we returned to our waiting men.

"What do we do, jarl?"

"We let them attack Coutances. When they have surrounded it, and begin to assault their gates, then we attack."

Lord Bertrand had a good mind for war, "Those were Breton horsemen who carried the javelins, Ragnvald. They are clever warriors. They ride close and throw their javelins. They ride off before you can close with them. When I was young I saw them in action. My father feared them."

I nodded, "Then we try to kill them before they can kill us." We mounted and rode parallel to the road. I was silent as I tried to work out what was happening. The world was a wider place than our little peninsula. We knew little of Frankia and Brittany and even less about the lands of the Saxons to the north of us. I needed to leave my home and find out more.

Our foes reached Coutances not long after the sun had reached its zenith. Once again, we found woods to the north of the town and waited there. I saw that Folki and Rollo One Ear had lined the walls with our men. I watched arrows flying from the walls. Their horsemen dismounted. Bertrand was with me again. "We wait until they commit to an attack on the walls and we charge them. If their Bretons are on foot then they are not a threat. Have your light horse drive off their horses and we will try to get to their lord."

"A bold move."

"Sometimes a single bold move can achieve victory. I waved my arm around them all. "When you hear me order you to fall back then do so!" I mounted my horse and said to Karl. "I need you to watch my back. The standard flies over the walls. Today you can use your shield and your sword."

I waited and I watched. They had concentrated all of their forces on the east gate. Had we wanted to we could have entered the town through either the west or the north gate. The Franks and the Bretons had some crossbows. They began to use them against the men on the walls. They were supported by warriors who hurled javelins and others who used slingshots. The archers behind the walls dealt with them. Then I saw them preparing men to march behind shields. They had larger shields and managed to get a little closer to the walls and then they found the caltrops my men had sown. In the confusion, my archers slew more of the enemy. I began to wonder if we would be needed to charge at all.

The Franks and Bretons withdrew. A heated debate ensued. A horn sounded and they moved forward again.

This time they followed the same path but went more slowly. Bodies lay over the caltrops and the ones which remained could be avoided. When they reached the ditch and the bridge they did not descend into the ditch. Instead, they used the large shields as bridges and a line of eighty men crossed to the walls. I saw that they had axes and logs. They began to batter the walls. Another eighty men waited to follow across when they had breached our walls. Now was our time.

I turned and raised my sword. "Now is the time of the Clan of the Horse!" I dug my heels in and led my men down the almost imperceptible slope. Behind me, my mailed warriors thundered. I saw Erik lead the lightly armed men for the horse herd which was grazing a mile from the main camp. Our hooves alerted the enemy. Lord Salomon or one of his lieutenants quickly turned their eighty men and the rest of their army to face us. It meant those attacking the walls were without support. It takes time to turn a line of warriors from east to north and we were approaching rapidly. They were not locked when we hit them.

Dawn's Light struck the shield of one Frank as I swept my sword across the head of a second. I raised my sword and brought it down onto the head of a third. Frankish horns sounded. I saw mailed men running towards their horses. Their horses were already being driven away, their horse guards, dead. Our attack had been so speed and our impact so great that we were through them and I began to wheel around.

I discovered then that the horns had been sounded to bring the whole army back to their lord. I held up my sword, "Reform!"

There were empty saddles, eight of them. Some of my warriors had suffered wounds. We still had ninety mounted men. Then I saw that the Franks and the Bretons had formed a triple circle of warriors around their lords. I recognised the third rank as the javelin men I had been told about.

"Do we charge again, jarl?"

I turned to Soren, "I think not, Soren. They have two ranks of spears and they are backed by javelins. We would not break through."

Bertrand pointed to the walls. "Folki could bring the men from the town. They have archers."

I said nothing but I waited. I had intended to make this raid to clear the way for our attack at Tvímánuður. We had not lost many men. If we attacked this band then I would expect to lose at least a third of my men and for what? Even if we destroyed them we could not take Saint-Lô. That had ramparts and would require a siege.

It was strange. There were three groups of warriors and we all waited. The deadlock was broken when, after a debate amongst the Franks and Bretons, two figures left their ranks and walked towards us. One was a priest and the other was a boy with neither helmet nor shield. I dismounted. "Lord Bertrand, it seems they wish to speak with us."

We took off our helmets and walked down to meet them. The youth, for I could now see that he was older than a boy, spoke first, "I am Wigo, son of Lord Salomon. My father wishes to speak with you."

I nodded, "And he sends a priest and a child in case I wish to continue to fight. He must not value you."

Wigo flushed but the priest said, "It is known than some of the Northmen married Christian women. The king thought that this might be greeted with less violence than if he came."

"Tell him that I will speak with him and he is safe so long as my helmet is with my horse." Wigo ran back to his father. "A brave boy."

The priest nodded, "He is. He said he was not afraid of a barbarian."

I gestured to Bertrand. "You know that Lord Bertrand is a Frank and a Christian. He might be insulted by the title you afford him."

The priest's eyes turned cold. "Then he is worse than a barbarian! You are a pagan and know not the error of your ways but for a Christian to fight for one is beyond the pale!"

I turned to see if Lord Bertrand was angry. He smiled, "Cluck in your own barnyard, priest! I am happy with the choices I have made. My lord here has more nobility than any Frank I have met."

Lord Salomon and his son reached us. He nodded and said, "You know who I am but who are you? I know you are Viking but you barbarians all look the same to me. What do you want in our land?"

"I am Ragnvald son of Hrolf the Horseman of the Haugr." I saw from his eyes that he recognised my father's name. "As for what I am doing here? I am finishing what we started when we

73

drove the Franks from Carentan. The Bretons took what we had captured. I am reclaiming it."

"This land was Breton before the Franks took it."

"You are not a Frank?"

"I am the cousin of Erispoe, Duke of Brittany."

"Yet Saint-Lô is ruled by King Charles."

He said nothing but smiled. I allowed the silence to stretch a little. He broke it. "What happens now, Viking? Do you bring your men from Coutances and we fight to the death?"

"My men would like nothing more. We have your horses and you have no baggage. When you came here what thought you? Did you believe we would simply ride away?"

The priest said, "You did the last time."

"And perhaps now we stay."

"You could be our allies." King Charles has great faith in me. One day I shall be King of Brittany. If you are my ally I may allow your people to keep their homes."

I laughed, "I am sorry but I trust not a Frank and a Breton even less. As for letting us live in our homes... your bones would mark your passage home if ever you tried."

I could see that my laughter had offended him. He coloured. "Then what will it cost to send you home?"

"We keep your horses and you pay us a thousand gold pieces each year. If you do so then I promise that the land around Saint-Lô, for twenty miles in every direction, will not be raided by my clan."

The priest snorted, "A thousand gold pieces? You could build a cathedral for that."

"True, priest, but would we allow you to do that?"

The Breton was beaten. His shoulders slumped, "Very well. We agree. Will you leave now?"

I laughed, "Do you think me a fool? Your son and the priest will be hostages until the first payment is made. The second will be on exactly the same date next year. If not then we put Saint-Lô to the sword."

Lord Salomon looked at his son. He put his arm around his shoulder, "Fear not, Wigo. You will have just a short time to endure the stink of a barbarian. The gold will soon be sent."

"One more insult and the price will go up!"

Lord Salomon nodded and headed back to his men. I said, over my shoulder, "Karl go and fetch a couple of horses for these two guests. We have plenty to choose from!"

Chapter 6

Folki was unhappy that they had not had the chance to fight the Franks and the Bretons. "Think of Cancale. You have a quarter share of the gold. You and your men will be rich. When we raid at Tvímánuður you will have all the fighting you wish and even more treasure."

"But this means I cannot raid south of my walls!"

"I do not think that they will pay us next year. I will keep my word but they will renege on the payment."

Taking everything of value and after burning the walls and the houses of Coutances, we headed home. I rode with the young Breton lord and the priest. They assiduously avoided speaking with me. That did not worry me. With only thirty miles to travel and plenty of spare horses, we reached home in one day. Folki and Rollo One Ear stayed one night so that we could share our bounty. They felt guilty having done less work than the horsemen.

"Your presence meant we did not have to fight. When the ransom arrives, I will send your share."

Mathilde was happy to have a priest in the hall but less so to have a Breton. Her family had suffered at the hands of the Bretons. I summoned Ragnvald. "I would have you and Arne keep our guest away from your mother. She does not like his presence. Treat him well. He is surety against the ransom we will receive."

He seemed quite happy about the task and he led Wigo, who looked to be just two or three years older than he was, away. His absence from my hall made my life easier and I had less to worry about. When Gilles' sons and Lord Bertrand left us my hall and my walls felt empty. I felt alone when I was with my son and my wife. I missed Rollo. I forced myself into action.

I visited Harold, my shipwright. "Will she be ready to raid in Tvímánuður?"

"She could raid tomorrow. Those two voyages did not harm her at all. She is a young ship. You can push her more than you do." Harold was an old-fashioned Viking. He has been brought up by Harold Fast Sailing and trained by Sven the Helmsman. He knew his business.

"And who shall captain her? I will be on my horse. I need someone to sail my drekar. I have others to lead my men."

He stroked the sheerstrake of the drekar and then looked up at the mast. I knew what he was doing. He was running through the warriors who might be able to handle such a large drekar. "When we came here from the Haugr there was a young man who helped Harold Fast Sailing; Magnús the Fish."

I nodded. He had been so named for his skill in swimming. When Harold Fast Sailing needed work below the waterline then Magnús took on the task. "I remember him."

"He did not like to live at the Haugr without Harold and Sven. He came with his young wife and son here a year since. He has a fishing boat and he catches fish now."

"He has not taken an oar?"

"No, jarl. He is no warrior but he knows how to sail. He was a ship's boy and served with Harold. I know that Harold Fast Sailing thought well of him."

I had learned, from my father, to trust the men who served me. "Then let us visit with him."

He was four hundred paces offshore. He had baskets at the bottom of the sea for crabs and lobsters. Harold waved and when Magnús saw us he waved back. He hoisted his small sail and was soon at the beach and jumping ashore.

"Jarl, this is an honour." He pointed to the blue crustaceans in his boat. "Do you wish a lobster?"

I shook my head, "I confess they are fine specimens but I came here to offer you the chance to be my helmsman when next we raid."

His eyes widened, "Helmsman on a drekar? It would be an honour. Do you think I can do it?"

"Harold Fast Sailing thought so."

He looked at Harold, "Truly?"

"I do not lie, Magnús and I think that you can do this."

He smiled, "I confess that I have sailed further in my little ship than my wife knows. I took her all the way to the islands off Cancale when the winds were favourable. If that is where you wish to raid then I know the waters there. I have sailed them."

"That is perfect then and shows that I have made the right choice. I will not be on the drekar but you will have Harold, Snorri, Leif and Haaken. They have more experience than

76

enough. You will be given a share of the treasure and we hope that it will be a good haul."

"Then I accept, jarl, thank you."

Our two hostages ate with us that night. Mathilde was still wary of them but the fact that one was a priest made her less anxious. She did not say much and it was left to me to make conversation. Ragnvald and Wigo appeared to get on. They were close in age. I spoke with the priest. "Did you come from the land of the Bretons with Lord Salomon?"

He shook his head. "I was a priest who served the Archbishop in Paris. I was bound for better things. The King himself sent me to act as God's messenger to Lord Salomon."

The priest was not only pretentious he was also a liar. He had been sent as a spy to make sure that this Breton obeyed his new master. If he was a Breton then he sought to oust Duke Erispoe. I nodded. I could play games too. "Then you have a great deal of influence."

He smiled and sipped my wine. "More than many priests, that is true. I will be rewarded one day. A bishop first and then who knows? Archbishop?"

He had a smug look on his face. I smiled at my wife, "What do you think, my love? We are dining with someone who may be an archbishop."

That appealed to the Christian in my wife and she began to speak with the priest. It allowed me to drink and to listen to the conversation between Wigo and Ragnvald. From it, I also learned much. Wigo was as ambitious as his father. I now understood why the Lord of Caen was wary of Lord Salomon. The Franks were at war with one another and there were different parties vying for the throne. The Lord of Caen supported King Charles' brother Lothair. Lord Salomon was attempting to gain the Dukedom of Brittany from his cousin Duke Erispoe. They were forming alliances to help them gain what they wanted. I could see why King Charles chose Saint-Lô. It was close to Brittany and would keep the Lord of Caen looking over his shoulder. Now that I understood everyone's motives, I was satisfied.

The ransom arrived two days later. The escort for the treasure took Wigo and the ambitious priest home. I sought out Ragnvald when the Breton lordling had left. "What did you learn from the Breton lordling?"

"The Duke of Brittany makes war on the King of the Franks. It is being fought far to the south of here. There will not be as many men for us to fight. Wigo hoped to be fighting alongside his father. He seemed to think that there will be a battle between his father and the Duke. His father will lead Franks into battle."

His voice told me that he had got on well with the hostage. "What did you think of the Breton?"

"I liked him. He will be a king one day. I would be king,"

It was not the answer I expected. "We do not have kings."

He shrugged, "Perhaps we should. You and grandfather rule like kings. You should have the titles."

Was this the curse again? This did not sound like my father, or me and certainly not Rollo. I left him and went to my stables. I found comfort in horses. I groomed my horses and found that I was calmer than I had been. What did I do about my son? My warriors thought he was a hero and yet I had seen a totally different side to him. He could never lead the clan. Rollo was my heir.

I sent the ransom to my jarls and lords. We still had a couple of months before we raided. My home did not need me and I felt lonely in my own hall. I left for the Haugr. I needed to speak with my father and Rollo. I had decisions to make before we raided. I went alone and I took Dawn's Light. I did not go the short way. I rode to Gilles' farm first. I did not visit. I just watched his men and his son working with the horses. That was my father's legacy. While we went to war, Gilles prepared horses for us. I rode up the coast to the Haugr. The church on the spit of land always seemed, to me, to symbolise our people. It was a Christian church but my father had made it for my mother. He would never convert but he respected my mother and her religion. I did the same for my wife. I could not see a Christian doing the same for us. Drekar bobbed in the harbour. Despite our horses, we were still raiders from the sea. We were still Vikings.

As I approached the Haugr from the east I was able to watch my grandfather and son as they rode along the beach. They both had spears and my father's servants had laid out hoops which they were spearing. My son was keeping pace with my father. His horse was the same size as my father's. My son had grown. Although he was not spearing as many as my father he was very impressive. I waited until they had finished before I dug my heels in and headed over.

Rollo saw me and galloped towards me. He threw himself from the saddle and leapt up to me. "Father! I have missed you!

Tell me all!" It was the welcome I wanted from Ragnvald and never received.

I clasped his arm. He was becoming almost as tall as me now. He was almost a man. I had not seen him for some time and he had grown. "We have had battles and we have defeated Frank and Breton. We have great stores of treasure in our hall and I have missed you!"

"Will you stay? I have much to show you!"

"A few days and then I prepare a raid on the Bretons."

My father came over, "Take the horses to the stable and I will speak with your father." When he led our three horses off my father said, "Rollo One Ear told me some of what happened. You need to tell me all for I believe there were things unsaid."

I nodded, "I fear that there are Franks and Bretons who play a game of thrones. We are pawns and we are in the middle. I need your advice."

"Then use my old ears and I will see if I can dredge some thoughts from beneath this thatch of white." I told him everything; including that which was speculation. He nodded when I had finished and Rollo had returned. "You have done well my son. You have power here and do not know it. When you raid you will weaken the Bretons but, as they make war on the Franks then you will have a greater chance of success. This Breton lord plays a dangerous game. I would avoid an alliance with him. It is better that you look to our people."

"Where is Jarl Thorbolt? His men would be an asset we could use."

My father shook his head, "He suddenly left. I blame myself. He wanted to be a powerful lord and he always saw me as someone who was above him. I never meant it thus. He wished to carve out his own land. He and Erik Green Eye had a falling out. I think that it was to do with me."

I put my hand on my father's arm. "You have no reason to reproach yourself. Some men have a streak inside them which destroys them."

"Ragnvald?"

I gave a slight shake of the head. It was not seemly to speak of such things while Rollo was there. I looked at Rollo. "And how is my son?"

"He is a horseman. As you can see he grows so fast that I wonder what is going on inside him. He is three fingers taller now than when you left him with me. This will be the tallest Viking I have ever seen."

I saw Rollo swell up with pride. I looked at him with new eyes. He was big. I hazarded a guess that he was now bigger by a hand than his brother and he would soon catch up with me. What did that portend? I smiled, "You are growing. Perhaps it is the air here or the food your grandmother feeds you. Would you wish to come home with me?"

He looked at my father and then at me. "I still have much to learn here and, if I am to speak from my heart, life is better here."

It was like a knife to my heart. It was confirmation of the hardship one brother had inflicted upon the other. They had common blood and that was all. It had even stopped him growing. Rollo's size was nothing to do with his grandmother's cooking, it was to do with Ragnvald. Freed from the tyranny of Ragnvald his body was making him the warrior he was meant to be. I forced a smile, "Of course, I will not be back here now until after Tvímánuður. I would have you return with me then." I put my hand on his shoulder. "But whatever happens it will be your decision."

Rollo nodded, "Aye, father, that would be good. My grandfather's hearth weru are teaching me how to be a better warrior. I will be able to handle myself... whatever happens."

When I returned to my home I threw myself into the raid. It helped me avoid a confrontation with Ragnvald. I knew that he was now very popular with all who lived in our stad. Ironically, I liked him less. Mathilde noticed my demeanour and, one night, as we lay in our bed with my youngest daughter mercifully asleep in her own bed, she asked me the reason for my behaviour.

I had kept it from her merely because we had rarely been alone. One or other of the girls normally shared our bed with us and at meal times Ragnvald was there. I was keeping no secrets from her. When I told her, she was appalled. "He should be punished!"

"He has been. What has been done cannot be undone. We must prepare for the time when Rollo returns here. Ragnvald is now strutting around the stad like a young cockerel. All the other young boys follow him. I do not want Rollo to be isolated. We will have to think of some way of protecting him without being seen to do so."

She cuddled closer to me. "I am sorry, husband. I did not know and I have been thinking bad thoughts about you. I will have to confess my sins to the priest."

I laughed, "I worry not about bad thoughts my love. You were not to know what was going on. I could not tell you earlier. I beg you not to change in your attitude to Ragnvald. If you do then it will drive him further from us. Perhaps, after this raid, he will have grown up a little more. He is not yet a man."

"I will. Women can keep secrets too."

I did not know enough about the land we would be raiding. I sought out Magnús the Fish. "You said you had sailed to the islands off Cancale." He nodded. "How long did it take you to sail there?"

"I was lucky with the winds. I was there and back in daylight."

"Could you take me?"

"I could but I would not be able to guarantee that we would be back in one day. We might have to either lay up or risk a journey in the dark."

"I am not worried about that. When you attack then you will be sailing in the dark."

He nodded, "True." He looked up at the pennant on his fishing boat. "The winds are set fair at the moment. If you do not mind leaving in the middle of the night…"

"I will be ready."

"Then I will see you at my boat."

I took neither mail nor helmet. I was a fisherman and I would play the part. I had a bow with me and my short sword. I had my best seal skin boots and my seal skin cape. Magnús the Fish's wife saw us off. He would soon be a father. His son would have a father who would be not only rich but highly respected. It was *wyrd*. The wind was from the east. It would serve us both ways. Coming back would be trickier but as that would be in daylight I did not worry overmuch. I had no chance to look at the land we had recently captured. It was a shadow to the east but, as dawn broke I saw the island that was Mont St. Michel ahead. This had an abbey but there was also a stronghold. The treasures which lay within would be riches beyond our wildest dreams but the price we would have to pay made it unlikely that we would raid. There were easier targets.

As the sun came up and we headed south and west, we saw other fishing boats. There were Breton boats and there were

Franks. As Magnús told me, they did not bother each other. They were farmers of the sea and there was an unspoken truce upon the water. I saw the two islands he had told me about. I saw a tendril of smoke rising in the sky. "Could you go further south? I would like to see the place whence that smoke rises."

"It will add to our journey but I can reach there."

We had seen a few collections of huts along the coast. They marked where families of fishermen, like Mathilde's family, made their living. The one I had spied looked a little bigger than the others. As we neared it I saw that the boats which used it were at sea. There were twenty homes but no wall and no tower. More importantly, there was a stream which emptied into the sea. It would not slow us down but it might delay pursuit.

"I have seen enough. Let us return home." Our voyage north was slower. Magnús the Fish took us due north to take advantage of the wind. I spied other islands on our way north. Smaller than Sarnia and Angia they were uninhabited. I wondered if they might make good places to build a stronghold. If there was water on them then they would be impregnable. We made it home a couple of hours after the sun had set.

"Thank you, Magnús the Fish. I now know how we will take this town."

"And I am more confident about sailing your drekar."

"You will do more than that, Magnús the Fish. You will lead our fleet!" I left him open-mouthed.

We would have more horsemen this time. The forty Breton horses we had captured were added to our herds and more of our young men chose to ride with us. Of course, they had no mail. All began to make the oval shield they would need. I made sure that our blacksmith made spearheads. We had plenty of swords. We had taken a great number from the dead Franks and Bretons. Lord Bertrand arrived first with his men. He still only had ten warriors who were mailed but the rest had a leather jerkin which was studded with metal. We had found it to be an effective way of protecting horsemen.

He sat with me in my hall and, as we drank, told me what he had been thinking. "Those Breton horsemen with the javelins, they will be a problem." I nodded. "I have come up with a solution. I have twenty of my men who have been training with javelins. They may not be as good as the Bretons yet but they are improving. We have to stop them destroying our mailed men. We counter their javelins with ours."

"Good. I have spoken with Folki and Rollo One Ear. We need to time our attack perfectly. There are two islands off Cancale. Magnús the Fish knows of them. They will stand out to sea with masts stepped and await our signal. Four miles south of Cancale is a small stream and a fishing village. It can be seen from the islands. We light a fire when we are there. That way we will arrive at Cancale at the same time as our ships. They will have to divide their forces. I intend to leave half a dozen men there with the spare horses. I do not fear pursuit from Cancale but there are other Breton strongholds. Even though there are many men with the Duke they will still leave a garrison."

Ragnvald had used the coins he had been given to have a helmet made. Of course, as soon as he did that then the other ships' boys emulated him. Magnús the Fish pointed out that they would not be able to wear them while working on the ship but they insisted that they would be useful, "Last time we were attacked when we moored. This time we can fight back."

The horsemen left before the ships. We knew how long both would take and timing would be all. We had spare horses. We did not have enough for every rider but enough for us to ride without exhausting our beasts. We rode fifty miles that first day. We passed through Lessay, Périers and Coutances. All were unoccupied. Our scouts found a small dell in a wooded area. There was a stream and there was grazing. I made certain that we had plenty of sentries. I was not particularly worried. Lord Bertrand had confirmed the rumour of war. The Bretons had defeated the Franks in a battle to the south of us at a place called, Jengland-Beslé. We had an opportunity to strike while they were distracted.

When we left, the next morning, we passed through a land devoid of any stronghold. There were isolated farms. This would be a good land for us to colonise. I would not break my word but when Lord Salomon did then we would take it. The huge island stronghold of Mont St. Michel was awe-inspiring. We could not hide from it for it towered high above the land. There were no boats in the small harbour. I wondered what they made of us. Perhaps, like the warriors from Caen, they mistook us for Franks or Bretons. Either way, I was unworried. We would be within sight of the town by dawn the next day.

The scouts reported that there were no warriors at the crossing by the river. It meant that we were able to take the town without a single blow being struck. I told the people there that if they cooperated we would do them no harm and we would be gone by the end of the next day. I told them that if they did not cooperate we would destroy every one of their fishing boats! They complied with our request.

I hoped that, by now, Magnús the Fish was heading for the two islands we could see to the north of us. I had my men collect dry wood ready for the signal fire. We waited until it was dark of night. There was no moon and there were clouds. The wood soon burned. It was like a beacon in the night. They would probably see it in Cancale and might wonder what it meant.

Karls' sharp eyes picked out the tiny pinprick of light which flashed three times. It stopped and then it repeated. I had four men hold a cloak in front of the fire and then lower it three times. Leaving the ten men who would guard our spare horses we rode the four miles up the coast to Cancale. The three drekar would be rowed thence by warriors eager for vengeance. We had new ships' boys but we remembered the ones we had lost.

When I had sailed with Magnús the Fish I had had the opportunity to study, at a distance, the defences of the town. The harbour had no wall but above it on a long ridge lay the main homes, the warrior hall and the wooden wall which surrounded the settlement. I had seen one gate which was close to the harbour. I guessed they had to have a second and so I was leading my horsemen towards the western side. I knew that the road from Saint Maclou came to the town. There had to be a gate. The cloud cover made the night especially dark. I knew that we could not approach silently. Our horses' hooves would be heard and they would snort and neigh too. The Bretons had horses too and they would give the alarm at the sound of strange horses. We were going to use a trick. I would use Lord Salomon's name. All we needed was for the attention of those on the gate to be fixed on us. Lord Bertrand had some of his younger warriors ready to scale the walls. The fact that we wore helmets like the Franks and the Bretons might buy us just enough time.

We found the road from Saint Maclou and I led my horsemen towards it. Lord Bertrand waved off his young warriors. As we neared the gate a voice shouted, "Halt! Who are you?"

"We have come from Jengland. We bring news of our great victory over the Franks."

"And who is your lord?"

"Lord Salomon."

"Lord Salomon? I thought he was north of here."

84

"He is. We fought for him." I was running out of answers. I sensed that they were becoming suspicious. How much longer would it take my men to scale the wall and kill the gatemen?

"I will send for the captain of the guard. Do not move. There are crossbows aimed at you."

Just then we heard a shout from the sea side of the walls. At the same moment, there was a cry as one of the guards was pitched from the walls. Another two men followed and then I heard the sound of the bar of the gate being removed. It was opened and we galloped into the town. The young warriors of Lord Bertrand waved cheerily as we galloped through the gates. My men needed no orders. We would ride as quickly as we could and get to the sea gate. Men ran from buildings as the sound of battle erupted. I leaned from my saddle to hack into the chest of one of the warriors who was rushing, sword in hand, from his home. Our horses drove others back into the shelter of their houses and halls. We had enough men following us to enable us to clear the homes later. Our priority was the gate.

There was a press of men before us. They were trying to gain access to the fighting platform. Our sudden appearance threw their plans into utter confusion. Soren and Karl flanked me and our three horses and swords drove a wedge into the mass of Bretons. Most had not had time to don mail. The greatest danger was to our horses.

I pointed my sword at the gate, "Get to the gate!" I pulled back on Dawn's Light's reins and stood in the stiraps. His hooves clattered down on a group of Bretons. Others moved out of the way of his snapping jaws. I leapt into the gap they had left. Karl and Soren followed me. Three of Lord Bertrand's men were also there and they turned their horses to enlarge the enclave we had created. I slipped from the saddle and ran to the two men who guarded the gate. I blocked a blow on my shield as I slashed at the thigh of the other. I brought my head back and butted the warrior who had hacked at my shield. His head went backwards and I lunged at him with my sword. He died quickly. With one man dead and one bleeding to death, I was able to sheath my sword, lay down my shield and lift the bar.

I shouted to the men I heard banging on the other side. "It is Jarl Ragnvald!" I did not want to lift the bar and then be trampled beneath the feet of my own men! The bar was heavy but I managed to manhandle it. I threw it to the side and then pulled on the gate.

Folki and his oathsworn stood there grinning. He raised his sword, "Now let us show the rest of the clan how we can fight!"

I stood back to allow the rest of my men to enter. I confess, lifting the bar had taken more out of me than I cared. Karl had dismounted and he led my horse over to me. He said, "We have them, Jarl Ragnvald!"

I mounted my horse, "We had best make sure."

Many of the Bretons who lived in the town fled. There were, we discovered, four gates. They could not use the sea gate nor the west gate for we had taken that first. Pursuit was impossible as we were having to fight our way through knots of men trying to buy time for their families. They died well for Christians. By the time dawn had broken we had taken the town. This time the treasure was worth the butcher's bill. Many warriors would not be returning home. The church was well endowed and had fine candlesticks and platters. There was even a golden goblet. We found three holy books. They had begun to collect in their wheat and we loaded a knarr with the cereal we took. We did not take slaves. We could not have carried them. Every ship was laden. We were lucky that there were three knarr in the harbour and we took those too. If we had not then the oar ports on our drekar would have been underwater.

The Lord of Cancale died well. Folki and Rollo One Ear killed him and his bodyguards. Our ships' boys were avenged. We found another twenty horses in the stables. We took those too. We left at noon. Our ships lumbered north and west. I heard the songs as the victorious crews rowed and celebrated their treasure. It was my father's song for, without him, we were nothing.

The horseman came through darkest night
He rode towards the dawning light
With fiery steed and thrusting spear
Hrolf the Horseman brought great fear

Slaughtering all he breached their line
Of warriors slain there were nine
Hrolf the Horseman with gleaming blade
Hrolf the Horseman all enemies slayed

With mighty axe Black Teeth stood
Angry and filled with hot blood

86

Hrolf the Horseman with gleaming blade
Hrolf the Horseman all enemies slayed
Ice cold Hrolf with Heart of Ice
Swung his arm and made it slice
Hrolf the Horseman with gleaming blade
Hrolf the Horseman all enemies slayed

In two strokes the Jarl was felled
Hrolf's sword nobly held
Hrolf the Horseman with gleaming blade
Hrolf the Horseman all enemies slayed

I knew that we would be in the most danger. Our ships would be safe from retribution but the Bretons would follow us. Horses left a trail which was easy to follow. Our horses would be tired. We were driving our captured horses and that would slow us down. All went well until we reached the island stronghold. Riders were waiting for us at Mont St. Michel. They blocked the road home. To pass them we would have to fight them... and defeat them. At low tide, it was possible to walk across to the mainland. Sixty horsemen had done so. We were lucky that our scouts spotted them and we had time to prepare. Leaving the ones without mail to watch our spare horses and captured horses I arrayed the other sixty in two lines.

I realised that we had parity of numbers but more than half of our men had no mail. They had the leather jerkins studded with metal. What we did have was a Viking behind forty of the blades. That would make the difference. I saw that the Bretons had ten of the horsemen armed with javelins. They too had no mail. I turned to Lord Bertrand, "Take ten of your men and take out the javelins."

Are you certain, jarl?"

I nodded. "I do not want our numbers thinned. Do not let them release their javelins. Do that and we have a chance."

"Aye jarl."

"Karl, leave the standard here with the spare horses. I have need of your right arm this day." As he handed it to one of Erik Gillesson's men I raised my sword. "These Bretons think we are barbarians. They think we cannot ride horses. We are Vikings! We are the Clan of the Horse. Today they will learn to give us more respect! Charge!"

I do not think the Bretons thought that we would initiate the attack or perhaps they were waiting for more men to join them. I knew that we would not be able to do as my father liked and hit them together. We did not have enough men who had that skill. We would rely on the fact that they did not have a Valhalla ahead of them. So long as we died with a sword in our hand then we would live forever! The Bretons we faced had spears. That did not worry me. A long spear is hard to control. I saw the Breton horsemen with javelins as they raced away from Lord Bertrand and his men. The Bretons relied on warriors not coming after them. They could not throw whilst they were running away.

I guessed it was a Breton lord who came for me. His horse looked expensive and his mail was burnished. I hefted my shield so that it was held close to my side. His horse was slightly bigger than Dawn's Light. He would be striking down at me. That made my head safer. I allowed him to choose the side he would attack. It would be shield to shield. I had to make him fight that way. If I did not then there was a chance he could end up spearing Karl and Karl was not as experienced as I was. The lord stood slightly and pulled his spear back. I saw the head wavering up and down. I had my sword held horizontally from my body. As the spear cracked into my shield and down towards my leg, I began my swing. My blade hacked into the back of his left arm and his back. His spear tore through the mail and into my leg. I had not killed the lord but Karl did. His sword sliced into the chest of the lord when his shield fell from his hand.

I forced myself to ignore the blood dripping into my sealskin boot and I rode for the next Breton. He had just seen his lord killed. Perhaps he was angry, I know not, but he rushed at me wildly. I easily took his spear on my shield. He hit it so hard that it shattered. He seemed taken by surprise. I swung my sword at head height and it sliced through his cheek and jaw. He fell sideways and died beneath the hooves of the horse which was following him.

I slowed down Dawn's Light. My mount was tiring and there were more enemies behind me. I rode at three Bretons who were trying to get at Soren Asbjornson. Soren was a wild man. He fought on the back of a horse the way he did in a shield wall. It was with reckless abandon. He used a sword, head, shield and his horse to get at any foe. He cared not how many wounds he took. I galloped into their backs. I struck my shield against the spine of one while I stabbed a second under his raised arm. Soren brought down his sword and split the head of the third.

"Watch out jarl!"

A Breton galloped at me with a spear aimed at my back. Even as I was turning my tired horse I knew I could not avoid it. Soren threw his sword. It spun end on end and embedded itself in the Breton's chest.

"I owe you a life, Soren."

He pointed at the two I had slain. "And I owe you two!"

That was the end of their attack. The survivors rode south. We had won. I looked around to see who had survived and saw, to my horror, that Lord Bertrand's body was being draped over his saddle. He had been slain. That was a cost which would be hard to bear. My father, I knew would be upset. I saw that Karl and Soren were unhurt. "Fetch the horses and our dead."

Lord Bertrand's men rode over. "He did as you asked, jarl but he was slow to react. One turned and hurled a javelin into his chest. He could not avoid it. We slew the man."

"I am sorry for your loss. We will take our dead and bury them at my hall."

We camped close to Coutances. I could not believe that the young Frank who had trained me to become a horseman was dead. Was it my fault? Should I have used some other to charge the men with javelins? I could look back all I liked. The simple fact was that I could not change what had happened. His thread had been cut. He was a Christian. What would his fate be?

It was a sombre column of horsemen who rode through my gates into my stronghold. The ships were all tied up and Folki, Rollo One Ear and my oathsworn were cheering as we rode up. As soon as they saw the cloak covered corpse on Lord Bertrand's grey they knew the worst. Had he been a Viking we would have celebrated for he would be in Valhalla. But a Christian?

My son and his band of boys were unaffected by the deaths. That was in the nature of youth. They thought they would live forever. Bertrand had been older than I was but he was a reminder that death was just around the corner. We divided the spoils. There was much to be divided. I told Rollo One Ear to wait until I was ready to travel. I would go and see my father and my son. I had to break the news of Lord Bertrand's death. I could not rid myself of the feeling that all of this was my fault. It was my curse. I had brought this tragedy upon the clan.

Part Two
Brother's Blood
Rollo grandson of Hrólfr the Horseman

Chapter 7

It had been four years since I had returned to my father's hall. It had been four years of constant trials and tribulations. My grandfather had not wanted me to return but I knew that I had to face my tormentors or forever hide in the Haugr and that was not my way. I did not return after the death of Lord Bertrand. My grandfather was too upset. My father recognised that. I stayed until the new grass and then I returned. In that time, I grew even more. I was now the tallest and broadest Viking in the Land of the Horse. I towered over all of them. Behind my back, my brother called me 'the Giant'. It was not a term of endearment. It was an insult intended to hurt me. My grandfather had had to buy a specially bred horse from Gilles. The others were too small and my feet trailed along the ground.

My mother had been pleased to see me. My father was most definitely delighted. All of the older warriors like Snorri and Harold were also delighted but Ragnvald and his band of crows, as I called them, were not. It was partly that I had outgrown all of them. My brother could not bully me for he could not defeat me. I was the better horseman and I was better with a sword. He knew more about ships but, as we raided, I soon picked up skills. He was galled when I was chosen to take an oar before he was. My size and strength made me an asset. He was still a ship's boy for he was the same height now as he had been four years earlier. He did not work as much with a sword and shield and it showed in his frame. That was the moment when he began to hate me. I had always thought he disliked me but after that, it was pure hate. He moved into the warrior hall with Arne and the others. There they could mock me and belittle me. They would not do it to my face but they would behind my back. They were inseparable. I stayed, happily in my father's hall.

Ragnvald then tried to make me look bad in front of others. He would get smaller youths to challenge me to combat knowing that if I defeated them then I would look like a bully and if I was defeated then I would look foolish. My grandfather had not only taught me how to ride and how to fight. He had taught me how to use my head. I made the bouts more like training despite the taunts I endured. That exacerbated the problem for Ragnvald was the one who ended up looking foolish. The defeated youths became sympathetic to me and Ragnvald began to lose friends. He stopped that. I knew he had something else planned but I knew not what. I was just pleased that I almost had a normal life.

All changed when my father decided to raid Lundenwic. The city had grown since the last Viking raid and was now a centre of trade for Wessex. The land of Wessex had grown rich and we wished to have some of those riches. The king of Wessex was Æthelred. He was not as strong as some of the other kings they had had. The Danes were making inroads from their Kingdom of the East Angles. We heard that there were other ships gathering for a raid. There was safety in numbers and the rewards so great that they were worth the risk. We sailed with five other drekar to Lothuwistoft where other ships were gathering for the great raid, as it was called.

Ragnvald had not grown much. He was still scrawny. I know that my grandfather thought that he had been cursed. He believed the curse was the reason he had not grown. For myself, I was not certain. He was still a ship's boy. Admittedly he sometimes helped to steer the drekar but he was just a ship's boy. He had to fetch us water and beer as we rowed. Even then he tried to make me look foolish. He would spill the beer and water on me. I just smiled and shook my head. I had learned that was the best way to defeat him. He could not get over that I was younger and yet I had an oar.

Lothuwistoft was a lively port. I had never seen anything like it. My father had told me that, in the past, Dorestad had been a dangerous place. This felt dangerous. There were Danish ships, Norse, Frisians and our ships from the land they were calling Normandia. While Ragnvald and his band of youths walked around the port together I stayed with Harold Strong Arm. I liked Harold. He had a good sense of humour and stories that I enjoyed hearing. I had been given him as an oar brother and I felt honoured. It also helped that my father was close by too. We went ashore without mail. The jarls had agreed that it would be better that way. I was disappointed. I had a fine byrnie. My grandfather had had it made by Bagsecg. He now made it quite clear that he did not like Ragnvald and the gift of a suit of mail had angered my brother. It was a well-made byrnie and a sword would not penetrate the links. It was not long enough to cover my thighs but I liked it nonetheless. Instead of the mail, I wore a fine kyrtle and a cloak. I had my sword. Grandfather had given me that too. Ragnvald and his band deliberately chose a different path from us as we left our drekar.

As we headed to an alehouse I saw a fight between a Dane and Norse warrior. It would end in death. They both had blades in their hands. That would mean weregeld. I determined not to drink too much. I was such a big warrior that many smaller men felt offended and would challenge me. Such was the way of little men. Ragnvald was a little man. Without too much drink I could be funny and end it peacefully. If I had had a drink then blood would be shed and I did not wish to let down my father.

"Why do we raid, father? The Bretons and the Franks are no threat and we have supplies aplenty."

"That is simple. Young men need to blood their swords. If they do not then they fight amongst themselves."

Harold Strong Arm said, "Besides the Saxons are little better than the animals of the field. Since they became Christian they are not even warriors."

"Do not let my wife hear you say that, Harold." He turned to me. "Keep your eyes and ears open. Oft times you can learn things when men are in their cups."

I nodded. My grandfather had told me much the same. The alehouse was full of warriors. Two were rolling around just outside the door. My father's four oathsworn ensured that we were not bothered. He pointed to a Norse jarl, "Come let us have an ale with Jarl Bjorn Arneson. He is as honest a man as you can ever meet. He is a friend of my father's."

The huge Norse jarl saw my father and jumped up to embrace him. "By the Allfather but you have grown! And who is this giant next to you? Surely that cannot be your son? Is your wife a giant?"

My father laughed, "I like that you never change! This is my son Rollo!"

The jarl looked at me. "He looks like a Viking but why give him a Frankish name? What is wrong with Hrólfr?"

My father shrugged, "I married a Frank. Hrólfr, Rollo, it is the same name and he is the same warrior." He waved over the ale wife and put down some shiny coins. "Ale for the table."

Jarl Bjorn shook his head, "Those are freshly minted coins. Why do you need to join this raid?"

"Young men must raid and they need to see other waters rather than their own. We have just fought Breton and Frank for some years. It is time my sons and my men saw Saxons. Who leads us?"

"Halfdan Ragnarsson. He is from Northumbria. He and Guthrum of the East Angles have been waging war against Wessex. He brings ten drekar to this raid."

"When do we sail?" Two men had begun a fight just outside the alehouse. We heard them being encouraged by other drunken warriors. "The longer we stay here the more chance we have of losing men before we begin."

"You are right." Our ale arrived and the alewife took some of the coins. Jarl Bjorn lifted his horn, "Here's to Hrólfr the Horseman!"

I raised my horn and drank deeply. It was a good ale.

"How is he? He must be getting old."

"His body might but his mind is still as sharp as ever. He rides each day and is still the arbiter of disputes through the whole land."

"That is good." He drank some ale and wiped the foam from his beard. "To answer your question, we are leaving on the morning tide. We sailed a long way to get here and needed supplies. Halfdan is making a longphort in the waters between the Isle of Grain and Canvey."

"Then we will follow you. We are well supplied and need nothing that they have here."

We talked of Halfdan and the other leaders. Jarl Bjorn came from the land of Norway and he told us of some of the other men who raided from that harsh land. "There is a clan there that is trying to take over the whole of Norway. We have no king but they would make one. Halfdan the Black is their jarl. If I stayed at home I would end up fighting my own kind. I think I will do as the Horseman did and seek a new land. I hear that there are lands to the north of the islands. I may go there. First I raid and make as much coin from the men of Wessex as I can." During a pause, he gestured with his horn towards me. "Does this giant fight or just row? I see few hairs upon his face."

I was not insulted. Ragnvald had often mocked me about my lack of a beard, telling me to put milk on it so that the cats could lick it off. He had a full beard. My grandfather told me that he had not had his first beard until he had seen seventeen summers.

My father answered for me, "He can fight although he has yet to blood his blade. My father trained him and I have practised against him." He punched me playfully in the arm, "I would not like to face him across a shield wall."

The jarl laughed, "If you fought him then you would always be in the shade. I look forward to watching him in a shield wall!"

We headed back to the ship when another fight broke out. This one was settled by Jarl Bjorn grabbing the two drunken warriors by the hair and smashing them together. We left in one large group and made our way to our drekar. Magnús the Fish had kept watch on our ship. Two of the ship's boys were his sons. They were too young to be of any use to Ragnvald and so they had stayed with their father. Magnús looked pleased to see us, "It has been lively this night. There are Danes and Norse here as well as our men." He pointed to a pool of blood. "Blood has been spilt. This does not bode well, Jarl."

My father nodded. I could tell, from his conversation with Jarl Bjorn, that he regretted his decision to raid. I wondered if this was the curse. However, we could not back out now. Our men would have felt it dishonourable. "Aye, Magnús, I think this will be our one foray into these waters. We sail on the morning tide and follow Jarl Bjorn's ship. Tell the other captains."

"Aye jarl."

As we made our way to our cloaks and our chests I saw that most were already on board. The exception was the four led by Ragnvald. My father noticed it. He spread his fur on the deck and said, "Your brother is not back aboard yet. I told him not to stray far. This is a dangerous port."

I laid my fur next to his and wrapped myself in it before covering it with my seal skin cape. "He will be back, fear not. Loki looks after his own!"

My father laughed, "Aye, your brother is more like Loki just as you are more like Thor! But then you were not cursed. You share the same blood but there the resemblance ends."

As I curled up and fell into a deep sleep my thoughts were on the curse. I had not known about it until I had stayed with my grandfather. He had told me about it just because it explained his distance from my brother. Since then I had felt more sympathetic towards Ragnvald. It had not been his fault. Our mother had allowed the priest into the birthing room. That had been the start of it.

That night I dreamed. It may have been the strong ale or perhaps it was meeting so many new people. Whatever the reason it was vivid.

I was falling. I tumbled from the top of the mast. I seemed to spin forever. I would surely hit the deck but I did not. I hit the water and I sank into its blackness. I went down and down. I saw skulls and bones. I saw dead men. Rurik One Ear lurched towards me. I saw, in the water, my father's back, when he turned I saw that his throat was cut and his hands were bloody. I heard the word, 'Ragnvald'!

I woke.

"Ragnvald!" I opened my eyes and saw my brother; Arne and the others were staggering aboard. They had clattered into sleeping men and woken them. The four were drunk. I heard Harold Strong Arm complain. As I sat up I saw my father rising.

Ragnvald shouted, "Be quiet old man! I am Ragnvald the Breton Slayer, my blood brothers and I do what I like."

My father had never been violent to us but Ragnvald had stepped over a line. He had insulted one of my father's hearth weru and he had abused his position. My father brought his hand back and punched Ragnvald so hard that he fell unconscious. He jabbed a finger at Arne and the other two. "Put my son to bed. I will speak with all of you in the morning when you are men again!"

The two younger ones nodded but Arne glared. This was not over.

I slept but fitfully. My dreams were pictures which came and went quickly. They were filled with the sight of my brother's bloody nose and my father's grazed knuckles. I knew that this was not a good thing. We woke with a cool feel to the morning. I had been wise to use my seal skin cape for there had been drizzle in the night. I had slept dry. I was one of the first awake. I hauled a pail of seawater and then made water over the side. I plunged my head into the seawater. It woke me. I would not need my mail until we raided and I left it in my sea chest. I stripped and changed into the kyrtle I would use to row. It was a thick and rough material. It also served as an undergarment when I wore my mail.

Harold Strong Arm joined me. I knew that I had been given a great honour when I had been chosen as his oar brother. As he

95

rubbed himself dry he said, "Anyone other than the son of the jarl would have died for insulting me. Your brother is a lucky man. Had it been any other than the jarl's son I would have ended his insults and it would have been with more than a fist. Your father saved your brother's life."

"I have never seen my father get so angry, so quickly."

"He has been patient with your brother. We all have. It is not his fault that he is cursed but a warrior and a man choose their own path." He put an arm around my back. "I am pleased I have the better brother as an oar and shield brother."

"I have yet to fight in a shield wall. What if I let you down?"

"You cannot. You have the blood of two heroes coursing through your veins and you are not cursed. Besides, I believe that you are destined to be greater than any of us."

"Are you Skuld now?"

He laughed, "No, for I still have all my own teeth but you are not only grown tall and wide, but you are also grown wise. Others your age, on their first raid, would have done as your brother and Arne. They would have swaggered with their swords and got drunk. You did not."

My father's voice rang out, "Rise and shine! We leave this cesspit and we go to war! Awake I say!"

There were grumbles but men rose.

Magnús the Fish shouted, "Ship's boys! Mooring lines."

I watched as Ragnvald rose. His eyes were already beginning to blacken and the dried blood was still on his face. His nose was broken. It would be forever twisted and disfigured. My father pointed to him and said, "We will put last night behind us but today, you make up for it by leading the boys to work harder than any other crew."

It was an attempt to make peace but my brother chose to ignore it. He just glared at my father and then shouted, "Ship's boys to me!"

Then Harold and I had to look to ourselves. We oarsmen went to our oars and picked them up. Harold and I were on the landward side. We would have to fend us off from the wooden quay before we were able to put them through the oar ports. We would have to row until Magnús the Fish found us a wind. With the mooring lines freed we pushed against the wooden quay as Magnús the Fish turned the steering board. The oars which were in the water on the seaward side sculled us around. As soon as we were far enough away Harold and I slipped our oar through its port and prepared to row. We would not use a chant yet. We just had to pull us away from the land. I looked up at the masthead pennant. The wind was against us. We would have to row. I saw my father speaking with Magnús the Fish. He nodded and then cupped his hands to shout to the other drekar. He ordered them to follow us. I could not see him but I knew that Jarl Bjorn was ahead of us and already heading for the longphort.

"Right my lads, let us have Siggi's song eh? He was a great warrior and his spirit will help us row." My father knew the right thing to say.

> *Siggi was the son of a warrior brave*
> *Mothered by a Hibernian slave*
> *In the Northern sun where life is short*
> *His back was strong and his arm was taut*
> *Siggi White Hair warrior true*
> *Siggi White Hair warrior true*
> *When the Danes they came to take his home*
> *He bit the shield and spat white foam*
> *With berserk fury, he killed them dead*
> *When their captain fell the others fled*
> *Siggi White Hair warrior true*
> *Siggi White Hair warrior true*
> *After they had gone and he stood alone*
> *He was a rock, a mighty stone*
> *Alone and bloodied after the fight*
> *His hair had changed from black to white*
> *His name was made and his courage sung*
> *Hair of white and a body young*
> *Siggi White Hair warrior true*
> *Siggi White Hair warrior true*
> *With dying breath he saved the clan*
> *He died as he lived like a man*
> *And now reborn to the clan's hersir*
> *Ragnvald Hrolfsson the clan does cheer*
> *Ragnvald Hrolfsson warrior true*
> *Ragnvald Hrolfsson warrior true*

Soon we were speeding down the coast. We did not have far to travel. The exercise would exorcise some of the ale from those who had drunk too much. Once we had the rhythm we were able to stop singing. I found some satisfaction in seeing my brother having to work hard. This would be his last voyage as a ship's boy. He had managed to grow a little and to become broad enough to take an oar. We always had a ready supply of boys but men able to row were rarer. This was a large drekar and needed a large crew. All of the boys who had served with Ragnvald were either dead or were rowing like Arne the Breton Slayer who was two oars behind me. It irked my brother.

"Have you raided the Saxons before, Harold?"

"Aye. It was many years since. We went with your grandfather. The men of Wessex build better burghs than we do but since they became Christian they are not as warrior-like. Many have mail. If you face a housecarl then they are the equal of our warriors." He grinned. "Do not worry you will be behind me. This will be your first shield wall. My fear is that you are a real target for them. You are a head taller than any other. It is a tempting target for a Saxon axe."

"Grandfather gave me his full-face helmet. He said he would need it no longer. It was made by Dragonheart's smith Bagsecg."

"And your mail shirt is a good one but a little shorter than I would have liked."

It was true, I was so big that my byrnie did not go all the way to my knees. It stopped at my waist. I had been promised a longer one but it took time to make a good byrnie.

A lookout shouted, "Longphort ahead!" We had reached our destination.

It was not long before the order to ship oars was given and we slid next to Jarl Bjorn's drekar and tied up. Jarl Folki tied up on our other side. There were drekar to our fore. After we had stored our oars Harold and I wandered to the steering board. "How many ships on this raid?"

My father pointed, "There are twelve of us here now and there were six more in Lothuwistoft. I heard there were more ships coming from Denmark. That will be over six hundred men."

"Will there be enough treasure for us all?"

"Lundenwic is the richest prize on this island. Paris has more treasure but that is harder to take because it is on an island."

I turned to Harold, "How do you know these things?"

"I spoke to other Vikings who have travelled further than we. Some have been all the way down the Issicauna. It is said that there are some Rus Vikings who sailed all the way to Miklagård.

They carried their drekar over mountains." He laughed. "They must all be giants such as you, Rollo."

My father laughed too, "I will go and see this Northumbrian jarl, Halfdan. Harold, Snorri, come with me. You have sharp ears and eyes."

I did not leave the drekar. Instead, I took out my mail and began to rub oil on it. This coast was notoriously damp. Once that was done I replaced it in its sack and took out my sword. My sword did not have a name yet. It was a well-made sword but it was no Heart of Ice. I think my grandfather would have given me his sword but he thought it might be unlucky. It had been made especially for him when he had lived in the Land of the Wolf. He had promised it to me when he died. I had said that I hoped I never owned the sword. The sword I had was the same length as the other warriors but, with my long arms, it looked and felt short. My grandfather said I needed a longer sword. He had promised me one.

Father did not return until dark. He had Folki and the other jarls with him. I was close enough to hear their words. "Halfdan is a man of action. We leave this night. Step the masts for we row. Any ship which has not reached us will miss out." Two more ships had arrived during the afternoon. None of the Danish drekar had arrived. Some of the crew, like Soren Asbjornson, said that was a good thing as he did not trust a Dane. The Danes were gathering in the east of the land of the Saxons. There were many bands of them. So far, they had just raided in small groups. Soren foresaw a time when they would band together. It did not worry me. We would make this one raid and then be back in the Land of the Horse.

I had already sharpened my sword and my two seax. I had one inside the bindings of my leggings. Grandfather had told me that they had a habit of slipping out of sealskin boots. The other was tucked in the back of my sword belt. The rest of the crew prepared their weapons. Then we stepped the mast. Once that was done I joined Harold and the others. We were drinking the ale we had bought in Lothuwistoft. We ate the salted cod and dried ham. It sustained us. Ragnvald and his band of crows kept apart from us. Their heads were together and whenever I passed them they were silent. They were plotting. I suspected that they had something unpleasant planned for me when we returned to the Land of the Horse. I had already planned on seeking my father's permission to move to the Haugr. He would be upset but I had decided I would be a horseman. Nothing I had seen thus far had convinced me that I would enjoy the life of a raider.

I slept until dark. I woke first and roused Harold. We washed in seawater and then donned our mail. Until we returned to the longphort I would wear it. Leaving the longphort was trickier than joining it. The last ships to join it left first and then we had to wait in the estuary. It was tricky for there were shallows where a drekar could be grounded. We needed the deep channel which led upstream. Halfdan Ragnarsson was leading the raid and his drekar had the honour of rowing first down the tightly twisting Tamese.

There would be no chant. We needed silence. Ragnvald and the ship's boys would have to be on watch. The last thing we needed was for two of our drekar to become fouled. That would be a disaster. It would take most of the night for us to row upstream. The river had a strong current and our helmsmen had to be careful. My father spent half of his time with Magnús the Fish and the other half at the prow. He was nervous. I knew why. He had normally raided with just those who were the Clan of the Horse. He had raided the coast he knew well. He had been forced to leave the comfort of what he knew best. We had many young men who clamoured for greater treasure than that offered by raiding the Bretons and the Franks. Unless we sailed deep into Frankia the pickings were poor. I knew from his demeanour that he was regretting giving into the younger warriors who had begged for the chance to go on a larger raid. Arne the Breton Slayer and my brother had been amongst the most vocal. I think Ragnvald had swayed my father. He always seemed to feel guilty about the rift between them. He had thought this a way to patch things up. He had been wrong. The blow the previous night had broken more than my brother's nose.

The river had different smells from home. The air felt damper. I could not see what was attractive about this land. There were many noises too. Above the creak of the timbers and rigging and the splash of the oars, I could hear animals in the fields adjacent to the water. I could smell wood smoke. What was absent was the sound of an alarm. No bells rang to warn them of the Vikings who were about to arrive in the heart of their land. We had managed to get into their land unseen. Would we escape the same way?

We were facing east, as we rowed, and I saw the sky growing lighter behind us. I was able to make out the river banks which had been hidden in the dark. I saw that the river was narrowing. There were lots of buildings. The smell of smoke was stronger. We were nearing Lundenwic. My father suddenly appeared down the centre of the rowers. "Prepare to ship oars."

I saw Magnús the Fish acknowledge the wave my father gave and he put the steering board over. We were landing.

"Steerboard ship oars!" We kept rowing as the other half of the drekar stopped. There was the slightest of bumps as my father said, "All oars in!"

Harold and I quickly withdrew our oar and then stacked it. We took our shields from the sheerstrake and I donned my helmet. The warriors who manned the steerboard oars were already swarming ashore. I followed Harold Strong Arm. There were twelve of us who would follow him. I was keenly aware that this would be the first time I had faced a foe and I did not want to let down either my father or my grandfather.

Ahead of me, I heard the clash of metal on metal as Halfdan Ragnarsson led his men into the heart of Lundenwic. There was no order to us. It was a mass of warriors. I stuck close to Harold Strong Arm as my father had instructed me. I wondered if they would manage to slay all of the Saxons. That illusion was shattered when there was a roar from our right and a warband of Saxons emerged from the old Roman fort of Lundenburgh which lay close to us. Harold shouted, "Shield wall!"

I almost panicked for I was not close to those I was supposed to be. I was the one who would stand behind Harold Strong Arm and lay my shield over his head. I lengthened my stride and caught up with him. I had followed him and was next to him as we turned to face the Saxons. I locked my shield with his. Soren Asbjornson pushed his in front of me. Behind me I heard Eystein Foul Breath grunt, "I cannot get my shield over your head, man-mountain!" He pushed it into my back. I remembered to put the weight on to my shield leg.

The Saxons were upon us before we knew it. I barely had time to poke my sword out before me. The Saxons clattered into us. A sword rang into my helmet. As the Saxon had struck from below me his blade spun up above my head. I moved my sword to the left. As I was taller and very strong, I was able to saw the sword across his neck. The blood spurted and then gushed over me.

Behind me, I heard Eystein laugh. "You have first blood, Rollo!"

Harold shouted, "Hold them and when I shout we push!"

An axe suddenly appeared before my eyes and was slicing down at me. Was I supposed to maintain the shield wall and endure the blow? Instinct took over and I brought up the shield to catch the axe on it. I lunged with my sword and it went into the eye of the axeman.

"Two! It is like Hrolf the Horseman reborn!" Eystein Foul Breath was laughing.

"Push! Now!"

We all stepped off onto our sword leg. I had practised this often. As we did so we punched with our shields. The two men I had slain and the ones killed by Soren and Harold had made a hole in the Saxons and a hole in a line was a weakness. We pushed them back. I stabbed forward. I knew that I was supposed to swing but if I did so then I risked hitting Eystein and Einar behind me. Because I was taller than the Saxons I was able to stab down over their shields. I sliced into the shoulder of one Saxon and, as the next man raised his shield to protect himself, Soren sliced under his shield and he fell.

Now that we had blunted their attack and lessened their numbers we were able to push them back. More of our men had joined our shield wall and I found the strength of twenty men behind me.

Harold shouted, "Their gate is open! Clan of the Horse, push!"

With swords held before us, we all stepped quickly forward. We had momentum. A Saxon slipped beneath my feet. I raised my seal skin boot and stamped hard on his face. I heard something crack. Soren and Harold stabbed and slashed before them. I realised that I had no opponents. I did not know why.

Eystein must have read my mind, "Rollo, they fear you! They think you are a giant!"

He was right. Men were attacking Soren and Harold rather than facing me. I used that to my advantage and hacked to left and right. With no one before me I had a full swing and the men facing Soren and Harold fell.

Harold Strong Arm shouted, "With me! We take the gate!"

I ran with Soren and Harold. I was certain that they must close the gate but there was no one there. Our shields were no longer locked and my long legs took me ahead of my companions. Two men ran to close the gates. I put all of my weight behind my shield and smashed at the four hands which held the two gates. The gates sprang asunder. I almost overbalanced. By the time I had regained my balance Soren and Harold had slain the two men and our warband was inside the walls of Lundenburgh.

Harold Strong Arm was one of the most experienced of my father's men. He did not allow our sudden entry to make us race headlong into what might be a disaster. "Hold and reform!" As warriors locked shields again he said, quietly, "You did well. Now you are blooded and now you are a warrior. Welcome to the clan!"

It was one of my proudest moments.

Chapter 8

I looked behind and saw that there were now thirty of us. Worryingly there was no sign of our jarl, my father. I knew that he trusted his four hearth weru and this was part of the plan but I would have been happier if he had been close to me. Many of the Roman buildings inside the fort had been destroyed but there was still one, lone solid stone structure. I saw, in the rising sun, that there were Saxons there. This time they were forming up. It would be a shield wall.

Harold said, "Wedge! Soren and Eystein, behind me. Let the Jarl's son occupy the third rank." He laughed. "Perhaps he will draw their blows!"

Eystein shouted, "They will need a long sword to reach him! I swear there is snow on the top of his head!"

I laughed with him and the others. I was one of them now. The banter and the ribald humour were part of the acceptance. It mattered not what Ragnvald did now. I had oath brothers who meant more to me than my blood brother. I stayed where I was and the others formed up around me. We stepped forward, chanting as we went.

> *Clan of the Horseman*
> *Warriors strong*
> *Clan of the Horseman*
> *Our reach is long*
> *Clan of the Horseman*
> *Fight as one*
> *Clan of the Horseman*
> *Death will come*
> *Clan of the Horseman*
> *Warriors strong*
> *Clan of the Horseman*
> *Our reach is long*
> *Clan of the Horseman*
> *Fight as one*
> *Clan of the Horseman*

Death will come

I sang as lustily and loudly as any. I felt privileged for I had a clearer view than those behind me. I held my shield above the heads of Eystein Foul Breath and Soren Asbjornson. I was so tall that Erik and Ragnar who flanked me were able to use their shields to protect the sides of our wedge. The closer we came the faster we moved. Never quite reaching a run when we struck the Saxon line, it was with four swords sticking out from the front. My reach was so long that my blade was level with Eystein and Soren. The four swords struck the leading two men of Wessex. They had spears and they thrust them at us but our shields were large and our helmets well made. Both spears came for my head. My grandfather's helmet saved me for although both struck they glanced off either side and the two men perished. Erik and Ragnar's swords came into action as did the two behind them. Harold was face to face with a warrior who had been in the second rank. Harold brought his sword up and into the Saxon's body and then there was just one man facing Harold.

"Break wedge!"

Eystein and Erik turned left and hacked into the sides of the two men there. Ragnar and Soren did the same to the right and I stepped forward and attacked the man who tried to stab Harold. I backhanded my sword across his chest. I am not certain if I broke his mail but I broke his breastbone for I heard it snap. He gasped for breath and I plunged my sword into his neck. I joined Ragnar and Soren. The men we faced had been at the rear of their line. They wore no mail and they were the ones reluctant to be in the front rank and face death. They died easily. The first man I had slain had died so quickly that I had not had time to think about it. With the men we faced, I did. I saw the fear in their eyes and knew I would win. They did not see an untried youth. They saw a giant in a full-face helmet. I watched their swords and spears come to me and I seemed to have all the time in the world to block the blow with my shield. When I feinted with my shield they took the bait each time and I was able to place my sword into soft flesh rather than shield or bone. The three of us worked along their line until they were all dead. I looked around for more Saxons. I wanted to kill more men!

Soren Asbjornson seemed to realise it. After sheathing his sword, he put his hand on mine, "Breathe, Rollo. The blood rushes to your head. Now is the time for you to become calm.

You have done well. Already you think you will rush off and slaughter every Saxon before you. That is for others. In here lies a treasure. We need that treasure. Sheathe your weapon and put your shield on your back you will need both hands."

I nodded and forced myself to do as he said. I took off my helmet for my head was so hot I thought it would boil. The cool morning air helped me. I sheathed my sword as I looked around. Our men were putting the last of the Saxons to the sword. Others were at the east gate and the last of the garrison were dying. I slipped my shield on to my back and saw that four of our shield wall lay dead. It calmed me more than anything. I had thought we could not be killed. I was wrong.

Harold pointed at the building. "Search it. They normally have valuables here. Rollo, keep your seax in your hand. In the confines of a building, it is a better weapon."

I nodded and reached behind me to pull out the viciously sharp weapon. I followed him into the building. I was amazed at the quality of the stonework. I had thought my grandfather's stronghold was impressive but it was as nothing compared with this. This was Roman stonework and that was the best. The wisdom of carrying a seax was shown when a hidden Saxon suddenly lurched out to try to impale me on his sword. He did not have enough room to swing and I grabbed his right hand as I ripped the seax across his throat.

"Well done. These Saxons are sneaky." We had reached a small room which was lit by a single candle. Harold said, "Help me move this table."

We pushed the table out of the way and Harold took the candle that lit the room. He leaned down. "Go and fetch the Saxon sword." While I did so he shouted, "Soren, Eystein!"

I returned with the sword and our two shield brothers appeared. Harold put the sword into a crack and began to lever the square stone. The stone almost came out but then the sword snapped. Soren must have expected this for he suddenly slipped his seax under the stone before it could fall back into place. When Harold put the broken sword under it a second time he was able to lift it up. When it was removed I saw that there were steps leading down.

Eystein laughed, "Well Rollo, I cannot see you fitting down there!"

Harold said, "Go outside and see if we are needed elsewhere."

The sun was up when I emerged. Ragnar and Erik were organising the men and tending to the minor wounds. "A good battle. We all made a kill and we lost few men." Ragnar held up a sack. "We took treasure from the dead. We will share it when we are back on the drekar. Has Harold found treasure?"

"He has found a hidden room."

"Then he will have treasure for all these Roman forts have such a room. The trick is finding them."

Our three companions joined us. They laboured with three large chests. They placed them on the floor. Harold said, "You six carry them. We will head back to the ship." He glanced around. The interior of the fort was filled with our warriors and the dead. He nodded, seemingly satisfied.

I saw more of our men heading back to the drekar. Some were carrying booty and others helping wounded comrades. I saw Snorri Snorrison. He ran up to Harold and me, "The Jarl is wounded. It might be a bad one. He is on the ship. I have a healer looking at him."

Suddenly the treasure seemed unimportant. Someone had placed a gangplank so that we could board the drekar. We ran up it. Men were crowding around my father. We dropped the chests on the ship and Harold Strong Arm shouted, "Move away from the jarl!" His voice had the desired effect. "Get these chests stored. Fetch our dead so that we can take them home!"

I saw that there was a priest seeing to my father. There was a bloody bandage around his thigh. Ragnvald was standing close by. In contrast to Magnús the Fish who looked worried, my brother just appeared to be curious. Harold said, "Priest, will he live?"

The priest's voice showed the terror the Saxon felt, "I have cleaned the wound but it is bleeding and I cannot staunch it."

"Then get off the ship while you still live." As the man ran off Harold took my father's sword belt and wrapped it around the leg above the wound. He looked first at Ragnvald and then at me, "Go and fetch a brand. We will seal the wound. It will hurt and it will smell but it will save both his life and his leg."

Harold had been with my father as long as any and I trusted him. I dropped my shield and ran from the drekar. We kept no fire on the wooden ship but there was one at the gates of the fort. I ran. Folki and others were coming back laden with boxes. He shouted, "She must be pretty if you run after her!"

I shouted back, without turning, "My father is badly wounded!"

I knew without looking that Folki would have dropped his treasure and run to my father's side. I reached the fort and took both brands. As I ran the air made them flame up. I roared, "Out of my way!" My huge frame helped to clear a path and I hurtled up the gangplank and on to the drekar.

Folki was leaning over my father. He moved aside when I approached. "Give me the brand. I have done this before." I handed him one of the brands. Without hesitation, he plunged it into the torn flesh. Magnús the Fish was holding down my father's upper body. Even so, I saw our captain rise as my father, although he was not fully conscious, arc his back with the pain. There was a smell of burning hair and flesh. I wondered how long Folki would hold it there but he eventually lifted it. He sniffed seemingly satisfied. He stood, "We have done enough here. Until Jarl Ragnvald recovers I will command the Clan of the Horse. Let us return to the longphort and thence home."

Soren pointed, "It seems that others are leaving already."

I saw the drekar of Jarl Bjorn Arneson, *'Storm Bird'*, with full sail, heading downstream. I looked at Harold. He shrugged, "We agreed to help Halfdan take Lundenwic. We have fulfilled our promise. We have enough treasure to take home and we have a jarl who is wounded. Stay with him, Rollo. Tell me when he wakes."

I knelt next to him acutely aware that Ragnvald had not said a word during all this. He had not offered to help. Now he grinned at me. "If he dies then I will be the new jarl." He leaned in closer, "I will make you an outcast. You had better hope that the Allfather saves him."

For the first time, I looked at Ragnvald and hate was in my heart. When we returned to our home I would end this feud. One of us would die. I would end the curse.

We had no need to row for the current took us and so I sat next to my father. I pondered Ragnvald's words. How could he hate his own father? Then it came to me; the curse. I looked up at my brother. He was kept busy by Magnús the Fish. With so many twists and turns, the sails needed constant adjustment. I contemplated taking off my mail but I was fearful of leaving my father for an instant. He was breathing but he had barely moved.

We were passing Uuluuich when his eyes opened. He smiled when he saw me, "I am alive then. I dreamt that I died."

Brothers in Blood

Harold Strong Arm appeared. His face broke into a smile when he saw that my father was alive, "Jarl, you live!"

"Harold took charge when you were unconscious," I added.

"Then remain in charge. I feel like a newborn baby."

"I will go and tell the men. They were worried. Your son did well today, jarl. I will happily follow him into battle."

Sometimes you can hear the Norns spinning. They were spinning new webs and preparing to cut old threads. I looked up and saw that Ragnvald had heard. He pretended he had not and scurried up the sheets but I knew that he had heard.

My father looked at me. "I am pleased. You are a true warrior. Your grandfather told me so. I knew that you were a horseman. Now I know that you can stand in a shield wall. The clan is in good hands."

Ragnvald was at the masthead. I said, "Ragnvald is older."

"But you are the warrior. You are my heir. You know that your grandfather visited a witch's cave and met a Norn."

I was sceptical that it was a Norn but I nodded. "He was told his line would be rulers of an empire."

He nodded, "You will be that leader." He looked at his leg. "This is a bad wound. I know that. I cannot stand in a shield wall any longer and riding a horse needs powerful thighs. It will be you who sails up the Issicauna and takes Paris. It will be you who defeats Charles the Bald. It may not be in my lifetime but I will be in Valhalla and I will be watching over you. I think this is the last raid for me."

I shook my head, "Father, the wound has made you delirious. We will get you home and you will heal. We will send for the priest who made Einar Bear Killer whole."

"This raid was a mistake. We should not have come save for one thing. You have become a man and you have become the leader of the clan. As soon as I knew that Danes were involved I should have sailed home. They have ever been treacherous."

"Peace. We will sail to the longphort. Jarl Bjorn will come aboard and he will speak with you."

"You are right. I am tired." He closed his eyes. I placed my fur over him. I now knew my future. He was right. My brother would destroy the clan. I had to save it.

Ahead of me, I could see *'Storm Bird'* as she headed for the longphort. There was a single ship we had left there. Her steering board withy had sheered. That was why she had not raided with us. She was a Dane. We had not needed her and, to be truthful, none of us wished to raid with a Dane. I looked up at Magnús the Fish. He was alone. His crew were busy trimming the sails. "If we get my father home I will make a blót. This wound is a bad one."

"Your father is tough. He will live."

I risked standing. The day was ending and the sun was sinking in the west. We were heading east into the darkness. The wind was getting up and the river was getting rougher. There might be a storm ahead. My father was asleep. My grandfather had told me that sleep was the way that the gods healed you. I hoped so. I saw that many of our warriors were curled up asleep. It had been a hard row up the river and we had fought hard. Halfdan and his men would be enjoying a night in Lundenwic without fear of a knife in the night for their enemies were dead. Only five boats had headed downstream away from the captured city. I had no doubt that the rest would gain more treasure than we but Harold was right. We needed our people safe. My father regretted the raid. I did not for I had a vision of the future. When I returned to the Land of the Horse I would set about claiming it. My brother would not have it without a fight. I would see my father healed and, with my grandfather and my father's oathsworn, I would make the clan one, once again.

The Norns were spinning and I knew not. My life was changing and I was unaware. Threads would be cut but I could not see them.

My father appeared to be sleeping easier. I peered ahead and saw that there were three Danish ships at the longphort. I assumed they were Danish for they had been the only ones which had not arrived before we left. They would have poor pickings for we had taken the best.

Harold walked back to us. "Magnús the Fish, lay us alongside *'Storm Bird'*."

"We could carry on home if you wish, Harold Strong Arm. There may be a storm coming. If we row we might beat it." He was a true sailor and knew the wind and the tide better than any man I ever knew.

Harold shook his head. I can still see it now twenty years after he did so. "We owe Jarl Bjorn a farewell. We will say goodbye and then leave."

The river was getting rougher moment by moment and the wind was increasing. Our men had taken off their mail. The battle was done. I wondered about taking off my mail. It was as we were nearing *'Storm Bird'* that Magnús the Fish shouted, "There are two more Danish ships coming from the other shore. I like not this!"

If my father had been awake we might have survived. Harold Strong Arm was not a jarl. He looked south as the Danes poured over the side of *'Storm Bird'*. It was a trap. The Danes had deliberately waited so that they could lure us close and take the treasure from weary warriors.

Harold was frozen. I shouted, "Magnús the Fish! Head for the open sea!"

He obeyed me and put the steering board over. The two Danish ships crashed into us. Harold reacted the quickest. "Repel boarders." He turned to me. "We need your sword! Remember Rollo, keep your feet wide apart when you fight. If you do not then it is easy to overbalance." He gave me a grim smile, "Pretend you are on a horse!"

The drekar was pitching with the wind and the rough water of the estuary. The sea and the river intertwined between these two islands. I drew my sword and glanced at my father. No matter what happened I would make sure that he was safe. The Danish drekar lurched into us and I almost lost my footing. I ran to the side and, using two hands, swept my sword into the guts of the Dane who clung to our stays. I held the stay with my left hand and stood on the sheerstrake. I raised my sword and I shouted, "If you wish this ship then you will have to get past me!" I heard the crew shout as they heard my voice. A Dane leapt at me. He did not even make our drekar. My sword sliced across his belly and he fell between our two hulls. A second drekar had attached herself to our prow and Danes flooded over her. I watched as Harold Strong Arm led our warriors to face them. I had eight warriors with me but my wide swing had stopped the Danes from gaining access across our stern. I brought my sword over my head and split the skull of another Dane who tried to board. A spear was hurled at me. My mail was too strong. The tip pricked me but that was all.

I heard a cheer from the bow. It was a Danish cheer. I saw Harold Strong Arm and Snorri Snorrison. They were both slain in the same instant. Even as I thought to go to their aid I heard a cry from Magnús the Fish. "Rollo!"

I looked around and saw that he had a spear in his shoulder. We needed someone on the steering board. "Soren, hold here!" I jumped down and ran to the steering board. I noticed two things.

Ragnvald was standing there with a bloody knife in his hand and my father's chest was covered in blood. His throat was bloody. I dropped to my knees and put my head to my father's mouth. He was not breathing. Ragnvald Hrolfsson was dead.

Magnús the Fish shouted a warning, "Rollo!"

I looked up and saw Ragnvald lurching towards me with his bloody blade. As I raised my sword to kill him my life changed forever. I was struck in the back by a blade and a third Danish ship crashed into us. I found myself toppling over the side. The sheerstrake was before me and I overbalanced. I was unable to stop myself. As I tumbled over the side I saw Arne the Breton Slayer with a sword in his hand coming purposefully towards me and then I hit the water. I was wearing mail and sealskin boots. I was going to die!

Chapter 9

Even as I hit the water I let my sword drop from my hand. I undid my sword belt and let that fall too. My mail was dragging me down. I knew that I had to remain calm and not panic. For the first time, I appreciated having a short byrnie. I reached down and lifted it above my head. My descent to the bottom of the river helped. The water pulled my arms and the mail shirt up and over my head. My feet touched the muddy, oozy bottom. I had been lucky and fallen onto a shallow part of the estuary. It was still and it was silent. There was no storm here. It was dark. It felt unreal. As I pulled the byrnie from me I kicked with both feet. I held my horse amulet and prayed to Njoror, the god of the sea, to save me. The seal skin boots had filled with water and the muddy bottom held them firmly. My feet came out of them. That saved my life for I began to rise through the water. I saw nothing above me. How far had I sunk? I must have been close to the shore when I had fallen for I had touched bottom. As I rose I felt the current taking me. The closer I came to the surface the stronger was the current. I was in the water that was a mixture between the river and the sea. The tide and the river were pulling me. Which way was I headed?

My head broke the surface. I sucked in air. I had just closed my mouth when a wave broke over me. I had made sure after my brother had first thrown me in the sea, that I knew how to swim well. I trod water and spread my arms. I spun myself around. At first, I saw nothing and then as a swell lifted me I saw the masts of ships. They were more than five hundred paces from me. Another wave broke over me and when I came to the top of the next swell I could see nothing. It was dark and night was coming. I was going to die and my father would be unavenged. As I felt the cold of the sea bite into me I knew that my brother and Arne the Breton Slayer would concoct a story about me which would make sense without warriors like Harold Strong Arm and Snorri Snorrison to refute it. At that moment I knew that Magnús the Fish was dead too. They could not allow him to live for he had seen Arne the Breton Slayer strike me in the back. He had seen my brother kill my father. Patricide! Was there a more heinous crime?

I was resigned to die and then the Norns spun. When the Danish ships had crashed into ours there had been a crash. Both the Danes and we had suffered damage and the Norns sent me a shield. I saw it bobbing on the top of the water a few paces from me. It was not from our ship for this had no metal boss. That would have sunk. I kicked my legs and swam towards it. I turned it so that the leather straps were on the top. I hauled myself so that the top half of my body lay upon it. I gripped the end with one hand while slipping my other hand through the leather strap. The wind and the sea took me north and east. I guessed it was north and east for that had been the wind direction as we had sailed from Lundenwic. The sea was empty. I saw crests and troughs as the choppy waters tossed me and my Danish shield about.

It was a long night and it was an empty night. The troughs and crests of the waves subsided as the storm lessened. I peered into the night but I saw nothing. The drekar would either be at the longphort or they would be heading south and east. We would be going in different directions. I reached under my kyrtle. I had not lost the metal horse I wore around my neck. I gripped it. "Allfather, help me to live that I might wreak vengeance on a murderer. My father should be in Valhalla with you. He cries out for vengeance and I am that instrument." My eyes were closed but I saw a light. I thought about that light long after. The light was inside my head and it was the answer from the Allfather. Gripping the horse seemed to bring me peace.

I must have fallen asleep for when I opened my eyes the sky was lighter. I knew I was being taken east for the sky behind me was still dark. Would I strike the marshy land of the Frisians? I doubted it. When we had sailed from Frisia to Lothuwistoft it had taken more than a day. I was just drifting. Salt had caked my head and my lips. I was so thirsty that I doubted there was a barrel of ale large enough to quench it. I dipped my hand in the sea and used it to wash my eyes. I heard the screech of sea birds above me. What creatures were there in the sea? Would I be a tasty meal for some denizen of the deep?

I could no longer feel my legs and I felt cold. Sleep seemed an attractive proposition. When my eyes closed I felt at peace. I slowly slipped into an uneasy sleep. I dreamed.

*My grandfather was piling stones upon a cairn. I knew
what that was. It was a memorial to me and my father. He
looked old. Even as I watched I saw a gleeful Ragnvald raise
his sword and strike the old man in the back. It all went black.
In my dream, I smelled smoke and I saw flames. It was the
Haugr and it was burning. Drekar were on fire. There were
Bretons slaying people I had known since childhood. I saw
Brigid the alewife as she was hacked by Breton swords. I saw
Bagsecg Bagsecgson with hammer defending his family until
he was cut down. It was the end of my world as I had known it.
I heard a laugh which filled my head and I woke.*

Opening my eyes, I looked up and there was a sea bird above
my head. Then I heard another sound. It was the creak of a rope
and the crack of a sail. Then I heard a voice, it was Norse, "Ware
ahead, wreckage in the water."

I raised my arm. It was a mistake for the move made the
shield flip over. My arm was still attached to the strap and I was
dunked beneath the waves. I struggled to pull my arm from the
strap and my head broke the surface. I looked up at a row of
shields and warriors staring at me. It was a drekar. Would they
leave me or end my pain? Would they take pity on me and haul
me aboard? I was answered when a rope snaked over. I grabbed it
with both hands and I was dragged to the side. Strong arms
pulled me over and I flopped like a floundering fish on to the
deck.

"By the Allfather, jarl, we have caught the biggest fish I have
ever seen! Look at the size of this giant."

"Bergil you fool, he is a youth. Give him some ale, his mouth
is covered in salt."

"A waste of good ale, jarl. From the way those birds were
closing in he might be dead already."

I croaked, "No, I live. The Norns have saved me for a
purpose."

I opened my eyes and looked into the face of a grey-bearded
Viking. He smiled as the young warrior called Bergil held a horn
of ale to my mouth. Beer had never tasted as good. The Viking
said, "I am Rognvald Eysteinsson. Njoror the god of the sea has
sent you to me. I will see you safe to my home in Møre." He
stood, "Get us back on course. Beorn, go to my son's chest and
fetch a kyrtle and his cloak."

The one called Bergil shook his head, "Your son was a big
warrior but not as big as this one."

"He needs to be out of the wet kyrtle. He needs warmth." He put his hand out to me, "Can you stand?"

"Aye." I took his outstretched arm and pulled myself up. I was a head taller than the old man.

The one called Bergil shook his head, "What did they feed you when you were growing up? Whole cows?"

I pulled off the kyrtle as the ship's boy brought me a dry one. As soon as I donned it I felt warmer but my teeth began to chatter. Why was that? Rognvald Eysteinsson put the cloak about my shoulders. "Come to the steering board. I have a canvas rigged there. I would hear your story."

"First I would like to thank you. I owe you a life."

"No, for the gods have sent you to me for a purpose. The Norns have been spinning. Your thread was not yet ready to be cut." He waved over Bergil. "Watch over him. That storm looks like it is returning to us."

Bergil draped the sealskin cape around my shoulders and, gradually, my teeth stopped chattering. "What is your name, giant?"

"Rollo."

He frowned, "I thought you were Viking! You speak our language well if you are a Frank."

"I am no Frank! I am the son of Ragnvald Hrolfsson, grandson of Hrolf the Horseman."

Bergil laughed, "Then you must be Hrólfr the Walker for there is no horse big enough to carry you!" The men around laughed. I was too busy eating the salted ham they gave me to correct them and that became my name while I served under Jarl Rognvald Eysteinsson. I became Göngu-Hrólfr. It was not meant in a nasty way. It was, if anything, a compliment. I was just grateful to be alive. Now I had to plan how to get home and wreak my revenge. We were travelling in the wrong direction. We were travelling north!

"Where have you come from?" I noticed that the oars were only single manned and there were some chests without rowers. They were not rowing yet; the oars were raised but it seemed under crewed. She was only a threttanessa but I would have expected more warriors.

Bergil's face darkened, "We were raiding the land of the Franks. My cousin Eystein Rognvaldson and half of our crew were taken and slain when we were ambushed. My uncle felt the loss deeply. Eystein was his only son."

"The jarl lost a son?"

He nodded, "I think that is why he is so concerned about you. You are some father's son and he has saved you."

"Hands to oars!"

"I must go. We will talk later. I would hear your story."

I saw that the oars were unbalanced. They had one more on the steerboard side. It would make the helmsman's task harder. I saw that the jarl was at the steering board. I stood and walked to an empty chest and, taking an oar pushed it through the empty port. I watched for the other oars and I joined them in rowing. They were rowing silently. This was a saddened crew.

Bergil was behind me, "You had no need to row, Göngu-Hrólfr, although we are grateful."

"This will warm me up quicker than anything and I cannot sit idly by while others work. It is not in my nature."

"We are grateful and the drekar moves quicker."

The man in front of me shouted, "Less talk and more effort Bergil Big Mouth." Others laughed. I saw that the man, who was bare-armed had two dragons tattooed on them. It was exquisite work.

"Ignore Sven Blue Cheek, Göngu-Hrólfr. He and the others are jealous because I tell the best tales."

"But you do not sing when you row."

There was silence until the man before me, Sven Blue Cheek, said, quietly, "Eystein used to lead the singing. No one has the heart."

"Göngu-Hrólfr, have you a song to cheer us up?"

"I have." I chose the one about my grandfather.

The horseman came through darkest night
He rode towards the dawning light
With fiery steed and thrusting spear
Hrolf the Horseman brought great fear

Slaughtering all he breached their line
Of warriors slain, there were nine
Hrolf the Horseman with gleaming blade
Hrolf the Horseman all enemies slayed

With mighty axe Black Teeth stood
Angry and filled with hot blood
Hrolf the Horseman with gleaming blade

Hrolf the Horseman all enemies slayed
Ice cold Hrolf with Heart of Ice
Swung his arm and made it slice
Hrolf the Horseman with gleaming blade
Hrolf the Horseman all enemies slayed

In two strokes the Jarl was felled
Hrolf's sword nobly held
Hrolf the Horseman with gleaming blade
Hrolf the Horseman all enemies slayed

Bergil shouted, "A good song. I feel power racing through my veins. That is your grandfather?"

"Aye, he slew the Dane, Black Teeth."

"Until we are clear of Danish waters we do not like to speak of them." Sven Blue Cheek appeared to be the leader of the crew. He was like Harold Strong Arm had been.

"I am sorry. I did not know."

We rowed until noon and then the wind turned enough to make life easier for us. We stacked our oars and drank ale. The crew gathered around me. "Now, tell us your tale."

I was not certain I wanted to share the treachery of my brother but these warriors had given me a life. I told them all. My story was greeted with silence. "So, you were betrayed, left without a father and oathsworn, you died and were then reborn. I can see, Göngu-Hrólfr, that there is more to you than a chest as big as two men and a height which would dwarf trees." Bergil handed me another horn of ale. "I like you!"

I was tired and so I rested my head next to the chest I had used for rowing and, with my cloak over me, I fell asleep.

I was shaken awake by Jarl Rognvald Eysteinsson. "We have made camp on a beach. Come ashore. It will be more comfortable sleeping on a beach than the hard deck."

"I was so tired, jarl, that I could have slept standing up."

He put his hand out and helped to pull me up. "Bergil told me your story. My nephew is loud but he means well. The Norns have been spinning their webs again. I lost my son not far from your home and you lost your father even as I was sailing close to Cent. Our threads are bound."

We were alone and so I said, "What will become of me?"

He looked at me quizzically, "Become of you? I do not understand."

118

"I am grateful that you rescued me. Do you intend to put me ashore at a port?"

He laughed, "From what you told my men your grandfather was Norse. We do not abandon our own besides, were you not listening? Our threads are bound. You will come to Møre and join our clan. What would you have happen?"

I shrugged. I had thought I was bound to die and yet I lived. I had been to the bottom of the sea and survived. "I would return home and kill my brother. I know that I cannot do that yet; I have nothing save this coarse kyrtle and my seax. What use am I to you?"

"My son is lost. He has spare clothes and weapons. You will fight with our clan. Let us not look too far ahead. Njoror saved you and the Allfather was watching over you. Let us see what happens. Now come. There is hot food. I am certain that you need that."

My story had touched all of the crew. The fact that they had lost so many of their own men made my salvation even more precious. I seemed to represent the dead warriors. *Wyrd.*

I was not asked to stand a watch. When I awoke I felt refreshed. The jarl took me to the chest which had belonged to his son. He took out the clothes his son had left behind. They were a tight fit but they would do. The Norse wear loose-fitting clothes. There was also a short sword. One of the other crew found me a scabbard and a belt in the chest of another of their dead crewmates. I no longer felt naked. I had a sword.

The wind was with us and I watched the coast of Denmark fly by our steerboard side. I had never been this far north. The land of the East Angles was as far north as I had travelled. I was heading for the land which gave birth to my grandfather. He had not remembered much about it. He had been taken as a slave when he had been young. I spoke with the other crew. I discovered that Bergil was but a little older than I was and his dead cousin had been his age too. They had been the youngest on the drekar and they had been close.

"How did the Franks ambush you?"

"Horses! My uncle had captured a small village. Eystein went with half the crew to take another settlement we had spied when we had travelled down the coast. The Frankish horsemen caught them in the open. It is hard to stand against charging horses."

I shook my head, "You are wrong, Bergil. My people often fight the Franks. Sometimes we fight on horses too and so I know these things. If you lock your shields and present a sea of spears then a horse will not try to breach it."

"They can jump!"

It was my turn to laugh, "Not over a shield wall! Your cousin should have made a circle and walked back to his father. They might have lost one or two men but that is all."

Bergil nodded, "You are young but you know much about fighting."

"Yet I have only just been in my first raid. But my grandfather has passed on his knowledge. He is wise." I suddenly turned my head to look south. What of my grandfather? He was now in danger. Ragnvald did not like him. Perhaps another would become Jarl. As soon as the idea blossomed in my head it began to wither and die. The rest of the clan had been seduced by the one brave act; the slaying of the Breton warrior. By the time I would be able to travel south then he would have power and I feared that my grandfather would pay with his life.

I was lying on the deck looking at the clouds above us when the ship's boy shouted, "A Danish drekar and she is armed for war!"

Jarl Rognvald Eysteinsson shouted, "Arm yourselves."

For me that meant little. I had a seax and a short sword. There were six of the crew who had mail byrnies. The rest did not. Bergil had a leather vest. I thought of mine which now lay at the bottom of the Tamese Estuary.

"Where away?"

"The steerboard side; she is off our bow."

I looked and saw the sleek lines as the Danish drekar raced to cut us off. We could not outrun her. We would have to fight. I felt the ship heel to larboard as the jarl put the steering board over. He was making it as hard for the Dane as he could. There were open waters to the north and west. Much could happen.

Sven Blue Cheek shouted, "Bergil, Göngu-Hrólfr, protect the jarl. May the Allfather be with you." He handed me a shield. "It is the one which saved your life." He shouted to the others. Take two spears with you!"

I had fought on the one raid but I had practised my whole life. If I was to die then I would take as many Danes with me as I could. My head felt naked without a helmet but one advantage was that there was nothing to block my vision.

The jarl pointed to the stern, "Help me tie off the steering board. This old man will need to wield his blade if we are to win through and see our home once more." The three of us managed to fix the steering board in position. He shouted up to the masthead, "Beorn, I rely on you and your brother to keep the sails trimmed."

"Aye jarl!"

"Do you not have bows?"

Bergil shook his head, "Our archers were slain in the ambush."

I saw that the drekar was larger than that of Jarl Rognvald Eysteinsson. She would have a larger crew. It was hard to see how we could win. My grandfather had told me that a real warrior never gave up. There was always hope. The dream I had had was of the future. It was not written yet. I would live and change the future. My descent to the ocean bottom had proved that the Norns had not yet done with me. I pulled the shield a little tighter to me. It was a Danish one. There was neither boss nor metal studs. The soaking in the sea had done it no good either but it would protect my left side a little. Although it was a short sword my reach would mean I could still fight an opponent with a longer sword. As the Dane drew closer I noticed many Danish axes. That gave me hope. Harold Strong Arm had told me that a Danish axe needed room to swing. There was precious little of that on a drekar. He had also advised me to keep a wider stance than normal. That was especially true for me. I was so tall that it would be easy to overbalance.

As I adjusted my feet Bergil said, "What are you doing?"

The jarl smiled as he said, "Showing me that he has been taught well. The deck of a drekar is never the easiest of fighting platforms. Do not overswing nephew. I would hate to have to tell my sister that I lost her only son at sea!"

The Dane was now two lengths astern of us. His bow would catch us amidships. That was where Sven Blue Cheek and the bulk of the warriors were waiting with shields already locked. If they could stop their warriors boarding then we had a chance. The ones who would attack first would be the bravest and the most reckless. If they died then the others might not be as confident.

"Your two flank me. Göngu-Hrólfr, on my right. Bergil my left." The jarl was encased in mail. His helmet was an open one but he had a mail hood beneath it. Bergil had a similar helmet but without the hood.

I could now see the eager Danes. They lined the side. Four stood on the gunwale and were holding onto the forestays. Had we had bows then they would be dead. All four wore a mail byrnie. Suddenly Sven Blue Cheek hurled a spear. It struck one of the Danes in the chest and he tumbled into the water. A second had been holding the same stay and as the first was struck, he lost his grip and he also tumbled beneath the waves. Here the bottom would not be obligingly close. The Dane was as good as dead already. Two more men took the places of the fallen warriors. These had leather vests and Danish axes. Sven shouted, "Spears!" fifteen spears flew. One of the men who was about to board was struck and the others clattered and fell into the well of the drekar. Some found flesh for there were cries. Then the Danish drekar stuck.

Our ship shook. Wood splintered on our gunwale and the dragon prow fouled our forestay. With a roar, the three jumpers leapt towards our shields. It was brave but foolish. Sven and his men had spears ready and the three were plucked from the air. Their bodies dropped between the two hulls which were beginning to grind together as the wind pushed the Dane closer to us. The bulk of their warriors would try to board in the middle where they could use the height of the bow to drop onto our lowest point. Their stern was swinging around but their greater length meant that we would have the height advantage.

The jarl saw this and he pointed to the spears which lay close to us. "Use those. Kill the helmsman and the crew around the steering board."

I sheathed my short sword and picked up a spear. Pulling my arm back I hurled it the ten paces to the stern just behind ours. My spear struck the helmsman in the thigh. The jarl might have been old but he had a good eye. His spear struck a warrior in the face. Bergil's managed to strike the shoulder of another. I glanced down our ship. Sven and the crew were holding off the Danes. There were four left by the steering board and the rest were trying to support the men attempting to climb across from the prow. I saw a chance. I climbed up on to the gunwale. The Dane was swinging closer to us. When it was just three paces from us I leapt. I do not think another could have made the leap for you needed long legs and none had longer than me. They were not expecting such a rash and reckless act from someone without mail.

I landed heavily on the Dane's deck and began to lose my
balance. I used my long legs and I strode towards the four men
who were unwounded. My speed saved me. The Danish shield I
held smashed into the hand and the face of a Dane. I slashed to
the side and my newly acquired sword bit into the thigh of a
warrior. Blood pumped from his leg. The pitching deck became
even more treacherous as the blood poured across it making it
slippery and slick. A spear flew past me and struck the shield of
the Dane who was advancing towards me. The weight of it made
his shield drop and I lunged and struck him in the chest. My
height helped me again. I whirled as I sensed someone coming at
my back. There were two of them. Instead of backing off, I ran at
them holding the shield before me. As the deck pitched they
slipped in the blood and both tumbled over the side.

There were three men left but they were all wounded. I
picked up a Danish axe and brought it back behind my head. I
swung it over to smash through the steering board, the withy and
the rope. The swing was so hard that the axe remained embedded
in the deck. The drekar was rudderless.

"Göngu-Hrólfr back!" Bergil was pointing. The Danes had
seen what I was about and some were rushing towards me.

I spied a fine helmet and I grabbed it. After I put it on I took
the long sword that one of the warriors had had. The Danes were
getting close. I took the shield from my arm and I threw it like a
skimming stone towards them. Even as they slowed and held
their shields to protect themselves from the missile I clambered
up onto the gunwale and slashed the backstay, Gripping the rope
and my new sword I swung out over the grey sea towards our
ship. I would not reach it. I let go and flew through the air. As I
neared the sheerstrakes I struck at them with my sword. It bit in
and I held on for grim death. Bergil raced down and threw me a
rope. Using the rope and the sword I climbed up the side.

"Look out Bergil!"

Two men had managed to get aboard our ship and were
racing to Bergil. He picked up his shield and bravely faced them.
I clambered over the side, wrenching the sword from the side of
the ship. The two Danes were so concerned with Bergil that,
when I suddenly ran at them with two swords in my hand, they
were taken aback. I used the short sword to fend off the Dane's
sword as I rammed my long sword through his side. My sword
came through and hit the other Dane whom Bergil slew.

Beorn the ship's boy had slid down to our forestay and was hacking, with his short sword, at the entangled ropes. The Dane's sail fluttered for I had cut the backstay when I had swung over. As the forestay was cut and without a rudder, it began to drift away. We still had the wind. There was a creak followed by a groan and we burst free from the Dane's clutches. The three men who were still aboard us were hacked and butchered by Sven and our crew.

The Danes waved impotent swords at us. I saw two of our crew drop their breeks and bare their backsides. The rest of the crew laughed and cheered. Sven Blue Cheek shouted, "Strip the bodies of everything and then throw them for the fishes. Get some water and clear this blood. Well done Beorn! That was smartly done!"

Bergil nodded to me, "I owe you a life."

"You pulled me aboard!"

"It is not the same. You could have easily pulled yourself up. I thank you." He shook his head and pointed to the drifting Danish drekar. "That was a prodigious leap. You are fearless. What were you thinking?"

"That the Danes had cost me my mail, my sword and my helmet. I wanted vengeance."

He laughed, "Come let us help my uncle to untie the steering board. I am sure he will wish to thank you too."

The jarl had taken off his helmet and was untying our knots. As we helped him he said, "You will be an asset to our clan, Göngu-Hrólfr. You had no need to do what you did."

We had freed the steering board and he pushed it over to resume our course. "I did for they had already managed to get men on board. The two whom Bergil and I slew would have aided the ones at their stern. It was a gamble." I smiled, "And I flew!"

The jarl laughed, "Aye you did!"

Chapter 10

Møre was a long way up the Norwegian coast. It was surrounded by islands and lay nestled in a fjord. I did not envy any raider trying to sail into it. It was as secure a home as I had seen. It needed no walls for nature was its defence. There was a wooden jetty. I saw another drekar already tied up there. Bergil said, "That belongs to my uncle, Bjorn Eysteinsson. He will be sad that my cousin died. He was my uncle's favourite. Everyone liked him. This will be a sad homecoming." He pointed to the women who were gathered on the side watching us arrive. They would be able to see that we were few in number. Mothers, wives and daughters would be looking for their men. Many would be disappointed.

Jarl Rognvald Eysteinsson wandered over to me. "We will take my son's belongings ashore and then his chest will be yours."

"Thank you, jarl. I know this must be hard for you."

"We could not bring back my son's body. The Franks displayed them on spears. We saw them as we sailed home. We need vengeance."

Bergil said, "You can stay with me. There is just my mother and me. There is room."

"Thank you but I would not wish to be a burden."

"A burden? There are tales and songs in you, Göngu-Hrólfr. I will milk you for them!"

I waited until the rest of the crew had gone ashore before I took my few belongings and stepped on to the jetty. Everyone else had a family to greet them. I did not wish to intrude. However, everyone was staring at me as I walked down the jetty toward the land.

Jarl Rognvald Eysteinsson raised his hand and shouted, "Everyone, this is the new member of our clan. We fished him from the sea and he repaid us by saving us from Danish pirates. He is a mighty warrior: Göngu-Hrólfr."

His words were greeted by cheers from the crew who had sailed with me. I saw a woman who nestled in the jarl's arms. She was weeping and I guessed it would be the jarl's wife. There was nothing I could say. Back in the Haugr, it would be my grandmother who would be weeping and my mother grieving in Benni's Ville. Who would comfort my mother? I doubted that it would be Ragnvald.

A smiling woman with grey hair hugged Bergil. It was his mother. He spoke to her and then she came to me. Her head came to just above my waist. She put her arms around it and hugged me. "You saved my son's life. I am grateful. You are welcome to my home but I fear we have no bed that is big enough for you."

"I need no bed, lady. Some straw in a sack will do."

She stepped back and looked appalled, "Straw in a sack! We can do better than that. We have goose feathers. Come let us get you home and I will need to get out my needles. You will need clothes!"

The houses were all perched against the rocks. I wondered where they farmed for there seemed to be just rocks with trees precariously clinging to them. I had come to a world which was totally different from my own home. It would take some getting used to. I paused and looked down at the fjord and the jetty. There were two drekar. If I could persuade the jarl then we could sail down to my home and retake what was mine. The longer I was away the more power would be in the hands of my brother.

My first few days in Møre were spent meeting people. The jarl's wife, Gefn, was a lovely lady. She had lost her only son and had grieved but as soon as she was able I was sent for. "The jarl has told me all that you did for him and the crew. But for you, there would be more widows in Møre. No one can replace our son but we believe that you have been sent here to fill his place."

I saw the jarl nod, "When we fished you out from that empty ocean I knew that there was something special about you. After the voyage home I am certain. We have another warrior in the clan."

The jarl's brother was also keen to show me that he held me in high regard. He presented me with a shield. It had a boss and was studded with metal. "This belonged to my son. He did not die in battle. It was two years since that he died of the coughing sickness. We buried him with his sword but his shield is for you."

"I thank you and I will bear it with honour."

By the end of the first ten days, I had a complete set of clothes including sealskin cap, fur cloak and even a pair of sealskin boots. As Bergil said, "The one animal we have in abundance is the seal. We sail to the islands each year and take many of them. Their flesh keeps us in winter."

"What are winters like up here?" I confess that I was worried. I could not remember us having snow which lasted for more than a day or two in the Land of the Horse.

"They are harsh and the days in winter are so short that we have some days when the sun appears for a brief moment and is then gone."

"What do you do then?"

He laughed, "We make more warriors!"

"And the raiding season?"

"We are in the middle of it. Our voyage to the land of the Franks was a scouting expedition. My uncle has been repairing his drekar. If we had been successful then we would have returned there now..."

I was disappointed, "Then you will not raid there this season?"

"No, we lost too many men. My uncle wishes us to be stronger. We will make alliances with our neighbours and take more ships. It will not be easy. We have had feuds with other clans. My cousin's death may be a good thing. Had he been killed by a Viking then we would have continued our feuds. Now we can put those arguments behind us. The head of our tribe has spoken of making war on the men of Sogn but that will not be this year. Now that we have you we have two mighty warriors: Göngu-Hrólfr and Sven Blue Cheek."

"Then we will raid the land of the Franks?"

"I can read your mind Göngu-Hrólfr, you wish to go to your home. Two or three years should be enough time for us to gather the fleet that we will need. We will be raiding again at the end of the month."

"And where will we raid?"

"The Danes. They keep pigs. They feed us well over the winter. It is not far to travel and we know the waters better than we did those of Frankia."

I was disappointed. It must have shown.

"Where would you raid?"

"There are churches along the east coast of Northumbria. They would be just as close and they would yield greater rewards."

"They have stronger defences. The days when they were like sheep to be fleeced are gone." He shrugged, "When you have

127

been here a while then your voice will be heard. My uncle does listen to his warriors. Sven Blue Cheek is the most important of warriors. He has defeated many other champions in single combat. He likes you. If you can get him to support your idea for a raid on the east coast then it may happen."

"But not this season."

"No. The clan decided where we would raid three days after you arrived. We held a Thing." He looked at me apologetically. "You are not yet one of the clan. When it is Yule you will be made one of the clan. After that, you can speak."

I had time before we raided to make a bow and some arrows. I had used a bow since I had been able to stand alone. Now that I was much bigger and stronger I could use a much longer bow. My grandfather had always said that the longer the bow the better. The hardest part was to find a yew. It was Bergil's mother who told me where to find one. I cut and shaped the bow over a period of three days. She also had plenty of goose feathers. When I had made my arrows, I used flint for the heads. I had no coin for metal.

Bergil saw me practising. "What do you want a bow for? A warrior fights with a sword or a spear."

"True but a bow can be useful and besides I have a mind to go hunting. I would like a deer hide jerkin. I am used to fighting in mail."

"Mail is expensive!"

"Most of my father's warriors had mail."

"I will come hunting with you. I know where there are deer."

Bergil brought a spear and he carried a water skin and a bag with food. That should have warned me that this would not be as quick as at home, in the Land of the Horse. I knew that it would be more difficult to hunt here than at home. At home, the land was largely flat. The trees were different and I knew my way around; also, I could ride. Here we walked, and in places, climbed. The deer were also different from the ones I had hunted. Their tracks were the same but they grazed different areas. If I had not had Bergil with me then I might not have even found one. As it was it took us most of the morning and into the afternoon until we found some. We were almost in the next valley when we did so. There were two of them.

I held an arrow ready to nock. I had practised with the bow but that had been without flint arrowheads. I held a spare arrow against the bow. Pine needles were a hazard. They crunched when you stepped on them and they were more slippery than I had expected. After I had made a noise and they had skittered some thirty paces from us then I changed my approach. I looked for the rocks and used those. It made my approach even slower. When I was just forty paces from them I nocked my arrow and pulled back. I had made a good bow. Grandfather would have been proud. I released and Ullr must have guided my hand. The arrow flew true and struck the doe. She managed ten paces before she fell to the ground.

Bergil slapped my back. "A fine hit. May I try the bow?"

"Of course." I handed him the spare arrow and the bow. He pulled it back. He could not manage to get half the distance I had.

"By the Allfather! How do you manage to pull back this beast?"

"You make a bow for the man who draws it. If we made one for you then it would be shorter." I shrugged, "I am a big warrior."

We reached the deer and while I gutted it Bergil rammed the spear he had brought through its body. It would make it easier for us to carry. I left the heart and kidneys in the animal but I put the rest by the spilt blood for Ullr to thank him for his help. The arrow was ruined. Had I been at home I could have re-fletched it and used it again. The flint had done its job but it had broken and the shaft with it.

As we carried the carcass down the twisting path I asked, "Have you a smith? When I get coin, I would have some arrows made and I will need metal for my leather jerkin."

"I would not worry overmuch about that, Göngu-Hrólfr. When we raid the Danes, you can take metal from them."

Bergljót, Bergil's mother, was delighted with the venison. I skinned it for I wanted the largest piece of deer hide I could get. When you are my size then you are aware of such things. The meat would be prepared in two ways. We would eat some of it and the rest would be preserved. I gave a haunch of it to Jarl Rognvald Eysteinsson. Gefn beamed, "You are such a kind and thoughtful young man." Her eyes welled up, "Your poor mother will be worried about you."

Jarl Rognvald Eysteinsson said, "You know, mother, that a Viking steps into the world knowing that he might never return home."

Gefn looked sadly at her husband, "And a Viking woman never ceases grieving and worrying."

She was right and I felt guilty. I had given little thought to my mother and her predicament. I had not finished preparing the deer hide before we left to raid. I had clothes now and I would have to use my sealskin cape as protection. At least I had helmet, shield and sword. I did not feel so bad when I boarded the drekar. There were others who were dressed as I was. Some had no helmets and many were my age. The difference was that this would be their first raid. I felt like a veteran. I put my belongings in the chest. As we rowed down the fjord to the sea I was able to admire the rugged nature of the land. I could see why they needed no horses here. The land would not support them. It explained why they thought I would be too big for a horse. They had ponies which were so small that they could walk between my legs without touching me. It was a lovely land but it was not mine. As we left the fjord and turned south I knew that this would be the first step on a long journey but that journey would take me home. I would be returning to the Land of the Horse.

It took two days for us to reach the seas of the Danes. I was relieved to see that this land was not like Jarl Rognvald Eysteinsson's. There were islands and the land was flat. The two brothers had raided here before and they knew where they wished to raid. Jarl Rognvald Eysteinsson took us away from the land so that we could approach in the dark. This was not like the raid in Wessex. There we had had many ships and a river to use. Here we sailed through the dark to a shadow. The jarl was a skilful sailor. There were no chants and no shouts. The ship's boys came down and spoke quietly with our orders. Two men were left to scull the last few paces as we shipped our oars, donned our helmets and took our shields from the sides. Some warriors had no sword but those carried spears. I noticed that none of these warriors donned colours on their faces and hands. Some of my grandfather's warriors did.

We slid up on a shingle beach. I was new and I knew my place. The jarl and his brother leapt ashore first followed by Sven Blue Cheek. The warriors with mail led the way. There were just ten warriors who wore mail. The rest of us, all forty looked ragged by comparison. Bergil ran with me. He had become my oar brother. Jarl Rognvald Eysteinsson and Sven Blue Cheek had moved us so that we rowed together. That made us shield brothers. The Danes had a stockade. Bergil had told me that when we had sailed south. The Danes thought that would protect them. The jarl believed that they did not keep a night watch.

We loped through the trees. They were more familiar to me
than the ones in which we had hunted. I smelled the smoke of
cooking fires. We were close. We halted when I could see the
solid shadow of the stockade. Sven Blue Cheek waved his arm
and we moved into a long line. The plan was to scale the walls
and fall upon them. The idea was a familiar one. Two men would
hold a shield and a third would use it to ascend. A young warrior,
Arne Larsson was with us. He looked a little slight to me. As we
neared the wall I realised that I could almost reach the top of it
with my hands. As Arne unshipped his shield I shook my head
and turned with my back to the wall. Bergil realised what I
intended. He put a sealskin boot in my hands and I lifted him up.
He put his feet on my shoulders and slipped over the wall. I
nodded to a surprised Arne. He did the same. The two were in the
stockade before anyone else. I stepped away and then ran at the
wooden wall. Arne and Bergil reached out and grabbed an arm. I
scrambled up the wall. I made a noise but it was not a loud one.

The three of us were the first on the fighting platform along
with Sven Blue Cheek. This was not the plan. The first ones
inside were supposed to be mailed, warriors. Sven pointed to the
gate while he helped his shield brother up. I led the way. Arne
hesitated and Bergil just followed me. We had not said that this
was what we would do but it felt right. I had fought more times
than both of them. I drew my sword and swung my shield around.
With the wall to my left, I would have the freedom to swing with
my right arm.

There was a sentry. A Dane was resting with his back against
the stockade. He must have been asleep but the vibration of our
feet along the fighting platform awoke him. He stood and looked
around him. That hesitation cost him his life. I swung my sword
so hard that it took his head which flew beyond the walls and the
headless corpse slid to the fighting platform. I climbed down the
ladder and reached the gate. I sheathed my sword and laid my
shield on the ground. I took the heavy bar and lifted it from the
gate. I placed it on the ground and, picking up my shield, opened
the gate. Bergil and Arne joined me as Jarl Rognvald Eysteinsson
led the older warriors inside the walls. He nodded his thanks.

He and his oathsworn took the lead. The jarl's brother
pointed to Arne and another young warrior to stand and guard the
gate. I think Arne was grateful. We had not reached the first hut
when the alarm was given. A woman came out of a hut and,
seeing Jarl Rognvald Eysteinsson, screamed. One of his warriors

slew her. I do not think he even knew it was a woman. It was a shadow which screamed but I saw her body as we passed. A warrior stepped out with a sword in hand. He lunged at me. I instinctively brought around my shield and the blade slid along it. He was so close that I could not swing my sword. I pulled back my arm and struck him in the side of the head with the pommel of my sword. He fell to the ground and Bergil stabbed him. We stepped into the hut. There were three children. I pointed to the door and shouted, "Run!" They looked terrified. Later Bergil told me that he would have been terrified if a giant had entered his world when he had been so young. They ran.

I saw the warrior's chest and opened it as Bergil searched the rest of the hut. He found the family's coins and took them. We emptied the chest of that which we did not need and added the coins. We placed the chest by the door. We would retrieve it before we left. Once outside we headed towards the clamour of sword on sword. The Danes had made a shield wall before their chief's hall. Our mailed men were in a wedge led by the jarl, his brother and, at the fore Sven Blue Cheek. We took our place at the rear of the line. I put my shield into the back of the next man and I pushed. I was big and I was heavy. The wedge lurched forward.

With mailed, experienced men at the front, our wedge hacked and slashed into the heart of the half-formed Danish shield wall. We, at the back, were just weight. Suddenly we almost lost our footing as the jarl slew their chief and we broke through.

"Break wedge!"

I turned and ran towards three Danes who were just five paces from me. Bergil ran at them with me. My height gave me an advantage. I had a longer sword than they did and my arms were longer too. I swung at them as they closed with us. My sword sliced through the head of the first warrior and the tip ripped the cheek of the second one. My shield smashed into him, knocking him to the ground. As he lay there, sprawled like a beached fish I plunged my sword through his chest. The third Dane was glancing fearfully at me as Bergil slid his sword into his ribs.

We looked around. There were no more Danes. Our warriors were searching for the dead Danes. We had three before us. Their purses yielded coins. We took their helmets, swords and daggers. They were metal and, as such, they were valuable. We left their hammers around their necks. It was bad luck to take a warrior's token. There was a hut nearby. We entered. The family had fled. The warrior's chest lay there. We opened it and discarded the clothes. After putting in the swords, helmets and daggers we searched the hut. There was a mail shirt. Too small for me it was a good fit for Bergil. His eyes lit up. "Mine?"

I grinned, "It might fit one of my arms. Yours."

We moved the sleeping sack. I found a sword. It was not just any sword. It was a long sword. It was almost the height of a man. The gods had sent it to me. When I moved it, I saw an area of soft earth. Using my seax I cleared it. The tip touched a box. We dug it up. It was the family fortune. There were coins. When I had lived in the Land of the Horse I might have given them to one of the servants. Now they represented the start of a fortune. If I was to lead men south and have vengeance then I needed coin. We put the coins in our chest and we carried it out. We headed back to the first hut. We put the first chest on top of this larger one and walked back to the drekar. I laid my new sword on the top. Others were making the same journey as well as the wounded warriors who were being taken back. We dumped the two chests on the jetty and then turned to return to the village.

We could see that the battle, if battle it was, was over. Warriors had taken off their helmets. They were drinking the villagers' ale. I heard the squeal of pigs and the lowing of cattle. Sven Blue Cheek nodded to us. He was always a hard man to please. "You did well. Your weight came in handy!"

Bergil shook his head. "We slew five warriors, Sven Blue Cheek. When we both have mail then you will see us next to you."

He laughed, "That will be the day!"

The Jarl and his brother walked towards us behind eight pigs and six young cows which were being driven towards the drekar. They both looked happy. "A good raid. We lost but one warrior."

Bjorn Eysteinsson nodded, "We caught them while they slept. They should have had a guard." He pointed at me. "And, of course, they did not know that we had a giant with us who could boost men over the wall. I believe that you, Bergil and Arne made it easier for us. Brother, you made a fine catch!"

The jarl looked sad, "The gods took my son and gave us Göngu-Hrólfr. The clan may be happy but I have still lost a son."

Bergil said, "I have no father. Now that I have a byrnie I will try to be the son you lost."

The jarl put his arm around Bergil, "Then between the two of you there should be a son for me eh? Come let us board the drekar. We will have a noisy and smelly journey home."

Bergil asked, "Do we not take slaves?"

"We do not have enough room. The chests and supplies we took and the animals will have to be enough."

Once at the drekar, we loaded our two chests below the deck along with the sacks of wheat, barley and oats. The other chests were placed there too. It seemed that the animals apart, the treasure remained the property of the one who took it. They were a different clan to mine.

The jarl was right, we could not have carried slaves. We lost one pig which became agitated when we put to sea. It ran around before using a chest to leap into the sea. The fishes would feed well. It was fortunate that the wind was from the south-west and we did not need to row much. It would have been hard to do so with the animals we had on board. The ship's boys were in constant demand to clean up after the beasts.

I got to know the rest of the crew. I knew Arne. He was relieved to have survived. I recalled that he had been happy to guard the gate. He was still to be blooded. Leif Jorgensen was older than Bergil and I but he had, unlike Sven Blue Cheek, a sense of humour. He regaled us with funny stories as we watched the grey seas scud by. Sven Blue Cheek seemed preoccupied with war and being a warrior. I learned, through Leif's words, rather than Sven's, that Sven had not been born into the clan. He had had a falling out with his shipmates and the jarl had discovered him on the island of Ljoðhús. Grateful not to be marooned amongst people he did not know he swore allegiance to the jarl. That had been five years since and in that time, he had made the clan stronger for he was a real warrior. He reminded me of Harold Strong Arm.

"Sven, the jarl's brother said that we gained access to the Danes too easily for they had no guards. They had a wall and we have neither wall nor guards. What if we were raided?"

Sven nodded and gave me a sideways look. Before he could speak, Leif said, "We are a long way down the fjord. It would take a determined enemy to find us."

I persisted, "But if they did then we might all suffer the same fate as the Danes."

Before Leif could speak again Sven put up his hand, "You are right. I have made the same point to the jarl. His clan never needed one and he sees no reason to build a stockade. Did you have one?"

"We needed one for our land is flat and close to the coast. It is fertile and ripe for raiding. My grandfather and my father built stone walls and my grandfather has a stone tower."

"The jarl likes you, Göngu-Hrólfr. He might listen to you. We did not slay all the Danes in the village. They know who we are and there are other villages on the island. We picked a rich one but one which we knew was poorly defended."

I was interested, "How did you know that?"

"Last year we took the drekar down and we traded with them. They like our seal oil."

"Then they will know exactly who you are. Perhaps you should have gone in disguise."

Sven laughed, "I can see that we have a cunning warrior here. Your size suggests that you are all muscle but that is not true. There is a sharp brain inside your head."

It took two days to reach the fjord. I was glad when we saw our home for it meant I would not have the stink of pigs and cattle in my nostrils. The animals were taken off first and the decks swilled down. We then lifted the deck. The cereal was taken ashore as well as the preserved meat we had taken. The Danes also made good, hard cheese and we unloaded the six rounds. Then we took the chests. We had all marked our own. Bergil and I had the luxury of being able to take our two chests to his home. We could examine our booty without prying eyes.

Bergljót was relieved that her son was still alive, "I have the venison bones. I have made a stew with them and some salted meat. We have pickled fish as well. You can show me what you have brought when I have added some vegetables and dumplings to the stew."

Bergil had eyes only for his byrnie. He waved a distracted hand at me as I took out the weapons and helmets we had collected. "Take whatever you wish. I have a mail vest."

I nodded, "Good. I will see if the smith will let me use his forge. I would melt down the poorer helmets and weapons to make arrowheads and studs from my leather jerkin and shield."

"Next time we raid you will get mail."

"No Bergil. I will have to have a mail shirt made and they are not cheap." I had sorted the coins out. "We both have money but there is not enough yet for a byrnie. Besides, Sven said that we would not be raiding again this year. We have no reason."

Bergil looked disappointed. "I wanted to wear the mail!"

"It takes some getting used to. If I were you I would have your mother make you a padded kyrtle to go beneath it. They chafe and, even with mail, you can still be hurt by a blow from a sword. The quilted kyrtle will soften it."

"You had a mail byrnie?"

"When I was younger and before I grew. My last one lies at the bottom of the ocean. I had a fine helmet too. When last I fought I had a byrnie which was more like a vest or jerkin."

Bergil laid down his byrnie, "This must seem like a poor and backward place to you. No wall, poor farms and warriors who cannot afford mail."

I shook my head, "No, Bergil for if it were not for this haven, I would lie at the bottom of the sea. It is not what I am used to but that is my challenge. I must make it stronger so that I can be returned to my family. You could come with me!"

"I could not leave my mother but I would like to see it. This Haugr you speak of sounds magical!"

"It is, Bergil, it is." I became sad when I thought of the home I had had and now had lost. What was happening there? Was my dream that which was happening or that which might happen?

Bergil was pleased with his find but I was even more pleased. I examined my long sword. It was a fine weapon. The hut we had searched must have been the chiefs. This weapon was too good for an ordinary warrior. From the hilt, I guessed the Dane had used it two-handed. The chief had not taken it for he needed to use a shield wall. Perhaps this was for those times when he fought others in single combat. I was tall enough to be able to use it. I had found treasure. I had a sword. Not only that I had a sword which only I could use. Once again, I realised that my thread was still being spun. The Norns' web was a complicated one. I was on the path to becoming a warrior once more.

Chapter 11

I discovered that winter came early when you lived this far north. We had much to do in order to prepare the two drekar for winter. We dragged them onto the small beach which was just upstream from the jetty. Stripped to our breeks we cleaned all the weed from the hull. It was a slow job. The barnacles and limpets had to be scoured off with a blade and I had bloody hands after a short time. Then we had to coat the strakes with a mixture made from pine tar and resin. In all, it took four days by which time the weather had deteriorated. We then had to make more pine tar to take with us when we sailed. While we waited for the coating to dry on one side, so that we could do the other, we went into the forests to cut down two spare masts and yards. I knew from my father's shipwright, Harold Haroldsson, that every ship needed a complete set of spares and whilst some of the smaller pieces of equipment could be quickly fashioned, masts and spars were specifically sourced. I enjoyed it.

"Give Göngu-Hrólfr an axe. I would like to see how he can use those long arms and broad back of his."

Sven was challenging me. I did not mind and I accepted it. Harold Strong Arm had shown me how to use an axe. He had taught me for war but the stroke would be the same for timber. We had long axes. They were not war axes. We had taken some of those from the Danes we had killed. This was a more functional axe. With a sharp blade and long handle, it was for one purpose only: to fell trees. The tree was not massive. It was as wide as my leg. I held the axe with my right hand closer to the head and my left at the end of the axe. I pulled the axe behind and above me. As I swung I slipped my right hand down the shaft to my left. The tree shivered when I struck it. The blade had bitten deeply into the trunk. The warriors watching gave an appreciative cheer. My second blow was struck horizontally and was just as fierce a blow. A large wedge of wood fell from the tree. I moved to the other side and repeated the two blows. They did this three more times. By then I knew that it would not take much to bring it down. The tree was already teetering. I pulled back my arm and struck my last blow. I stepped out of the way as the tree crashed through its lesser companions and hit the ground.

Sven took the axe from me. "You have earned the right to watch us try to do the same. When next we fight, try a Danish axe. I would like to see that!"

We had taken hatchets and side axes as well as saws. I could not let my shield brothers do all the work and we all joined in trimming the tree to the right size. We then sought smaller ones for two yards. We carried them back down to the village. Four days later we launched the drekar again and the figureheads were repainted. All was finished as the first flakes of snow fell. As a reward, the jarl had laid on a feast. I found that I was happy here. It might have been perfect save for the fact that I needed to have vengeance and I was worried about my home, my family and, most of all, my grandfather.

At the feast, I was seated close to the jarl. He had asked me to join him. I am not sure that his brother appreciated the honour for he was seated on the other side of Gefn. "Sven is not easily impressed, young giant. Yet he is impressed by you. He says you believe we should build a stockade and keep a watch."

I nodded, "Winter is coming, is it not, jarl?"

"Yes, the fjord often freezes. The world becomes white and our nights are so long that we have no days."

"Then if I were a Dane I would choose that time to come and to raid. Darkness can hide killers and men can use the ice as a roadway." I saw the jarl take that in. I had my arguments prepared. "And what will the men do in the winter? Bergil says that they will make new warriors. From what I have heard that will take but the blink of an eye." The jarl laughed and nodded. "I know that the ground is too hard now to build a stockade. All we need is two men in a wooden tower to watch. We have fifty men. That is a whole day or a long night of watchers. Each pair could do one hour. The Franks use candles which are marked so that they can measure time."

"And the stockade would be built when the snow melts?"

"That would be a good time. It would help to prepare the warriors for raids. In my experience men become fat and lazy in their halls in wintertime"

"I will give it consideration and I will talk about it to my brother and my wife. It is not without merit."

Brothers in Blood

Sven had been listening and, as the jarl went over to speak to another warrior Sven Blue Cheek leaned over. "How did you manage to persuade him when I could not?"

"I just gave him answers to questions he had yet to think of. He did not agree to build a tower. He said he would consider it."

Sven laughed, "But he will. More ale for Göngu-Hrólfr!"

Sven was right and, from then on, all of us were given a duty. First, we had to build the tower. That was easy for there was plenty of wood left over from the mast and yards. It rose ten paces into the air and a ladder was made to allow the sentries to climb. It had a roof and there was a cow's horn. It had come from the cow we had slaughtered for the feast. It would be sounded if there was danger. Sven took charge of the manning of the tower. He reminded all of us of the Danish village. We were paired off with our oar mates. We drew lots for our first duty. There were enough of us so that the duty would change over a period of time. Those that had the dark hours at first, would eventually have either the brief time of dawn or the flash that would be sunset.

As luck would have it Bergil and I drew one which entailed being woken. It was hard to leave the comfortable goose down bed, get dressed and go into a night where our breath froze before our faces. On that first duty, I took my bow and arrows as well as my sword.

"Why the bow?"

"If I see someone then while you sound the horn I can try to hit him."

We settled into the tower. We had a fine view of the fjord. It had yet to freeze. We could see the drekar and the halls and houses. Sven himself had picked the site for the tower.

"How far can you send an arrow?"

I tested it not long after I made it. "I can make an arrow travel more than two hundred paces along the flat."

"And from a tower?"

I shrugged, "I have yet to try that out. But I would guess further."

We settled into a routine. Despite some misgivings, none of the warriors seemed to object to the duty. It was not long. It gave us a chance to talk to oar brothers. I told Bergil all about my home and he told me about the village and his dead cousin. He told me of his other cousin, Bjorn's son. He told me how it had affected the whole clan. He had been a popular warrior. Some had said he would be able to lead the clan.

When we met the other sentries, we were able to compare our duties. Sound travels at night and the young men in the warrior hall were the closest to the tower. The noises which emanated thence were a great source of amusement and embarrassment. The tower became a focal point of our day and that helped us grow closer as warriors.

I found the smithy and the smith was more than happy to let me use his forge in exchange for some labour. I did not mind. I was still growing and it made me stronger. When the weather turned colder it was the perfect place to be. Working with Farmaðr gave me new skills. I melted down my scrap metal and used the moulds I had made from river clay for the arrowheads and the studs for my jerkin and shield. I made simple arrowheads. They were narrower than hunting arrows. I wanted something which would penetrate a mail ring. In the long nights leading up to Yule, I made arrows and fashioned my jerkin. That too was made simply. I did not have enough to cover my arms. I used the hole where the head of the deer had been and used thongs for the sides. That way, if I continued to grow, it would still fit. There would just be increasingly large gaps at the side.

Yule came and went. They celebrated Yule differently to the Clan of the Horse. I knew why. They had no Christians living amongst them. I enjoyed Yule. It was nature which was celebrated and the power of the gods. It was not the birth of a baby in a faraway land. The sea ice which I had been promised never materialized and the waters remained free for our fishing boats to catch fish for us to eat.

After Yule, the nights became shorter. Not by much, it was imperceptible at first but the duties became a kind of timepiece we had something we could use to reference its passing. We knew that the new grass would show when the snows melted. Already the lower slopes were more mud and slush than snow. Bergil and I had just come down the tower after a middle of the night duty. It had been a night with a bright moon. Bergil's mother always left a good fire and a jug of ale. We used to reward ourselves by putting a healthy knob of butter in the ale along with some juniper berries and then plunging a hot poker into it. Sometimes we added cream. The hot drink helped us to sleep. We just took off our cloaks when we saw the table with the ale and the cheese. We both wore our armour. Bergil liked to wear his new byrnie and I was always warmer in the deerskin jerkin. It looked so appetising we did not change. We ate and we drank.

Even though we had been talking for most of our watch we talked as we drank our ale.

When we were together Bergil called me Rollo. It seemed more appropriate than Göngu-Hrólfr. "Rollo, do you have girls in your land?"

I laughed, "Of course! How do you think we make babies?"

"No, I meant are they pretty girls? Are they the kind a warrior would like to lie with?"

"I suppose." I drank some beer and thought about it. "We are lucky. We have women who were once slaves. They are Saxons, Hibernians, Welsh, even Franks. It means we have lots of different types of women, why?"

"I don't know if you have noticed but we do not have many girls here and those we have are guarded by their fathers and brothers. I regretted not getting slaves." He patted himself between his legs. "I wish to use this more than just to make water."

"You are young."

"Hark at old father time! My father was younger than me when he sired me."

Our conversation was ended by the sound of the horn. We were under attack! I still had my sword strapped to my belt. I slipped my shield over my back and I just grabbed my bow and four arrows from my pouch as we raced from the hall. Bergil lived in the upper part of the settlement. The ones closer to the fjord were the poorer people of the clan. I saw the mast of a large drekar. It was approaching the shore. There would be just four men to slow down the attackers. Us and the two who were on duty. Sámr and would be hurrying down the ladder. The men who would be disembarking were lining the sides of the drekar. They had helmets and, in the moonlight, I saw the glint of mail. It was a big drekar, it had perhaps twenty oars on each side. It could have up to eighty men on board.

I had elevation. The drekar was less than a hundred and fifty paces from us. I ran another twenty paces and stopped to nock an arrow and draw my bow. I took aim at the prow. There was a warrior in mail with raised Danish axe. I let fly and nocked another. I drew and sent this one into the press of men. I saw the Dane with the axe fall backwards into the men. I sent my third and fourth arrows quickly into the confused mass of men.

Dropping my bow, I swung around my shield, drew my long sword and Bergil and I ran down to join Sámr and Ragnar who were waiting for us.

Sámr shouted, "Fine arrows, Göngu-Hrólfr. Perhaps our bodies may slow them down and allow Sven Blue Cheek to organize our warriors."

Ragnar shouted, "Lock shields."

Bergil went on my left side Sámr and Ragnar on my right. Men had clambered over the side of the Danish drekar. Their weapons and their shields told me that they were Danes. Behind us, I heard Sven's voice as he shepherded our men down to the fjord. The Danes just ran at us. They saw four men. None of us had helmets. Our shields hid our bodies and they must have assumed that we wore no mail. Although only Bergil had a byrnie the other two wore, like me, metal studded leather. They might kill us but we would die hard. I held my long sword over my shield. With my long arms and a sword which was a hand and a half longer than any other my blade would strike the first blow.

The Danes obliged us by racing at us in an untidy and disorderly mass. Harold Strong Arm would not have approved. I pulled back my arm and, as the leading Dane ran at me I rammed the sword forward with all the power that I had. My hand was quicker than his. Even as he moved his shield up the tip of my sword rammed into his open mouth. His speed and my arm drove it through the back of his skull. He flopped like a fish and dropped from my sword. His body fell across us.

Ragnar shouted, "Step back!"

It was a clever move. By moving backwards, the dead body became a tripping hazard. They would be slowed down. I heard the rest of our warriors as they hurried from their huts. The next Danish attack was a little more organized. Five men carefully stepped over the body and then advanced upon us. Instead of stabbing with my long sword, this time I swept it across our front. My long arms and the long blade meant that they all had to protect themselves. Their shields came up and their heads went back. They slowed and each moment was precious to us for it brought help a step closer.

The Danes were all ashore now and someone organised a wedge. We had retreated up the side of the path to the jarl's hall. It was steep. Their heads would be below ours. The five men clashed with us. My swinging sword smacked into the side of the helmet of one warrior. Another was stabbed by Ragnar. A spear darted up at me. I almost forgot that I had no helmet and the spear gouged a line along my cheek. Unable to swing I punched my sword into the face of the Dane who faced me. He lost his balance and tumbled backwards. He rolled down the slope and the Danish wedge was forced to halt. The body of the dead Dane had slowed them already.

I felt a shield press into my back and saw that Sven Blue Cheek was now next to Bergil. Others joined both Sámr and Sven. We had bought the time. A scarred cheek was a small price to pay. Sven's sword stabbed into the side of one of the two Danes who were still before us. The last brought his axe to smash into Ragnar's skull before Sámr ended the Dane's life. Eystein pushed Ragnar's body to block the Dane's advance and he stepped into the gap. We would mourn and honour Ragnar later. He could still serve the clan, even in death.

The Danish wedge was not as tightly packed as it should have been. They were stepping over bodies and that left gaps. They were also coming for me. I had now become the centre of our line. My height meant that they were drawn to me. I saw the chief with a Danish war axe. He was the tip of the wedge and he marched to me. What he did not know was that I had such a long sword. He could only use his axe two-handed if he put his shield behind him. He could not do that for he was the tip. He held his axe just below the head. He would stab with it. He would see that I had no protection for my head. I heard him order the charge and I jerked my sword forward. He had an open helmet and I saw his eyes widen as he saw the sword come towards him. I had power in my arm and even though his shield came up I was able to drive the sword into his right shoulder. I twisted and the axe fell from his fingers. Bergil brought his sword up and under the Dane's arm as Sven blocked the sword which was aimed at Bergil. The chief was badly wounded. More importantly, he could not fight. The tip of the wedge was blunted and the Danes were forced to stop.

Sven showed his skill as a war chief. He shouted, "Push! Drive the Danes into the fjord!"

I heard the jarl's voice, he was behind Bergil, "On! On!"

I felt the weight of the clan behind me. I had been taught to step off with my right leg so that I could use my shield as a weapon. As the chief's hearth weru tried to pull his wounded body from the fray I punched, with all my might into the face of one of them. The boss caught him squarely on the side of the

143

head. The skull is weaker there. He fell to the ground and the Danes behind had another barrier. Our men had brought spears and I saw a line of them stab over our heads. Two of the Danish hearth weru fell along with three others. The last two hearth weru pulled the chief's body from the press and forced their way through the warband. For the Danes, it was a disaster. It brought the front of our line closer to them and we had the advantage of the slope.

Bergil and Sámr slashed and stabbed. Sven hacked and chopped. I had no enemies before me for I was following the hearth weru. Sven shouted, "Break wall!"

I began to run down the slope. My long legs began to catch the hearth weru. When we were twenty paces from the drekar one of them left the others and turned to face me. "You may be a giant but you will fall to Guthrum Skull Crusher!"

He was mailed but I was a good head taller than he was. He swung his sword in a sideways arc. I blocked it and brought my own overhand. He blocked it with his shield but he had no metal rim on his shield and my blade found a joint. The shield cracked asunder. He looked at the boss which was all that was left. I punched with my own shield and my boss hit him under his chin. As his arms spread to regain his balance I drove my sword deep into his body. Around me, Danes ran to get aboard the drekar. Even as I withdrew my sword the mooring lines were being cut and Danes were hurling themselves at the departing drekar. Behind me, I heard the last of the Danes as they were slaughtered by Sven and the rest of the clan. We had won! The tower had saved us.

The Danes who had survived made no attempt to surrender. They had come to win. There would be no honour in surrender. They would die with their swords in their hands and go to Valhalla. After they were killed Sven Blue Cheek organised the stripping of the Danish bodies while the women came to see to our wounded. Bergljót came to see to her son and when she saw that he was without wound she looked at me. The blood was pouring from the wound in my face. Her eyes widened, "Bergil fetch me a cloth and my needle. This wound needs stitches!"

The jarl came over. He clapped his hand around my shoulders, "Once again we owe you much. Your tower worked and you braved our enemies in the front of the shield wall. It was you and Bergil who defeated their chief."

144

Brothers in Blood

Sven came along, "I have my men bringing the best two mail byrnies. Our smith will combine them. You shall have a mail shirt! I am honoured to have you and Bergil as shield brothers."

I pointed to Ragnar, "Our other shield brother died well."

"And we will honour him."

Arne shouted, "What do we do with the bodies of the Danes, Sven Blue Cheek?"

"Throw them in the fjord. When we feast on the crabs and the prawns we will be feasting on our dead enemies!"

Bergil had brought cloth, gut, and a brand. Bergljót carefully cleaned the wound. In my land, they would have used vinegar. Here it was in short supply and so she used the stale ale which Bergil had brought. I bore the stitching stoically. A Viking did not complain of pain. When it was done she said, "Your ale is cold. Come I will heat it up and fry some dried ham for you. You are both heroes and deserve a hero's meal."

I picked up the Danish two-handed axe. It was a fine weapon and I would have it for Bergil and for me. We trudged back up the hill. The women had pails out and were already swilling away the blood and the gore from the battle. By morning there would be no sign. The dead would be laid out in their homes and we would bury them when the sun rose.

As we ate and then quenched our thirst Bergil said, "You were right about the tower. Perhaps you were right about the stockade."

I nodded and swallowed, "When we fought I saw that it would not need to be a large gate. There are rocks on both sides of the jetty. They would be hard to scale. With a gate and a wall, two men could safely watch."

"And you will have a mail shirt."

"But not for some time. I know how long it takes to make one. I am patient. We will not be raiding until Einmánuður. That is two moons away. By then my scar will have healed."

"Many men put charcoal in the wound as it is healing. It makes them look fierce!"

His mother snapped, "Bergil you have not the sense of a lemming! You think women find such things attractive?"

I nodded, "Besides I think my height and my width are enough to attract attention in a battle. What do you think?"

He laughed, "True and you are so big that they miss me. We make a good pair of shield brothers. You strike high and I strike low."

145

Bergil only came up to my shoulder. I knew that we made an incongruous pair but as we had shown with the Danish chief that sometimes worked to our advantage.

The next day we buried our six dead. The Danes had lost twenty to our weapons and another eight to the fjord. We saw their bodies in the fjord. They were not the ones we had thrown there for these had their clothes yet. The mail was duly delivered to the blacksmith and, after measuring me he worked out it would take a moon for it to be made. Although the clan had promised me the gift for my efforts I gave him some of the coins I had accumulated. I reasoned that I would have had to use them for mail anyway and this made a friend of the blacksmith.

A week later I was summoned to the jarl's hall. His brother was there along with Sven Blue Cheek. There were also the ten hersirs who made up the council. It was a little intimidating. Unusually Gefn was also there. Women rarely attended such meetings. They were normally called to punish a wrongdoer or to arbitrate on a dispute. Bergil had not been invited and that worried me.

It was the jarl's brother Bjorn who spoke. "The council is here to thank you, Göngu-Hrólfr. You and my nephew saved the clan when the Danes sought vengeance."

He sat. Jarl Rognvald Eysteinsson stood and he smiled. "Know you that the sons of our family are dead and there is none to follow us save our sister's son. Bergil Svensson. I have decided to adopt you as my heir. From this day you will be Göngu-Hrólfr Rognvaldson. When I go to the Otherworld, you will be jarl. I hope that will not be for some years. I ask the council to endorse my decision and ensure that my wishes are obeyed."

I noticed his brother said nothing. I also realised that the jarl had said his heir. Did he really mean I would be jarl? His brother's eyes said not.

All of them stood and banged the table with the daggers. I was pleased to see that Sven Blue Cheek did so as enthusiastically as the others. If he had not then I could not have accepted. I knew I had to accept the jarl's offer. I still had a mother, grandfather and grandmother. If I was going to find men to follow and reclaim my land then I had to accept this offer for it gave me power. I would have a drekar and the jarl's men if they would follow me. I had, in the twinkling of an eye a warband. I would not be able to attempt the reclamation for some time. I

146

intended to increase my wealth and buy warriors to follow my banner.

I knelt. Half of my body still rose above the table, "I accept your decision and henceforth I shall call you father. I have lost one and one was found. Your son was lost and one was found. It is *wyrd*."

Although most of us had thought this no one had vocalised it yet and, as I stood I saw that all of them clutched their Thor's hammer. This was the work of the gods, or the Norns and either way we were their playthings.

Gefn came to me and I saw tears streaming down her face. Her head barely reached my sword belt. Her arms would not go all the way around me. I put my huge ham-like hands around her back and squeezed. Neither of us said anything. There was no need. The words were in the tears and in the hugs.

She stepped away, "I will have ale fetched."

Jarl Rognvald held his arm out in a warrior's handshake. "I know you have a family but they are two oceans away. The clan will help you reclaim your land." He gave me a knowing look. "I know that it is in your heart. That will happen when we are stronger. Since you have come we have not been defeated. Our raids will make us stronger. Those who live further up the fjord will send warriors to join the band led by Göngu-Hrólfr Rognvaldson. We will build a bigger drekar. We will raid and make our warriors stronger." He pointed to Sven who was watching me. "Sven believes that you are the warrior who will make this clan great. I believe him and we believe in you."

Again, I saw that his brother had distanced himself. He had said little.

The ale came and we raised our drinking horns to each other. The beer had been brewed especially for the occasion. It was not watered down. It was a strong ale for a momentous decision. When I left I felt the effects of the drink but I knew that there was something I had to do first. I returned to Bergljót's hall. She was, as usual, sewing and Bergil was carving a piece of bone. They both looked up and smiled.

"You know?"

Bergljót nodded, "The jarl and Sven spoke with Bergil and me when you were hunting six days since."

"And you are happy?" I was looking at Bergil when I spoke. He was the nephew of the jarl. Had I taken his birthright?

"Rollo, I am happy for you. I am not the leader. I am a warrior you are *the* warrior. I never expected to be a leader nor did I wish it. I am a man of words. I will tell the tale of Göngu-Hrólfr Rognvaldson. People may remember the man of words who fought by your side," he laughed, "and often in your shadow. If not then I am happy to be part of your journey for I believe that a thousand years from now Rollo, or Göngu-Hrólfr Rognvaldson will be remembered."

I was happy. I could see beyond the horizon and I could plan for the death of my treacherous brother. I was more of a brother in blood with Bergil than with Ragnvald!

Chapter 12

I might have been the heir to Jarl Rognvald but it was still Sven, the jarl and Bjorn Eysteinsson who made the decisions. I did not blame them. I was still young. The difference was that I was informed of those decisions before anyone else.

"We will raid the land of the Picts. They are our closest neighbours save for the Vikings of the islands. The Vikings of Orkneyjar are kin and we would not raid those."

I must have looked confused. Sven said, "The Picts have poor weapons and little that we might want from them save that they make good slaves. We need women for our young men to seed. By bringing in hardy women from outside the clan it makes the clan stronger. They are also Christian and that means that their priests may have treasure. We will raid the land around the north-eastern corner of that land."

"What about Northumbria? They also have hardy women and better churches."

They looked at each other and Sven Blue Cheek laughed. Bjorn Eysteinsson frowned and shook his head, "Do you read minds, Göngu-Hrólfr? That is what Sven said."

"And we have decided to raid the Picts first and if that is successful then we will consider a raid on Northumbria."

"And when do we sail?"

It was the jarl who answered me. "In seven days. First, we visit with our relatives at Hafrsfjord. I wish them to know of my decision to adopt you. It lies south of here and the jarls of Møre meet there at this time of year." I had discovered that Møre was not the name of the village, it was the name for the whole area.

His brother said, "We tell each other our plans. We do not like to raid where another of the tribe has raided. It can cause bad blood. This way if another has an idea to make a big raid then others in the tribe can join. If they do not approve of you as heir then it will not be so." Was there a threat in those words?

It seemed like a good idea. As it was peaceful and we would only be travelling thirty miles down the coast we took one drekar and she just had one man to an oar. We were not going to war. We were going to talk. I now knew why Bergljót had been sewing so much lately. She had been making me clothes which would not disgrace the jarl.

We took no shields. The drekar looked naked without them. *'Fáfnir'* was a fast drekar but without the weight of shields, she flew. We did not need to use the open sea and so we had the sail furled. The jarl found it easier to steer using the crew of rowers. For us, it was a hard row. We had to respond to commands instantly or risk fouling the oars on unseen rocks. When we reached Hafrsfjord, there were already eight drekar moored there. We did not go ashore directly. We were sweaty from the voyage. Men swilled water over them. To their amazement, I dived overboard. I had often been asked if I feared the sea. I did not. I had survived and I knew that the sea was not my enemy. I had touched bottom and I had risen. The water was still icy from snowmelt but it made me feel alive.

I climbed back aboard and rubbed myself dry with an old kyrtle. I then dressed in my newly made clothes. The breeks were made of a sturdy fabric dyed red. My shirt, in contrast, was a dark green and the kyrtle I wore atop them both was a rich embroidered brown. Bergljót had embroidered a dragon on the front and a horse on the back. When she had given it to me Bergil had told me that she had begun work on it the day after I arrived. It was finer than anything I had ever worn in the Land of the Horse. With my hair combed and tied back and my beard also groomed I strapped on my long sword. My grandfather had a sword which was magical. It was called Heart of Ice. I had always wanted a named sword. After our battle with the Danes Bergil had said, "It has given you its name Longsword. Why make life hard? You are the only one who can wield the blade with one hand. The sword was meant for you."

He was right and I had looked at the sword differently now that it was named. I replaced the grip. I went to the blacksmith and had the blade engraved with runes. The runes said simply, 'I am Longsword, Göngu-Hrólfr is my master'. From that day I fought with no other weapon. We waited on Jarl Rognvald Eysteinsson. We would be making an entrance. It was important to do such things well. The Jarl led followed by his brother, me and Bergil. A few paces after us Sven Blue Cheek led the men we had brought. The head of the tribe was Hálfdanar the Black. He had built up the power of the tribe slowly. He had eaten into the lands of other tribes and clans. They had been absorbed. He would be king.

The hall was huge. Men were drinking. We marched to the table where a Viking with long white hair and a long white beard was drinking. The others with him, with one exception, were also older warriors. Jarl Rognvald Eysteinsson looked almost young in comparison. He bowed, "I have come to pay my respects Jarl Hálfdanar Svarti and to introduce a new member of my clan and my family." He held a hand out and I stepped forward. "Göngu-Hrólfr Rognvaldson."

The jarl laughed, "By the Allfather I have never seen a bigger Viking. What do you feed him on? Whole cattle?" Everyone laughed. He turned to the young warrior, "What say you, my son?"

The younger warrior who was even younger than Bergil and me smiled, "He is a father. I can see we will have a tale tonight instead of the same family stories I have heard my whole life."

His father shook his head, "You should respect the past, Haraldr Hálfdanarson." He waved a hand and said, "Welcome Göngu-Hrólfr Rognvaldson. When we have finished with our family business we will get to know you better."

Jarl Rognvald Eysteinsson took his place at the jarls' table and a chamberlain took us to a side table. I had never been to such a gathering and I was fascinated. I drank sparingly and listened to all that was said. We were there until after the moon had set. Others had to be carried to their beds but Sven and I, along with Haraldr Hálfdanarson, did not overindulge and we helped to carry both our jarl and Jarl Hálfdanar Svarti to bed.

Haraldr said, "It is late but I would speak with you in the morning." He clasped my arm and we headed to the warrior hall.

Sven said, "That will be the jarl of our tribe soon. His father is old. I hear he is ambitious and would be king of the Norse Vikings."

"There is no king of Norway!"

"And he would have himself as the first. Did you hear that story they mentioned?"

"The raid on the Franks? I did. Will Jarl Rognvald not join it?" If he did then I would have an opportunity to confront my brother sooner rather than later.

"Were you not listening? Haraldr does not wish that to happen. I told you he would be King of Norway. His father was a clever jarl and I hear that his son is too. If others raid the Franks

151

then it makes their homeland weaker. Many will not return. Our tribe will take over their lands. Haraldr Finehair would eat up Norway piece by piece."

"Haraldr Finehair?"

"That is his nickname. Did you not notice his fine flowing locks? When you talk to him do not be deceived by his youth. He is an old man in a young man's body. Let him plot and plan we will sail our own course."

Sven was wise and I heeded his sage advice.

I was up early and I took the opportunity of walking around the town. It was a town. We lived in a collection of huts but this was a mighty town. A double stockade surrounded it. It was on an island and without a hill. They had made one by digging ditches and planting a palisade. Within it, they had stables, smithies, bakers, tanners. They had workshops making beads and weapons. They had potters turning out dishes. They had halls in which were stored the goods brought by sea. I could see why Haraldr Hálfdanarson had plans to become king. More than half of the warriors I saw had mail byrnies. This was the rich part of the tribe. We were the poor relatives.

Haraldr saw me when I went back aboard *'Fáfnir'*. He hurried over to me. "I have been looking for you all morning. I am keen to hear your story."

I nodded. I knew that it interested every Viking. The treachery of a family member was not uncommon but surviving a whole day at sea was. I told him all.

He grinned when I had finished, "A fine saga. If I had not spoken to my cousin Bergil I would have thought it made up." He held up his hand as my face darkened. "I do not call you a liar. It is just such a fantastical story. And the battles you fought since then... remarkable. Would you serve with me? I could use a war chief like you."

"I am flattered but I have but one aim. I wish to return to the land of my birth, kill my brother and reclaim the Land of the Horse."

When I said, *'kill my brother'*, he touched his Thor's Hammer. The killing of a family member was not to be undertaken lightly. "I am sorry for that but the offer remains. I will be the King of Norway." His eyes challenged me to say other.

I nodded, "I can believe it and I will bow my knee to you if I am still at Møre."

"But you do not think that you will be."

"No. I was saved for a purpose." He seemed to accept what I had said. At least I would not be a rival to his power. The Land of the Horse was a long way from Norway.

We left for home two days later. None of the jarls was going to join the raid on the Franks. That was disappointing for me. I rowed in silence as we headed home. Bergil broke my silence as our fjord hove into view. "You do not really want the tribe to retake your land, do you?"

"Why not?"

"Because we owe allegiance to Jarl Hálfdanar Svarti and his son. If we took your land back it would become part of his land." He smiled and lowered his voice, "You want our clan to retake it for you."

I felt naked as though someone had seen into my heart. Bergil was right. Would my father have harboured such thoughts? My grandfather? I had changed and it was Ragnvald who had changed me.

Bergil smiled, "Do not worry. Our fjord is a backwater. We can never grow for the mountains are too close. Our numbers have never been great. The children who are born each year are likely to die in battle. That is why Sven suggested the raid on the Picts. We need their women. They will breed the warriors that you need."

"But I cannot wait for them to grow and become warriors."

"No, but the more women we have the more we will attract other warriors from the other members of the tribe. Sven has spent the last two days telling the other war chiefs of his plans. Some will choose to help my cousin become a king but others will see our clan as the one where they will become rich and have women."

I had underestimated Sven Blue Cheek. He was a planner and a plotter. Perhaps his plan would help me to get home.

The drekar had shown no signs of problems on our short voyage and, upon our return, we began to load for the raid on the Picts. We would be away for more than seven days. Sven Blue Cheek had planned on securing one village and raiding the ones around it. There were seven he had heard about. He had discovered that at the family meeting. We would not have to raid and run. We would be able to live off their lands for a few days. We would be able to slaughter some of their animals and use the

Picts' salt to preserve it. I was learning how to be a war leader by watching Sven.

Our two ships were almost fully manned as we headed across the grey seas to the island of Britannia. My mail was not yet ready but it would not matter. The Picts did not use mail. The jarl was able to use the wind for much of the voyage. It came from the south-east. Our drekar was a good sailer. It was only a wind against that meant we had to row. If we were chasing or being chased then we would row.

We sailed beyond the headland which hid the seven settlements. We ran a sea anchor out to hold us south of the Picts. We took down the mast and the sail. We would row in after dark. Those who had it donned mail. Bergil was wearing his into battle for the first time. We watched the sun descend in the west. It lit up, in the distance, the bay into which we would sail. I knew that this would not be as easy as the raid on the Danes. Then the jarl had known the waters and the landing site. Here we were almost sailing blind. The warriors who had told Sven of the settlements and the bay had never landed. He had been told that it was a wide bay with a sandy beach. The warriors we would face might not be as fierce as the Danes but their land was.

As soon as the sun became a thin line to the west we began to row. We had Beorn at the prow and we rowed slowly. Speed was unimportant. We edged toward the entrance to the bay. If our information was correct then it would widen into a huge bay once we had passed the two headlands. The resistance grew against the oars as we neared the narrow entrance. Then we were through into the flatter, calmer, almost fjord-like waters of the open bay. We turned to steerboard as soon as we were through and crept towards the beach. Beorn gave a low whistle and we all raised our oars. We moved forward until we heard the sand beneath our keel and we stopped. The ship's boys leapt ashore and wrapped our mooring lines around the largest rocks they could find. I picked up my shield and took my sword from my chest. I hung my helmet from the hilt.

Once ashore Sven sent out Arne and Valbrandr, our two scouts. Both had proved themselves to be both quick and able to hide. Both were small; they were smaller than Bergil. Everyone had agreed that I would make the worst of scouts. I would be seen too easily. We waited until all of Bjorn Eysteinsson's men had landed and then we followed the footsteps in the sand. They led up the sand towards the grass which rose to the first of the settlements just above the sea. We could not see it but we could smell the smoke from their fires. The only sounds which we made were our breathing and the creaking of leather. Those with mail had coated them liberally with seal oil. It stopped them rusting and ensured that they made no noise.

Arne and Valbrandr met us and, by using signs, told Sven where the village was and how many men were there. It was obvious that this was a large one. There was no palisade but they had a ditch and a rampart. They were useful when you were fighting behind them but they could not stop warriors striking from the night. Sven pointed to the northeast and Bjorn Eysteinsson led his men that way. He waved at the men he would be leading and they went to the south. That left the jarl with twenty of us. I stood on the jarl's right and Bergil his left. Without Sven and the rest of his oathsworn, the two of us would have to protect him.

As we neared the settlement, over the springy turf, we could hear the noises of their herds and flocks. They were penned. Then we heard the noise as the Picts talked with each other. We heard laughter. The jarl suddenly froze as there was a movement before us. We were on one of the grass filled ditches and the rampart rose above us. A shadow appeared. None of us moved. We heard the splash of water. It was a warrior making water. As soon as the shadow disappeared the jarl led us up the steep bank. Had there been defenders there and if it had been daylight, then we would have struggled. As it was we easily made the top and we lay there.

The settlement was laid out before us. There were one long hut and twenty smaller ones. There was a large fire in the middle but I could see the glow of smaller fires through the doors of the others. The jarl slid his sword out. He was about to raise when there was a shout from the north. His brother led his men to attack. They were early. It did not matter overmuch as we were all in position but I knew that Sven would be unhappy. I drew my sword and we raced down the bank. I did not bother with my shield. That was still covering my back.

The Picts grabbed their weapons and ran at us. We must have been a terrifying sight for the Picts just fought in breeks. When they went to war, they limed their hair and relied on raw courage to defeat their enemies. They had not been expecting an attack and so they had small shields and short swords and spears. They charged us.

My long legs took me ahead of the rest. I held my sword in two hands and slightly behind me. My experience of riding came to the fore. My grandfather had had me practice swinging a sword as I galloped. It was much easier just running. A warrior ran towards me and I veered slightly to my left. He might have thought I was afraid of him. I swung my sword. The tip struck his small shield but the mighty blade chopped his body in two. I allowed my sword to swing around and then I raised it above my head. Two warriors stood to block my path. I made a figure of eight with the blade and brought it down horizontally. One held up his shield and my sword turned it into kindling and ripped through his arm and side. The other saw his chance and he darted forward to stab at me with his short sword. The tip slid off one of my metal studs and then the side gouged a line across the leather. He was so close to me that I could smell the fish he had eaten. The hilt of my sword struck him in the side of the head and he was knocked to the ground. Bergil stabbed him.

When I looked around I saw that it was over. The rest of the warband had had as much success as I had and the warriors were all slain. The women surprised me. They were not screaming. They were not cowering. They stoically stood with their children around them. The children were afraid. The older boys had all been slain and I could not see any boy older than six summers.

Sven Blue Cheek shouted out his orders. "Separate the old. Put them in one hut. Put the mothers and the children in the large hall. Have the girls who are not mothers in another." He turned to Bjorn Eysteinsson, "Lord, have your men search for treasure." He could not criticise the jarl's brother but he was unhappy with the shout which had alerted our foes.

Bjorn shrugged, "The Norns were spinning. A warrior made water and saw us. He shouted before we could slay him."

"It mattered not." He turned to me. "You and Bergil take Arne and guard the young women. Make sure they do not harm themselves. Only one sleeps at any one time.

"Harm themselves?"

Bergil said, "Some women try to kill themselves rather than be taken by a Viking. I have never seen it but I have heard of this."

I nodded but I did not understand it. We took slaves but they always seemed to embrace the Clan of the Horse. Then I realised that our slaves had come from the Welsh, the Hibernians and the Saxons. We had never raided the Picts. It was Olaf Two Teeth who was guarding the young women and girls. He had lost his two front teeth when young. Quite old now, he had a comical look when he smiled. In war, he was a terrifying warrior. He grinned as we approached. "You had best keep your weapons in your breeks. They are some comely lasses here."

Bergil nodded amiably, "When we get home we can choose one as our payment. We will be able to decide which one is the right one."

Bergil said, "You slew more men than I did. You may sleep first."

"I was not counting."

"I was. I slew but one. The others told me that even Sven Blue Cheek killed but two. You have earned your rest." I lay down at the door of the hut. That meant none could leave without waking me and it would allow Bergil to stretch his legs and walk around the hut.

Bergil woke me. It was still dark. "Sven came around in the middle of the watch. We raid again tomorrow. We will be leaving at noon. Wake me at dawn."

He was soon asleep. I wrapped my cloak around me and looked out over the settlement. I saw movement but dismissed it quickly. It was rats feasting on the dead. The fires crackled. Sven had left two men tending them. There was a wind which presaged a change in the weather. I took all of that in. I was about to sit down when there was a movement. Someone had stepped over Bergil's sleeping body. I strode over. I saw a figure stepping out of the hut. It was one of the young women. She did not try to run.

I said, quietly, "You must go back into the hut." She looked at me blankly and mimed something. She seemed to half sit. I tried again in Saxon. She repeated the move. Brigid, the Alewife in the Haugr had some slaves from Hibernia and that was not far from here. I tried speaking Hibernian.

She smiled. She said, slowly, "I need to make water."

Now I understood the mime. I looked around. The rampart was just ten paces away. I pointed and she nodded. She walked that way and I followed. She stood and said, "I cannot go if you watch."

Was this a trick? Was she going to run? I almost laughed. She was half my size. If she ran and I could not catch her with my long legs I would give up being a warrior. I nodded and turned my back. I heard the splash of water and smelled her water.

She tapped me on my shoulder. "I am done." She walked next to me. "Thank you. What is your name and how did you get so tall?"

"I am Göngu-Hrólfr but I was born Rollo."

"Rollo." She seemed to roll the word around her mouth. "I am Kaðlín. I do not come from here. My father is King of the Caereni. It is a land to the west of here."

"Caereni? I have never heard of them. I thought this was the land of the Picts."

She shook her head. "That is what you barbarians call it but we do not. This is the land of the Cornovi."

"And what is a princess of the Caereni doing here?"

"I was meeting a man who was going to be my husband."

"Going to be?"

"As he was a warrior I am guessing that he is dead. I have not seen his body so I do not know."

"I am sorry."

She shrugged, "I did not like him. He was a small man and he smelled of fish." She squeezed the muscles in my arm. "Now you, I like."

I felt uncomfortable. "Come, you should be back in the hut."

"But I like talking with you and you have a kind voice and a gentle look."

"Bed." I pointed.

She did as I said but giggled and said, huskily, "Of course." She went inside the hut. I stood. I felt uncomfortable and I felt myself growing. I was aroused. Perhaps I would take her as my slave when we reached home. The night went quietly and my thoughts were filled with the young woman, Kaolin. She had smelled of wild thyme. She had been slight but her breasts and hips were those of a woman. She had red hair. I had seen it flash in the firelight as she had entered the hut. I found myself becoming more aroused and so I put thoughts of her from me. If she was a princess then I would have to tell Sven. Of course, a princess of such a primitive tribe was not the same as a Frankish princess or even a Saxon one but she might be worth something.

I woke Bergil at dawn. I curled up and slept. I seemed to be asleep for a short time and then I was awoken. It was a grey, damp day which greeted me. I made water and then ate the food and drank the ale which Bergil had for me.

Sven Blue Cheek came along with Olaf Two Teeth. Olaf was older than the other warriors. Sven said, "Olaf will watch the girls. We go to raid." He turned to walk away.

"One of them is a princess of a tribe to the west."

He turned, "How do you know?"

"She made water and she told me."

"It could have been a trick to help her escape."

"She did not try."

Sven looked thoughtful. "When we come back from today's raids we will speak with her. She could bring us coin. You disobeyed me but good may come of it."

I shook my head, "I did not disobey you, Sven Blue Cheek." I heard the intake of breath from Bergil and Olaf as I challenged the war chief. "You said to watch them. You said to stop them harming themselves. You said nothing about speaking or letting them make water."

He glared up at me and I thought I had gone too far. Then he smiled, "You are right. Next time I will give clearer orders!"

The warriors were all gathered together. Jarl Rognvald Eysteinsson spoke to us but I knew that the plan was that of Sven Blue Cheek. "The gods smiled on us and the Norns were kind. We took the largest village in this corner of the land of the Picts." I did not correct the jarl. "We killed the man they called the chief and his son. That means the others are smaller than this. We will divide into seven groups of warriors. I will lead one, my brother another, Sven Blue Cheek a third, my son and my nephew will lead a fourth." That was the first time he had called me his son. It sounded strange in my ears. "Sámr the Stout will lead a fifth and Pétr Pétrsson will lead the sixth. He pointed to an older warrior, Stig the Bold, you can take the seventh."

Sven quickly allocated the warriors we would be leading. I had nine men with me. I was grateful that most were young. Half were younger than me. Sven gathered them around him. "You will follow me and Sámr. Our villages are to the north-west of here. Göngu-Hrólfr, try to avoid talking to them too much eh?"

Bergil laughed.

"Aye Sven Blue Cheek."

We loped off. None of the villages was more than a couple of miles from the central one. The grey drizzly day would make it easier for us to approach them. All of them were obligingly along the coast. As I had the youngest of men I was given the one

159

which was the furthest northeast. Before Sven led his men north he pointed northeast. "It is a mile or two in that direction."

"How do you know?"

He grinned. I saw water dripping from his helmet and down his nose. "I too can talk. I asked an old man. It cost him two fingers but he told where the villages lay."

I led my men into the open land which appeared to be getting murkier with each step. When I saw cattle and sheep I realised that there would be shepherds and cattle herders. I stopped and turned, "Haddr Iverson, take two men and kill the shepherds and the cattle herders. Drive the animals back to the camp." I saw then why Sven had picked me. None would argue with the giant who wielded the two-handed sword. They nodded and ran off.

Knowing that the village lay ahead I waved my arm the other five spread out. I spied the smoke. The village lay over the rise. As we reached the top I looked down and saw a small bay. The ten huts were in a hollow. I took out my sword and raised it. We moved down the slope. We had gone but ten paces when a female screamed. We were discovered. As the men of the village grabbed weapons to defend their families I swung around my shield. This was the first time I had been given the responsibility of leading an attack on my own. I had a handful of men but I would not let down my adopted father.

There were twelve men and youths in the village. They had two shields between them but every man held a weapon. Three ran at me and two at Bergil who was just behind me. My long legs outstretched the rest. One of the Cornovi had two throwing spears. He hurled one at me and I batted it away with my shield. As I bared my chest a second risked his only spear and he hurled it at me. The fire-hardened tip hit a metal stud and fell to the ground. Before he could reach for his dagger I had taken his head and my long sword had bitten into the upper arm of the next warrior. It scraped along the bone. The third ran with a short sword at my right side for I was still pulling my sword from the Cornovi arm. As I pulled I turned and brought my shield across. His sword struck the wood of my shield. I punched him hard in the face with the hilt and he fell to the ground. Bergil had slain his men but Leif Siggison had been wounded by one of the two men he had been fighting. He had killed one but his right arm was bleeding. I ran at the Cornovi warrior who was about to hack at Leif's head. I brought my sword from on high. It hit his skull and split it. Such was the force that it continued to tear open his neck and his chest. I twisted it so that I could get it out. As Bergil slew the last one all that was left were their wounded.

I shouted, "See to Leif!" Then I spoke in Hibernian. Kaðlín had seemed to understand it. "Do not run and you will live. Stand close together." Perhaps it was my words or my height but either way they obeyed. The man I had knocked out, stood groggily. Bergil took his weapon. An older woman took a brand from the open fire and plunged it into the arm of the warrior I had wounded. It hissed and the smell of burning flesh filled the air. She had saved his life, if not his arm. The drizzle continued to fall.

"Bergil, search the huts. Arne, start them back to the camp. Keep your swords in their backs but do not harm them. They are valuable to us."

We found little in the huts. The weapons were poor and the few coins would not buy a horn of ale in Dorestad. We took the two warriors back with us. I did not want them to run and bring allies. We had raided the furthest village. We would be able to leave, the next day and be home in five more. It had been a good raid.

We were just two miles from our camp when we saw a warrior running west. He was a Cornovi. He was too far away for us to catch and I knew that we would regret the escape. He would bring more men. Our fight was not quite over.

The drizzle showed no sign of abating. We were the last to reach the camp and I saw Sven Blue Cheek berating Sámr. Sámr stood and took it. Sven saw me and pointed at me, "Göngu-Hrólfr may be the youngest but he has managed to bring back the men he did not kill. You let one escape and now we will have to prepare to do battle!"

Sámr nodded, "I am not fit to lead, war chief!"

The apology accepted Sven nodded, "Put the young women in the hut with the others. Göngu-Hrólfr and Bergil, Arne can help you watch them again this night. Just try to avoid talking eh?"

Olaf and the other men who had been guarding the camp had slaughtered four sheep and made the women cook them. We had hot food.

It was still raining and so the three of us ate inside the hut. Most of the girls pressed themselves against the far wall. The exception was Kaðlín. She did not move and ate her food while studying me. I looked at her and saw that she was dressed differently to the others. Her clothes were better. Her hair was combed and I saw, in the firelight, that it burned as red as fire.

She saw me looking and spoke to me. Arne and Bergil did not understand her words, "Do you like what you see, Viking?"

I blushed and turned back to my friends. As we ate Arne pointed at my leather vest. "How did that stop a spear? I thought you would have been wounded at the very least."

"It hit metal and it was only fire hardened. A fire-hardened spear is only good for flesh or killing a fish. They would have been better to use flint."

Bergil nodded. "There were just two swords in that village and six knives. None were worth bringing back. The sword which struck your shield was bent."

"I am surprised that these are not raided more often."

When we had finished I said, "They will need to make water. I will speak to them. Arne, go to the right of the hut and Bergil the left. I will let them stand on the ramparts. Do not watch them as they make water."

"What if they run?"

I laughed, "Arne, do you think they can outrun us? Where would they go? Yonder is the sea. If they were going to try to harm themselves they would have done so already. They might try to escape but I will speak with them. Now go."

After they had gone I said to the young women, "You can go outside and make water or whatever you need to do. Then you will have to stay in the hut." I looked at Kaðlín. "None will leave the hut tonight. My men will be there. They will not watch but if you run then we will catch you." I paused, "And you will be punished."

I saw a few of them looking confused. Kaðlín said, "They did not understand all of your words. My people have more to do with those from across the sea to the west." She spoke rapidly and the girls nodded. There would be no trouble.

"Thank you."

As she passed me she deliberately pressed close to me and I had the whiff of thyme once more. I felt myself becoming aroused again. They obeyed me and trooped back inside once they had finished.

Night did not fall; darkness crept up under the cloud of drizzle. We were all soaked. I took off my mail. I took the decision to sleep inside the hut. The warrior on watch would have to endure the rain but we would be dry inside the hut. I chose the hard watch. I chose the one in the middle of the night. My two companions would lose sleep but it would not be broken.

Bergil woke me, "It has stopped raining. The night is surprisingly mild."

I took my cloak and stepped out into the night. He was right. The rain had stopped but the clouds kept the air warmer than might be expected. I did a circuit of the hut. I saw nothing and I returned to stand guard. I saw Sámr feeding the fire. That had been his punishment. The rest of our men were inside the huts. The jarl, his brother and Sven had taken the chief's hut. We were at the very edge of the settlement. Beyond us were the ramparts and then the sea.

I began to think of my home. Perhaps I was distracted but I was suddenly aware of a movement. Before I could react, a hand slipped around my waist and fondled me. I turned and stared into the eyes of Kaðlín. She put her fingers to her lips and then reached around my neck and pulled herself up to kiss me. I had never kissed a girl's lips. I had never kissed any woman on the lips and I found myself growing. She pulled away and, taking my hand, led me to the ramparts. To my shame, I let her. I had been given a duty and I was not doing it.

Once we were at the ramparts she lowered herself to the ground and, still holding my hand pulled me on top of her. She fumbled at my breeks as she kissed me. I was aware that her dress had opened and, with her other hand, she took mine and placed it on her breast. She leaned up, nibbled my ear and whispered, "Viking, I want this." I succumbed to my body and I took her.

When we had finished we lay there for some time. I was trying to work out which was the greater crime. Neglecting my duty or damaging the value of a princess. I rose from her and took her hand. I led her back to the hut. She reached up and kissed me again. Her eyes were wet and I knew not why.

I felt confused. However, that moment changed me. I had no idea why she had chosen me to make her a woman. I am guessing that my appearance and size had something to do with it. When we took the slaves back to our home I would ask the jarl for Kaðlín. I liked her and it seemed she liked me. I might even make her my wife. I spent the rest of my watch going over every moment of the encounter. I found myself smiling. When I saw the first grey of dawn I realised that I should have woken Arne. I woke him and rolled in my fur. I thought I would not sleep but I did and I enjoyed the most delightful of dreams.

When Arne woke Bergil and I Bergil said, "Are all the girls here?"

I nodded, "Of course, why?"

"I was certain that one of them passed me in the night." He shrugged, "Perhaps it was a dream."

I glanced over and saw Kaðlín peering with bright eyes and smile from behind her fur.

Sven Blue Cheek came through the village like a winter storm, "Everyone! We need to begin loading the drekar! The cereal and the slaughtered and salted animals first. Leave the slaves until last. The young girls will be aboard *'Fáfnir'*."

I could not help smiling. I would have Kaðlín all the way home. I would be able to see her. We left Arne to watch them along with Olaf Two Teeth. The slaves were more agitated than we had seen. Sven had to post six warriors to watch them. That meant it took us longer to load. It was afternoon before we were able to replace the decks and to consider loading the slaves and the animals. We would be leaving the tiny bay after dark.

We were on our way back when Sámr ran to fetch us, "Come quickly and bring your weapons, there is a warband approaching!"

Sámr did not look happy. His lack of vigilance would cost us warriors. We would have to fight our way out. Sven Blue Cheek was not one to dwell on mistakes. Even as we raced up the turf to the ramparts he was organizing a shield wall. No matter how many barbarians came at us we would be able to repel them for we stood on their own ramparts. We might lose warriors but I did not think for one moment that we would lose the battle.

Sven saw me, "Göngu-Hrólfr. Your band anchors the right side of the line. That way you will have room to swing that mighty weapon of yours!"

"Yes, Sven."

By the time we had donned our helmets and held our shields the warband was closer. I stood on the far right, as ordered. Behind me, Olaf and Arne still guarded the girls. Sven had the men begin banging their weapons against our shields. We did not have a chant but the effect was intimidating. The warband stopped. I was able to count them. There were just a hundred warriors. They barely outnumbered us. Few had helmets although more had shields than the ones we had fought and killed. I saw two banners. That meant two leaders.

I watched as two men took off their helmets and left their weapons on the ground. They walked towards the ramparts with open palms. Jarl Rognvald Eysteinsson and Sven took off their helmets and, leaving their weapons on the ground walked to meet them. They were too far away for me to hear their words and it rapidly became apparent that they did not share a language.

Jarl Rognvald Eysteinsson shouted, "Göngu-Hrólfr, leave your weapons; we need you."

I took off my helmet and left my shield and sword. "Bergil, watch them."

I towered over Sven but he was taller than the two men we faced. I saw them looking up at me. One of them spoke, "I am Áed mac Cináeda. I am King of the Caereni. This is my ally from Hibernia, Beollán mac Ciarmaic."

The Irishman said, "You speak our language?"

"I can speak your language but not as well as I should."

It was a polite answer and they nodded. The king said, "You have my daughter?"

"Kaðlín? Yes."

"Is she harmed?"

I was glad he phrased the question that way. I did not need to lie. "She is unharmed and she is not distressed."

He looked relieved. They both looked relieved. "Ask your leader how much he wants as a ransom for her."

"You do not come here to fight?"

The king shook his head. "My daughter came here to see if she might be happy wed to the prince of the Cornovi. They are a poor people, as you discovered. My new ally would like her as a bride. I care not what happens to these people. We could fight you but we would lose warriors and you have armour. There would be little honour. If you will not sell her back to us then we will fight!"

My heart sank. For a brief few hours, I had been happy with the thought that I might marry Kaðlín. I turned to the jarl. "They do not wish to fight. They wish to buy back the princess."

Sven looked at me and smiled, "Your conversation has helped us then."

The jarl said, "How much are they willing to pay?"

Sven said, "They look poor and whatever they offer we will take." He looked at me. "They just want the one girl?"

"Just Kaðlín."

The jarl said, "Then say we agree." He lowered his voice, "Pretend to negotiate but take whatever you can get. This is an unexpected profit."

I did not negotiate hard and they paid us, thinking they had a bargain. When Kaðlín was brought and it became obvious that she was leaving there was a wail from the other women. They had thought that they were to be delivered. The chest with the coins was brought and the princess delivered.

When her father took her hand she turned and said, "Thank you for your kindness Rollo also called Göngu-Hrólfr. I will always remember you." There was a mischievous glint in her green eyes. I felt a pain deep within me that took some time to disappear.

The king said, "And I thank you too. When I saw a giant before me I feared the worst but I can see that you are a man of honour. May God watch over you."

We watched them leave and then Sven clapped me on the back. "The bounty of your arrival never stops!"

Chapter 13

On the voyage home, I was lauded by all for my skills both in languages and in battle. The crew were in ebullient mood. We had slaves and we had coin that was not expected. I found myself questioned at length. All thoughts of Kaðlín were driven from my head. When I slept, however, she haunted me. I knew that she had been sent by the Norns but I could not perceive the purpose. Perhaps they were punishing me. They had offered something sweet and delicious and they had torn it from my grasp. The accolades of the crew felt empty.

When we returned home I was offered my choice of the slaves. I was not the one given the first choice. That honour went to the jarl. He declined. His brother, however, chose the youngest. She had the look of a wild vixen. Sven Blue Cheek chose one who looked homelier. I was given the next choice. It was like being offered a kyrtle having lost a mail byrnie. When I deferred to the others it was taken as yet another quality in me. It was not. I had tasted something fine. I would not make do with oat bread. That evening, after we had eaten, Bergil took me to one side. "Göngu-Hrólfr, you did not choose a woman. You are not one of these men who prefer other men are you?"

I blushed and shook my head, "Of course not! I will take a woman but I do not want one of those women as the mother of my children."

He looked relieved, "Good, then I can tell the others. They were worried!"

Two eventful occurrences happened after we reached home. We had not known it but Gertha, Bjorn Eysteinsson's wife, had developed the coughing sickness. It had crept up on her slowly and our short absence had made it obvious to all. The volvas had tried all that they could but the illness worsened. She was dying; little by little from within. It coincided with Bjorn Eysteinsson sharing his hall with his captives. He said it was to nurse his sick wife but the one he took, Ailsa, was the prettiest of the captives. The one Sven had taken would have made a better nurse for she was older. Ailsa was younger than me. It soon became apparent that she was his concubine. He began to change that day. It was subtle but, looking back, I can see that was the moment when he ceased to be one of my supporters.

We spent some months at home. Many of the slaves became the women of the warriors while others were put to work. I lay with a couple of the women if only to silence those who questioned me as a man. I could have used my strength to quieten them but that was not my way. It was a pleasurable experience to lie with them and they seemed pleased with me but it was not the same as with Kaðlín. I still dreamt of her at night.

One of the jarl's cousins paid us a visit. He brought news from Jarl Hálfdanar Svarti. We were told that when we visited for the next annual meeting we were to bring all of our men. We were going to war. The jarl was going to subdue some of his neighbours. The Vikings of Sogn were going to have a new overlord. The tribe was expanding. It did not please me for that took me further away from my goal of going home.

The jarl also brought news of the land of Northumbria. There had been a great battle between the Danes and the two kings of Northumbria, Ælla and Osberht had fallen in battle. In addition, most of their men had been killed. The Danes now ruled Jorvik. South of the Tyne was Danelaw. North was ruled by King Ecgberht. He ruled only with the permission of the Danes. He was a figurehead.

I was present when Jarl Rognvald received the news. Sven was there too. Jarl Halfgrimr leaned forward, "This means that the whole of Northumbria is ripe for the plucking. Ragnar Lodbrok's sons lead the army and they have left Jorvik to take the rest of the Saxon lands which lie to the west of the Danelaw."

Sven had asked the question which was in my mind, "Why do you and the other jarls not raid Northumbria?"

"It is not that we are afraid, Sven Blue Cheek, and I am a little offended at the question. If I did not know how high a regard my cousin has for you I might draw my sword."

Jarl Rognvald pleaded, "Peace, cousin, Sven means nothing do you?"

"No jarl, it is just that this seems a golden opportunity. I cannot understand why more of our family are not taking advantage. I am sorry if you took my words the wrong way. I am a bluff warrior and used to speaking plainly. I cannot help my tone."

Mollified the jarl said, "I accept your apology. It is simple; next year we take the lands which lie far from the sea. They have few warriors but Haraldr Hálfdanarson believes that if we subdue them and take their best men as warriors then we can take our men to sea when we take Sogn."

Sven nodded, "That makes sense."

Jarl Rognvald said, "Thank you cousin, and I will make our drekar available to you and my uncle when the family raids."

He stood, "Good and make sure you bring your son with you. We have heard tales of his prowess. I am looking forward to seeing him in action. For one so young he has done much!"

After he had gone Jarl Rognvald chastised his war chief. "Sometimes, Sven, you forget yourself."

Sven did not back down, "I do not believe that they are going to spend summer fighting farmers! There must be another reason they do not raid Northumbria."

"Do not question my cousin's honesty."

His brother said, "I cannot see what we have to lose, Sven Blue Cheek. If the Saxons are north of the Tyne and the Danes raid further south then who is there to stop us?" He cast a sideways glance at me, "Besides, we have this mighty hero now! Who can stand against us?"

The words seemed sarcastic. Bjorn had been drinking and his wife was ill. I dismissed his words. It was a mistake.

The jarl was still ill at ease. The death of his son had affected him. It was one thing to raid the Picts but the Saxons were a different matter. They had strong walls and mailed men, "That is the trouble, I cannot see and that worries me. Göngu-Hrólfr, you have a clever mind; what say you?"

I did not lie but I did not look at it as objectively as I might. I wanted to go home. I needed the treasure which Northumbria would yield. I took the easier route, "Like you, Sven, I cannot see how this can hurt us but, perhaps, if we take it slowly and scout out somewhere that is rich we might end up wealthy and not lose too many men."

He smiled, "You are right. What was that place he mentioned? The one with an abbey."

I had been listening when the jarl had told us of the land of Northumbria, "Streanæshalc. It is south of the river called the Dunum. My grandfather told me about the river."

We all looked at the jarl. He nodded, "Then we are in agreement. We raid Streanæshalc."

The Norns were spinning and threads were about to be cut.

169

My mail was ready. Bergil's mother had made me a padded kyrtle to wear beneath it. This one was not like the one I had left in the ocean. This one went to below my knees. The smith had riveted the rings. It had taken longer but it was stronger. Sven gave me the idea of putting straighteners in my sealskin boots at the front. They were simple, thin pieces of pinewood but they were effective. They would not stop an axe but a thrust from a spear or a slash from a sword was less likely to penetrate. What I did not have was a mail hood but as my helmet came down below my ears, then I was well protected. As Bergil pointed out, there were few warriors who could reach high enough to get at my neck. My legs were more vulnerable.

Bergil had spent more time with one slave girl than preparing for war. I realised early on that she had decided that it would be better to be the wife of a Viking rather than a slave and, seven days before we sailed, he told his mother of his plans to marry. I could see that she was disappointed. The girl, although pretty, had a sly look about her. She had manipulated Bergil. His mother would have preferred a Norse girl but they were homelier. I could see the attraction in the Cornovi girl. The result was that I had to chivvy him up to prepare for the voyage. Our positions had changed, subtly since I had been plucked from the waters of the Tamese estuary. He now acknowledged me as his superior. I was the jarl's adopted son and I had won great glory and respect in war.

We left at Sólmánuður. Even in Northumbria, the nights were short. We would have to time our raid well for they had watchtowers along the coast. The Saxon king might be a shadow of the former rulers but there would still be Saxon warriors who would protect their church and their land from Viking raiders. We were fully crewed and so I shared my oar with Bergil. Sámr and Arne were considered part of my band. We generally drank together and got on well with each other. Sven put the four of us on the same side of the drekar.

We talked as we rowed across the sea. This time we were heading south and it was getting warmer. The three of them all had a slave girl and I had none. They began questioning me about that. "I thought you and that princess would have made good children."

How do you come to that conclusion, Sámr?"

"You are so tall and she had fine hips and breasts. Your children would have made good warriors or perfect mothers."

"I take it that you have been busy trying to make children."

Arne had laughed, "Of course! A warrior needs children. A man who just has one risks losing him."

He suddenly realised what he had said. The jarl, his brother and his sister had each only had one child and now Bergil was the sole survivor. We were silent. I changed the subject. "Have any of you fought Saxons before?"

"No. What are they like?"

"They are similar to us. They use swords, axes and shields. They have mail and good helmets. They fight in shield walls. There the similarity ends. They sometimes ride horses to war and I have heard of some who fight on horseback. However, they have no archers and their shields are smaller. Their biggest weakness cannot be seen."

"Why not?"

"Because, Bergil, it is inside them. They are Christians. They do not believe in Valhalla. Our warriors fight to the death knowing that death is just the passage from this world to the next. They believe that they have to be without sin to get into heaven. What man is without sin?"

They laughed, "Then this will be as easy as the raid on the Picts!"

The jarl took us towards the coast of Northumbria and then we sailed down it. I saw the watchtowers flame and flare as we passed their Holy Island and their castle of Bebbanburgh. They would be worried that we were going to attack them. We had many leagues to travel. It was coming on to dark as we approached the sands of the Dunum where the seals basked. We had passed three villages and their beacons burned. It did not affect our plans. These lights were north of the Dunum and we were going south. We dropped a sea anchor in the estuary. I could see that the marshland around us would prevent any from getting close to us. Sven had decided to wait at this estuary until dark and then sail the last part of the journey at night. There was a village upstream, we had heard. They might think we were going to raid that one.

A party of warriors slipped over the side and slaughtered half a dozen seals. We ate them as we waited for darkness to surround us. We donned our mail as we ate and while we waited. We had been told that the monastery stood on a high cliff above the fishing village of Streanæshalc. We had been told that there were twenty huts and no warrior hall. It all seemed easy, perhaps it was, too easy. As we spoke of the raid none of us could see where the problem might lie. There would be slaves and treasure. Monks and nuns did not fight. There was no stronghold.

The jarl stood with me, "I am worried about my brother. I think that he is paying more attention to Ailsa than Gertha. It is not right. Nor do I like some of the comments he has been making about you. You are my heir! I thought he agreed with that but lately..."

I smiled, "Father, you are still jarl. You are still hale and hearty! There is little chance of me becoming jarl. Besides I am too young yet."

"And you still wish to go to the land of the Horse." He smiled, "I know that. Fear not, my son, you have my blessing."

"Thank you. It means much to me that I can be honest with you. Do not worry about your brother. He will tire of the girl eventually and return to his wife."

The jarl shook his head, "My wife has spoken with the volvas. Gertha is close to the Otherworld. She may not be there when we return. If it were me I would not have left. I did not say goodbye to my son. I would wish to say farewell to my wife. My brother seems unconcerned. We share the same blood but lately, I do not understand him."

I said, with feeling, "I know what you mean."

Once night fell we rowed. When we were clear of the pull of the river then we used the sail. I prepared myself for the raid. The last two had been relatively simple. The Cornovi had been poor warriors and the Danes were not expecting us. Vikings had been raiding this coast for almost eighty summers. The Saxons would be expecting us. They would have plans in place. The fyrd would be ready with their weapons to respond to the summons of a beacon or a bell. I stood on the steer-board side and watched the landslip by. It was night but you could still see the beaches and the bays. There were five bays we passed before we reached Streanæshalc. I stored that information.

Arne had asked me how the jarl would know when we had reached our destination. I had smiled, as we had eaten our seal, "Simple. We look for a high cliff and we listen for a bell. If the wind is right, and that I doubt, then we could smell their incense and their candles."

I had not brought my bow. I would have had the only one. I did not think that the jarl had enough archers but this was not my drekar yet. The sounds we heard were the creaking of the stays and sheets and the water surging beneath our bow. Then we heard the sound of breakers on rocks. We were close to shore. I cocked an ear. I could hear the tolling of a bell. The monks were being called to prayers. I hurried to the steering board. "We are close. I can hear the bell."

Beorn was at the masthead. He suddenly slithered down the forestay. "Jarl, the entrance to the river is coming up!"

The jarl began to put the steering board over and said, "Beorn, get the crew to reef the sail."

"Aye jarl."

"Sven Blue Cheek have the men ready on the larboard side!"

"Aye jarl!"

"Bergil, go and signal your uncle to turn!"

Bergil ran down the centre of the ship with the hooded lantern in his hand. It was his task to let the second drekar know our movement.

I had my helmet hanging from my sword. I knew that I was the only one who could wear such a long sword from his waist. The Dane I had taken it from had a scabbard he wore over his back. My shield had been taken from the side and was now across my back. I had added a seax to the inside of my shield. I now had three weapons as well as my sword. The jarl had been sailing longer than I had been alive and he put the steering board over perfectly. We slid into the middle of the channel. We had learned they called this river the Esk. It was very narrow! I saw lights glowing above us. That had to be the monastery. There was neither jetty nor quay. We would have to land on the beach. The beach was tiny and there were savage rocks at the southern end of it. We would have to land the two ships prow on. It was pitch black and we would be reliant on the sharp eyes of the ship's boys. Sven hurried down to the prow as the jarl turned the steering board to head into the beach.

Sven shouted, "Hold!" But it was too late. I heard the crunch and crack as our bow rode over a beached fishing boat. Beorn had not given us any warning. It was too late for us but not for the other drekar. The jarl shouted to them and they stopped. We would use our drekar as a bridge. Sven disappeared over the prow and we all followed him. As we landed, men ran from their huts above us. The alarm was raised. Sven was decisive and, without waiting for the rest to disembark, he led the ten of us who had followed him quickly, across the sand towards the Saxons.

He swung his sword into the middle of the Saxon with the axe. I saw a second lunge at him with his spear. I jerked my shield arm out and the spear hit my shield. I was travelling too quickly to bring my sword around and it was my mailed body which hit the man. He fell to the sand and I was able to skewer him there. Bergil, Sámr and Arne were with us and we quickly dispatched the Saxon men. The men who had been killed had bought time for their families who now fled up the cobbled track which led to the church and monastery at the top of the cliff.

A bell tolled urgently above us. The monks knew we were coming. Sven turned, "Move, you lazy whoresons! Are we to do all the work?"

I had never seen such a steep track. Normally they twisted and turned but this one went directly up. Some of the older folk were ahead of us and they screamed as we approached. We ignored them. The monastery was the prize. As had happened before, the ten of us outpaced the rest of the warband. I kept pace with Sven Blue Cheek rather than opening my legs and reaching the monastery first.

When we reached the top, I saw that there were a number of buildings. There was the church. It was a huge wooden one. There were two halls. I later learned that one housed the monks and one housed the nuns. There were three other smaller halls. It was the church which would yield us the greatest treasure. Someone had gone inside and barred the door. As other warriors arrived Sven sent them to gain entry to the other buildings. He turned to me and grinned, his teeth white in the moonlight. "Göngu-Hrólfr put your shield before you. The rest let us make a wedge behind our human ram!" Sven led me twenty paces from the door.

As they formed behind me I heard Bergil begin to chant.

Hrólfr the giant two men tall
Hrólfr the giant broad as a wall
Hrólfr the giant leads the clan
Hrólfr the giant I am your man
The rest joined in and it helped to get the rhythm.

Hrólfr the giant two men tall
Hrólfr the giant broad as a wall
Hrólfr the giant leads the clan
Hrólfr the giant I am your man

Brothers in Blood

"Now!"

I stepped off on my sword foot and we ran at the door. I held my shield before me. Sven and Rurik held their shields in my back. We hit the door hard. I heard a loud crack as the bar broke and the doors flew open. It was so sudden that I almost lost my balance. A monk stood waiting for me and he lunged at me with his spear. It hit me but the monk was no warrior. Our smith's skill showed for the mail held. I saw the monk's eyes widen and then his life ended as Sven took his head with one mighty blow. The candlelit church was filled with monks and nuns. As we ran towards them they fled for the two doors at the other end of the church.

One or two tonsured monks turned to try to fight us. We slew them. Others fell in the doorway and they were killed too. The nuns were spared. They would make slaves but the monks and priests who remained were slaughtered. It was not long until dawn and when the sun did rise from the east we had the monastery in our hands. We had great quantities of treasure. It was fortunate that I was on hand for some of the others were all for burning what they saw as books of Christian magic.

"Hold, these books are worth much gold and silver. We can sell them."

Sven Blue Cheek gave me a quizzical look, "Where?"

I pointed west. "Hibernia. There are Vikings at Dyflin, Veðrafjorðr and Veisafjorðr. There is a market there and one for slaves."

He grinned, "Once again we are grateful to you. We might have wasted that which is valuable." He turned to some of Bjorn's crew, "Take them down to the drekar."

Once we were outside we saw that the jarl and his brother had emptied the two halls. I saw Bjorn waving the brand. Already flames were licking at the buildings. I frowned, "That is a mistake, Sven Blue Cheek! You might as well ring a giant bell and tell the whole of this land that Vikings are raiding."

"You worry too much, Göngu-Hrólfr. We will be long gone before any help can come to these priests."

As if to confirm the view flames raced up the church. That had been fired too. The clan was leaving its mark but I heard the Norns spinning. I alone trudged silently down the hill to the ships filled with foreboding. The others were in high spirits.

My fears were realised when we reached the beach. *'Fáfnir'* was down by the bows. The tide was on the ebb and the two

175

drekar had been pulled into the river. The fishing boat had sprung some strakes. The ships' boys were looking helplessly at it.

The jarl reacted first. "Drop the treasures get ropes and pull her on to the beach!" We all obeyed instantly. We could not sail home on our treasure. With two crews pulling we soon had the drekar on the wet sand. The wreckage of the fishing boat could be seen drifting out to sea. The jarl and his brother went to examine the hull. I fingered my horse amulet. Behind me, a pall of smoke rose in the sky. That and the ones who had escaped us would now bring the wrath of the Saxons upon us. Danes had taken their land. Our destruction would be their vengeance.

"Beorn get aboard and fetch the pine tar."

"Aye jarl!"

"Erik, there must be sheepskins in the huts. Find one."

"Aye jarl."

"Get the water out of the drekar. We can save her but we must work quickly."

Bjorn Eysteinsson climbed aboard *'Fáfnir'*. He waved to his crew, "Six of you come with me. We will pull our drekar on to the sand. The rest of you move those fishing boats! We will not risk my ship too!"

We all raced to the boats and pulled them high up the beach. Jarl Rognvald shouted, "Fire them! We need a fire to make the pine tar liquid."

This time I understood the need for the fire. By the time *'Dellingr'* had been drawn up on the beach the fire was going and we had our wool and pine tar. The ships' boys were given the task of teasing out the wool and taking it to the jarl. He knew his ship. He packed it along the sprung strakes. At the same time, we began to load *'Dellingr'*. We were all working quickly. The tide was still on its way out. We had the chance to repair the sprung strakes and give the pine tar and wool time to set.

Sven Blue Cheek pointed to the west, "Arne and Sámr, get yourselves up there on the ridge and keep a watch for Saxons."

They nodded and ran off. Sámr was keen to get back into Sven's good graces. I was tempted to take off my mail, as I toiled carrying supplies to the *'Dellingr'*. The monks and nuns had been well supplied. We had grain which would last us many months. We also had wine, vegetables and other foods which they had produced at the monastery. There was fresh bread, cheese and butter. Even without the items from the church, the raid would have been worthwhile. We had twenty captives. There were twelve nuns and the rest were young women who looked like they had child-bearing hips. I kept my mail on and endured the sweat.

When the tide was fully out and *'Fáfnir'* lay canted at a strange angle the jarl finished applying the tar and the wool. He had used our entire supply of it but the damaged section was well coated and the gaps filled with teased, oiled wool.

He nodded and glared at Beorn, "You have let down the clan, Beorn. We could have been heading home."

"I am sorry, jarl."

"You are just lucky that we did not lose any men as a result."

I clutched my amulet as the jarl spoke. I saw Sven do the same. You did not speak of luck until you were safe in your hall. Then you toasted the Norns and you spoke of luck. Here, it just antagonised those three sisters. The tide had just begun to turn and the stern of the drekar floated in the river when the jarl and his brother walked along the strakes which had been repaired. I saw him run his finger along the repair. He seemed satisfied. The remaining captives stood forlornly huddled around the nuns.

"Start to load *'Fáfnir'*."

We placed a gangplank so that the captives could climb aboard. Two men went first to watch them. It would be some time until *'Fáfnir'* was refloated but we would be able to leave as soon as it did. My heart sank when I saw Arne and Sámr racing towards us. I picked up my shield and helmet for I knew what their speed meant.

"Jarl! Saxons! They have mounted men and they have raised the fyrd!"

Sven Blue Cheek was not a man to dwell on misfortune and mistakes. "Those with mail, form a shield wall. Those with bows get aboard the drekar. You will shower death upon the Saxons."

We had thirty men with mail. Not all had a byrnie such as I wore. More than half had just a mail vest. The ones in the second rank took spears. Arne and Sámr joined those without mail in the third rank. We had to hold off the Saxons until the drekar refloated.

Jarl Rognvald stood between Sven and me. "Jarl, you should be aboard *'Fáfnir'*. Your brother is at the helm of his drekar."

"Sven Blue Cheek, I will fight alongside you. Too often I have let you and Göngu-Hrólfr bear the brunt of the fighting. I am not too old to stand with my shield brothers and oathsworn."

Then we saw them. They appeared on the skyline below the smoke from the burning monastery. They had twenty men on horses. None were mailed. There were, as far as I could see, just ten men with mail and they were on foot. But there were over a hundred other Saxons armed with a variety of weapons. They were the fyrd. They were warriors for the day and farmers for the year. I saw that the horsemen rode small horse little bigger than a pony and they did not use stiraps. That was the good news. The bad news was that we were outnumbered and *'Fáfnir'* was yet to be totally refloated.

The Saxons just launched themselves as a horde. They poured down the hillside. The huts and the buildings meant that they had to come at us piecemeal but that meant our handful of archers and ships' boys with slingshots had less opportunity to thin their ranks. The horsemen reached us first. I held my sword above my head. I brought it down as the first horseman, with spears outstretched, tried to skewer the jarl. My long sword hacked his horse's head in two and the Saxon flew over the horse's head. The Norns were spinning for his helmet-encased head struck the jarl square in the face. As Sven ended a Saxon's life the other Saxons saw their chance and they headed for the gap. Our shield wall was broken and so I did the only thing I could; I left the shield wall and stepped before it. I had to buy time to move the jarl to safety.

I slid my shield to my back and held my sword in two hands. I swung it in an arc before me. I knew that men were pulling the jarl to safety. Others were filling the gap. I had to stop their horsemen from reaching us. Our archers and slingers could do nothing about the mailed men and, as I started my swing, I saw their arrows and stones falling among the fyrd. I did not use a flat arc for my swing. I swung in two loops so that none would be able to approach. My blade tore into the throat of one horse and, as my sword rose it slashed into the shield of a Saxon. On the backswing, it ripped into the arm of another Saxon and then into the head of a horse. Their lack of stiraps was their undoing. Our shield wall was repaired and their horses baulked. As riders were thrown they were butchered by our front rank.

"Göngu-Hrólfr, get back in line!"

I shook my head but did not turn. "I cannot swing in the shield wall. This is a good day to die!"

Bergil shouted, "Do not go berserk, Göngu-Hrólfr!"

I laughed, "Fear not little shield brother. It is the Saxons who will find it a good day to die."

It was their mailed men who were advancing. They were the ones the Saxons called housecarls. Their thegn led them. He was as old as our jarl and his armour was made of overlapping metal plates. He looked like a fish.

Bergil banged his shield and started the chant.

Hrólfr the giant two men tall
Hrólfr the giant broad as a wall
Hrólfr the giant leads the clan
Hrólfr the giant I am your man
Hrólfr the giant two men tall
Hrólfr the giant broad as a wall
Hrólfr the giant leads the clan
Hrólfr the giant I am your man

The ten mailed men were backed by the fyrd but their numbers were diminishing even as they advanced. Sometimes a warrior needs to be reckless. I did not want to die. I wanted to see the Haugr and my grandfather again. To do so I had to get off the beach and the Saxons were in my way. I did what the Saxons did not expect. I stepped towards them. My long legs covered the ground quickly and I was swinging as I did so. This time there were no horses' heads in the way. As I swung they brought up their shields. My sword smashed into a shield and knocked one man over. He stumbled into the man next to him.

Behind me, I heard, "Break wall!" as my sword smashed into the helmet of a third Saxon. A sword, wielded by the thegn, was thrust at me. I turned but it still struck me. My mail was good but I felt the blade rasp through the links.

Bergil and my oar brothers fell upon the housecarls. The two who lay prostrate were butchered. I used the hilt to punch the thegn in the face. He reeled backwards. The Saxon next to him lunged at me but Sven Blue Cheek blocked the blow with his own shield and I was able to swing my sword overhand. The thegn looked up and saw his own death as my long sword hit his helmet, splitting it in two and then slicing through his skull. As the last housecarl was killed the fyrd took to their heels and ran.

The warriors behind me cheered. There were none left to kill and no one wished to chase after men whose bodies would yield neither honour nor treasure.

Bergil came up to me, "That is worthy of a song, Rollo, my friend. That was the stuff of legend."

Sven Blue Cheek said, "You are making a habit of disobeying me, Göngu-Hrólfr!"

"I am sorry but I could think of nothing else."

"One day you will try that and someone will have a longer sword!" Sven sheathed his sword and put his arm around me. "Come let us see how the jarl fares."

Just then Beorn came to the prow and shouted, "Sven Blue Cheek, the jarl is dead!" I watched as the drekar bobbed afloat and I swear I could hear a thread being cut. The Norns!

Chapter 14

When we looked at his body we saw no wound but I saw that
the front of his helmet was dented. As Sven removed the helmet
we saw that his skull had been crushed. The flying Saxon had
killed our jarl. Any joy at our victory disappeared like early
morning mist. We covered his body with his cloak and kept it by
the steering board. Sven took the helm. Like the rest of us, he was
bereft of words. The jarl had died with his sword in his hand but
it had not been a glorious death. The winds were with us and we
did not need to row. I wanted to row. I wanted to exorcise the
memory of his death. Instead, we had to look at the cloak covered
corpse. It made it worse.

Bergil and I were on the night watch. We did not stop for the
dark. Olaf Two Teeth steered and Bergil and I watched.

"This means you are jarl now. You were my uncle's heir."

I had avoided that thought. Nor was it true. I was his heir and
that was something different. I did not want to be jarl. If I was
jarl then I would not be able to go home. I shook my head. "Let
us not talk of that. First, we have to bury him. Gefn will mourn.
She has lost a son and a husband in a short time."

He nodded, "And soon my uncle may be mourning the loss of
his wife too. We have had great success since you joined us but it
has been at a price."

He was right and that sent my spirits even deeper into my
sealskin boots. I had thought that being saved was a good thing
but the clan I had joined was paying the weregeld for that
salvation. We made it back in two days. Perhaps the Allfather
took pity on us. We arrived back at dusk as the sun was setting
over the western waters.

I had been adopted by the jarl and so I took on the
responsibility of telling Gefn of her husband's death. While his
oathsworn carried his body, I preceded them. "Mother, your
husband is dead. He died in battle."

She took it better than I had hoped. She closed her eyes and
mouthed something then she opened them and smiled. It was a
sad smile. It was the smile of regret. She reached up and hugged
me, "He was never the same after our son died. You brought a

little light into his life. He will be pleased that the clan is in your hands."

I said nothing. The Norns would decide my fate. I knew that as certain as I knew the sun would come up each morning.

Gefn and the other women of the family prepared the jarl's body. Only Gertha was absent. He was laid out in his mail which we burnished. He had his sword in his hand, his helmet on his head and his shield on his chest. He was laid on the table in his hall. He would be buried the next evening at sunset. His passage to the Otherworld was not the same ritual as that practised by the Clan of the Horse. They still used a burning ship to take a jarl to the Otherworld. I had not known it but he had had his burial ship made when he had returned from the raid where he lost his son. It was a miniature version of *'Fáfnir'*. A shipwright had built it on the beach where we had repaired our drekar. The whole clan came to see him off. The warriors wore their mail and their helmets. They carried their shields on their backs. The women had their hair braided and wore their best. We waited until the sun began to dip at the mouth of the fjord.

His body was laid in the bottom. Gefn positioned his hands about his sword and then kissed his lips. His helmet hid the horrific wound which had killed him. I had the honour of loosing the sail and releasing the mooring lines. I lowered the sail and the lithe little vessel tugged at the mooring ropes. I released one and it began to drift away. As I released the second, Bjorn, his brother, Bergljót, his sister and Gefn, his wife threw the burning brands into the kindling filled boat. The wind caught her and she seemed to leap towards the west. The flames licked around the bottom of the mast and then flickered up the sail where they caught. By then the tiny drekar was well down the fjord. We saw her silhouetted against the sunset and then, as the sun disappeared, the glow of the burning boat sank beneath the waves. The jarl was dead.

We retired to his hall. We left our helmets and shields outside. It was just the family. Sven Blue Cheek was the war chief. This was not his jurisdiction. Gefn had had food prepared. We sat around the table, picked at the food and then toasted the jarl. Gertha Eysteinsson barely made it through the toasts. She began to cough and Gefn had her servants take her home. Her husband barely acknowledged her departure. I saw the displeasure on the faces of the two women. Jarl Rognvald would not have acted in the same way.

Bjorn Eysteinsson stood. "Now we come to the legacy my brother leaves." He smiled, "Gefn, the hall remains with you. It is your home for as long as you shall live."

Bergil stood, "Uncle, what is this? You talk as though it is your right to give away my uncle's goods. You are not the heir of the jarl. His heir is Göngu-Hrólfr."

"That is where you are wrong. I am jarl of this clan by right of blood." He turned to me, "My crew and many of the crew of *'Fáfnir'* support me as jarl. If you fight me then there will be much blood spilt. My brother would not have wished that."

"And I do not wish that either." He smiled. He thought he had won. I would leave the clan. We had planned on going to the island of Hibernian to trade. I would ask to leave the drekar there.

Suddenly Gefn stood. Her face was cold with anger and her voice, when she spoke, showed her scorn for her husband's brother. "You, Bjorn Eysteinsson, threaten to destroy the clan and yet my son does not. He has more right to be jarl that you have." He shrugged and drank some more ale. I saw a cold smile appear on Gefn's face. "This hall is not yours to give or take at your whim. It was my husband's. You know the law of our clan. The title of jarl may be stolen by you but you cannot steal my home."

He spread his arms, "I told you that you can keep the hall!"

"And what would you when I am dead? You would take it." She turned to Bergil, "Go and fetch Sven Blue Cheek. Tell him the wife of the jarl needs him!"

Bergil left eagerly. Bjorn shook his head, "He is a war chief and has nothing to do with this."

"True but I do not send for him as a war chief. I send for him as a witness."

Bjorn turned and stared at me. I saw his hands bunch. If this came to a fight between the two of us then I would win but if it spilt into the clan I would leave for I would not tear apart this clan. Sven arrived and I saw, from his face that Bergil had told him all.

Gefn said, "Sven Blue Cheek. Were you present when my husband made Göngu-Hrólfr his heir?"

"I was."

"Bjorn Eysteinsson claims the title of jarl."

I could see Sven choosing his words carefully. He nodded, "But Jarl Rognvald intended Göngu-Hrólfr to be his successor."

Bjorn turned and almost spat the words at Sven Blue Cheek, "Mercenary, I have more than half of the clan on my side. Would you make war on me?"

Sven laughed, "If I did then you would lose."

I stood, "Stop. I do not wish to be jarl. I will not have this clan destroyed by me."

Gefn smiled although tears coursed down her cheeks, "And that one statement shows that you are the true successor to my husband. Göngu-Hrólfr, my adopted son, this hall is yours, my husband's treasure is yours and," she stared at Bjorn Eysteinsson, "*'Fáfnir'* is yours. They are not Bjorn Eysteinsson's to give. They are mine as the wife of the jarl."

Bjorn stood. "Then have the drekar but you will not find a crew to sail it!"

"We shall see." Sven's voice cut through the silence. Bjorn stormed off.

Bergljót said, "It is that whore, Ailsa. She has him twisted around her finger. Since she came and he bedded her he is not the same man. She has turned his head."

Gefn said, "No, my husband believed that there was a bad seed in him. It is why he named Göngu-Hrólfr as his heir. He did not trust the clan to his brother. I fear this means the end of the clan."

Sven and Bergil sat and talked with me long into the night. Sven told me much that I did not know. We would speak to the clan the next day. The Norns were spinning. When we rose, we discovered that Gertha had died in the night. Many said it was the sickness but Gefn did not believe it. She thought it was something more sinister. Nothing could be proven. Out of respect for her, we did not speak with the clan that day, as we had planned, but soon all knew of the rift and men chose sides. I kept apart. I would not be the one who destroyed this clan. The delay went on for Bjorn Eysteinsson married Ailsa and it soon became apparent that she was with child.

The day after their wedding Sven Blue Cheek took it upon himself to blow the horn at the top of the tower so that the whole clan came to see what was happening. I saw that Bjorn was less than happy with Sven's actions but Gefn and Bergljót were with him and they were still the matriarchs of the clan.

Sven said, "Bjorn Eysteinsson has declared himself jarl of this clan. Göngu-Hrólfr was chosen as heir by Jarl Rognvald." People turned and spoke to their neighbours about this. It had been gossip but with the funerals and the wedding, nothing had been confirmed. "Göngu-Hrólfr does not want war and he accepts that Bjorn Eysteinsson is jarl of this clan." There was another buzz of conversation. He then unleashed his thunderclap. "However, Göngu-Hrólfr does not wish to serve this jarl. Nor do I."

Bergil, Sámr and Arne stepped forwards as one. They all said, "Nor do I!"

Bjorn's face was red and angry.

Gefn said, "Göngu-Hrólfr is master of the hall and master of *'Fáfnir'*."

There was uproar. I had been seated on a barrel. That was as small as I ever managed. I stood and silence fell. "I will not fight the clan but any warriors who wish to follow me are welcome to an oar on my drekar, *'Fáfnir'*."

The result shocked even me. Forty men chose to follow me. Bjorn was defeated. More than half of the warriors chose to follow me. The numbers he thought would support him were not there. There would be no war but I knew there might be treachery.

Matters came to a head months later at Haustmánuður when Jarl Halfgrimr Halfdansson arrived to ask us to take part in a winter war against Sogn. He made the mistake of addressing me. I shook my head, "Bjorn Eysteinsson is jarl. He did not honour his brother's wishes. I am not part of this clan."

Halfgrimr turned to Bjorn. "But the tribe acknowledged Göngu-Hrólfr Rognvaldson as the next jarl."

"Well he is not and I am!" Bjorn sounded petulant.

"Then I must ask you to come with me to swear allegiance to the leader of our tribe."

Bjorn had no choice. He had to agree. He and his crew left the next morning.

Gefn and Bergljót had been talking, behind my back, with Sven Blue Cheek. As *'Dellingr'* sailed down the fjord in the wake of Jarl Halfgrimr's drekar Sven said, "And now we must sail to Hibernia. We have holy books and captives to sell. And you need the coin to buy another drekar and crew."

"What?"

"Your mother knows that you wish to return to the Land of the Horse. She and Bergil's mother are happy for you to do that. You cannot return to fight your brother with just one drekar. We have your father's treasure. Come. We must tell the crew."

I felt as though I was in a maelstrom! I no longer controlled my own life. Events were happening too quickly for me to comprehend. I just went along with the plans which had been hatched behind my back. Those who supported Bjorn Eysteinsson had sailed with him. Those who supported me prepared my drekar and those either too timid or too careful stayed to protect our hall.

I stood on the jetty and said, "We sail to trade our goods in Hibernia. Know that the profit we make will be returned here and shared out amongst the whole clan: my crew, those who stay behind to watch our homes and the crew of the *'Dellingr'*." I saw the two matriarchs nod their approval.

I stepped aboard and we cast off. Olaf Two Teeth had the helm but next to him stood Beorn. He would never make the same mistake again and I had chosen him to train as my new helmsman. From my mast flew my new banner. Gefn and Bergljót had sewn it. It was a dark blue banner with my longsword sewn in grey thread. It looked a little like the standard which Alain of Auxerre had flown. I liked it. It was simple and the sword had now come to represent me. Many men called me Longsword. I had more names than Loki!

Our voyage would be a long one for we would head west around the north coast of the land of the Picts. We would be passing the land where Kaðlín lived or, at least, the land where her father ruled. *Wyrd*. It was a hard voyage. It was the time of the storms. We had completely repaired our drekar and I believe that saved us. I had made a blót before we had left but the waves were so high and the troughs so deep that there were times I thought I should have made a bigger one. The coast had savage teeth which threatened to tear out our keel. Finally, as we turned south, disaster stuck. A crack appeared in the mainmast. We managed to beach her in a small bay in the land of the Caereni. It appeared to be deserted.

We had the captives brought ashore first and I set a good watch upon them. We were close enough to their home for them to risk running. While the rest of the crew took the sail from the damaged mast and prepared the new one I went with Bergil and Sven to scout out the land around the bay. I did not want to be attacked. The land was bleak and desolate. I saw no sign of habitation save a single path which wound along the coast. We spied no horse droppings nor any footprints. We were on a deserted part of the coast. We returned to the beach. Night was falling and we had still to attach the sail. We would have to camp on the beach.

"When we have traded, what are your plans?"

Bergil looked at me as Sven asked the question which had been vexing me for some time. "Take the treasure back and share it."

Sven shook his head, "Honesty. We have supported you but we would have you speak honestly to us too."

I sighed, "I am bound to sail back to the Land of the Horse. I would do so sooner rather than later."

"With just one ship; a threttanessa?"

"Sven, I would take a knarr if that was all that I had. I have a father to avenge. If it means my death then so be it. I cannot escape this web."

Sven smiled, "Good. That is what I wanted to hear. When you did not take on Bjorn I thought I might have made a mistake with the choice of the man I would follow." He swept a hand around the camp. "These men will follow you anywhere."

"But what of Bergil's mother and Gefn?"

"They are Viking women. They will come with us but that will be when we have won. We do not go there to lose Göngu-Hrólfr."

I was a lucky man to be surrounded by such warriors.

We could not leave at first light. We rigged the sail but a storm blew up. The wind was blowing directly into the bay and we would have to wait until it abated or turned. We could not row against it. The Weird Sisters were still spinning. I spied a small ship. It looked like the Hibernian version of a knarr. It was trying to avoid the bay but it was as though it was being drawn into it. Eventually, the captain gave up and he stopped fighting the sea. We hurried down to the shore. I think the crew thought we were going to fall upon them but we did not. We helped them to beach the boat.

The captain, a Hibernian, fell to his knees in the sand, "Thank you, master! I pray you do not harm us. We are simple sailors."

He spoke our language, "Rise. We are all sailors. Where were you running in such a hurry?"

"I deliver a message to Áed mac Cináeda, King of the Caereni. It is from Prince Beollán mac Ciarmaic."

I felt the hairs on the back of my neck prickle. "What is the message?"

"The king's daughter is married to the Prince. I am to tell her father that she is about to give birth to a child. It is cause for great celebration."

"How so?"

"The Prince has had wives before but none conceived. The princess conceived immediately after their marriage. God has smiled on their union. The Prince wished the king to know that."

I nodded. The child was not the prince's. It was mine. *Wyrd.*

It took two days for the storm to abate. We managed to make all our repairs as did the Hibernian. We left at the same time. We headed south and he headed north.

Bergil saw that I was distracted. He took me to the side and asked me why. I could not keep it a secret from him and, besides, there was no reason to do so. I told him. "It might not be your child."

I tapped my chest, "Something in here," I tapped my head, "and here, tells me that it is."

"Will you do anything about it?"

I shook my head. "I have one quest. Save my land and find my grandfather."

I looked astern as we sailed towards Dyflin. Family was more important than any seed I might have sown. I was determined.

The winds were precocious. They had blown from the west and kept us in the bay. Now they had swung around to the south and east. They made life hard. We had to both row and tack. This was my drekar but I rowed. Bergil laughed, "I do not think that the gods wish you to get to Dyflin."

I shook my head, "This is the Norns. They are spinning. I can feel their web."

We ended up close to the Land of the Wolf. I had never been there but my grandfather had told me so much about it that I felt I knew it. My back was burning from the constant effort of rowing. Olaf said, "Jarl..."

"I am not jarl!"

He smiled his toothless smile, "Lord then. We have come far enough south. If we turn west we will have enough wind to make Dyflin."

"Then make the turn." As soon as he put the steering board over I shouted, "In oars! Rowers we will broach the barrel! We can buy more in Dyflin!"

The men cheered. They had worked hard. We did not get to open the barrel of ale. We had new ship's boys and the one at the masthead was Ragnar's son. He was keen to become a warrior. He wished to emulate his father, a hero. "Ships ahead!"

"Where away?"

"To the north and west, lord!"

"What are they?"

"A knarr, she looks Norse is being chased by a drekar."

Sven looked at me. "A drekar means a Viking."

I nodded, "As does a knarr. We can sail further south and close our eyes or we can go closer."

He cocked his head to one side, "We have captives and treasure on board. Why do we risk losing them?"

"I said we can sail south and avoid them."

He laughed, "That is what you said but that is not what was in your head."

I nodded, "You are right. The storm broke our mast and that meant we met the Hibernian. We were forced south and now we find a battle. We are meant to intervene."

"You are right. Following you may be a short life but it will not be dull."

I turned to Olaf, "Head for the drekar." I shouted, "Prepare for battle!"

I had my mail on but some of the others did not and they hurried to arm themselves. I walked down to the prow. We could have avoided this battle but something deep inside told me that I had to intervene. I looked up at the mast. "Erik Ragnarsson, will the knarr escape?"

"No, lord. The drekar is rowing. They are gaining."

I peered ahead. The ships were sailing on a south-west to northeast course. We were gaining rapidly for we had the wind and we would close with them. I hoped that the drekar would not see us. Their attention would be on the helpless little knarr. Olaf Two Teeth had grown to understand the drekar on our voyage around the coast of Britannia. Our ship was getting faster. He was teasing speed from the sails and the hull.

I walked back down the ship to make sure that everyone was armed. I would not be using my long sword. The pitching ship of a drekar was not the best place for such a large and long weapon. I took a pair of short swords. Men nodded and grinned as I passed them. They were ready. I reached Olaf and Sven. "Try to lay us along their steerboard side. That will keep you safe and let us disable the ship."

When Sven Blue Cheek nodded appreciatively I knew that I had made the right decision.

Erik Ragnarsson shouted, "Lord, they are about to grapple the knarr."

The small ship was hidden from us but the drekar was just two lengths from us. Sven knew ships. He had sailed far and wide. "That is a ship of Man."

"How do you know?"

"The standard they fly from their mast. It is the four legs which radiate from the centre. They are from Man."

I felt better. The men of Man were known to be without honour. They were pirates. All Vikings were pirates but there were degrees of villainy. They were amongst the lowest. The knarr was a victim. "Olaf lay us alongside them!"

"Lord they are boarding the knarr!"

Just then there was a shout from the drekar as she realised we were closing with them. I ran to the larboard side. I kept one sword sheathed and I stood on the gunwale and held the backstay. "These are pirates! No quarter!"

My men cheered. Olaf put the helm over and our ship crashed into the side of the drekar. I was about to lose my balance anyway and so I leapt. Most of the men of Man were trying to board the knarr from the larboard side of the ship. I ran for the steering board. Drawing my second sword I blocked the sword of the Viking who lurched at me and gutted him with my other. The helmsman saw a giant and he leapt overboard.

"Beorn and Olaf guard the ship and the captives. Erik Ragnarsson, come and take this helm!" I ran down the ship, shouting to my men who were scrambling over the side, "To me!"

I hurtled down the drekar towards the press of men trying to board the tiny knarr. The first four men died without even knowing that we were aboard. Then their jarl, who was on the deck of the knarr, realised that his ship was under attack. He yelled, "Back!"

As he did so I recognised the warrior he had just killed. It was Erik Green Eye. Then I saw the helmsman. It was Harold Haroldsson. Slumped on the deck next to him was my grandfather. The knarr was the *'Kara'*! My grandfather was here! The Norns had indeed spun. I just prayed that my grandfather's thread had not been cut.

Brothers in Blood

The warriors of Man tried to climb back aboard their drekar. It was higher than the knarr and I slashed and stabbed at the ones whose hands appeared. My men arrived and a terrifying battle ensued. It was a fight to the death. The drekar was bigger than mine and had a bigger crew. We had to kill them all. They needed to kill us to regain control of their ship. The chief, I recognised him by his warrior bands, hit his sword against Sámr's helmet. My friend slumped to the deck and the chief sprang aboard his own drekar.

"You have bitten off more than you can chew giant. I will have the knarr and your ship."

I said nothing. He was mailed and he had a shield. He had a sword but he had killed Erik Green Eye and for that, he would die. I blocked his first blow and, instead of aiming at his shield or his body, I slashed at his knee. His byrnie did not cover it. I had a short blade but it was a sharp sword and I ripped open the flesh of his knee. He roared in pain and I punched at his sword arm with the hilt of my second weapon. He had to take a step back and that made his leg bleed more. I lunged with my sword at his middle and when he brought his shield around I lunged at his shoulder with the other. I found flesh and his shield dropped a little. He was pressed against his gunwale. Blood pumped from his leg and seeped from his arm. I whirled the swords above his head and he appeared mesmerized. I brought them together and the two of them took his head. It fell to the deck of the knarr.

His crew were being attacked by my men and the handful of crew left on the knarr. It would be bloody but the outcome was no longer in doubt. As my men slew the last of them I leapt aboard the knarr and ran to my grandfather. His eyes were closed. I could not see a wound. Had he suffered a blow to the head as Jarl Rognvald? That would be truly ironical. Was I too late? I laid down my swords and cradled his head.

"Grandfather, it is Rollo! Come back to me! Do not go to the Otherworld!"

His eyes opened and he smiled at me, "Not yet for I have searched two years to find you. I have come to take you home." Then his head slumped and he fell backwards. I saw that his leg was bloody. I saw the wound. I had to save him.

Hrolf the Horseman

Epilogue

When we had left Dyflin I had felt old and I had felt weary. I had sailed the seas, it seemed, forever. In my heart, I knew that my grandson, Rollo, was still alive. There had been enough stories and legends from the north to keep me searching. The giant who had descended upon a Danish village, the warrior with the two-handed sword who had captured a kingdom in the far north, the warrior who had sacked Streanæshalc; all of these told me that my grandson was still alive but it had been a hard search. I had never believed Ragnvald and his story. Perhaps that was because I did not like him anyway but there was something in his eyes and in his demeanour, that told me all was not as he had said. All of those I trusted, my son's hearth weru, were dead. The witnesses were warriors like Arne the Breton Slayer and they were Ragnvald's men. I could not bring myself to say, grandson.

Folki had been the only one I could ask and he had told me that he had seen little in that confused night. He had gone to the aid of my son and found young Ragnvald defending my son's body. The fact that there were no Danes nearby was suspicious enough. Of Rollo, there was no sign and Ragnvald had said that Rollo had fallen overboard and been dragged down by his armour. That I did not believe. Who could have slain my son?

Ragnvald was now jarl and I could not bring myself to abandon Rollo. I had asked for warriors to come with me and search for Rollo. We had filled **'Kara'** with trade goods and set sail pretending to be simple traders. That had been more than two years ago. We had sailed to Cent and the Isle of Grain. As we had sailed over the waters I had not sensed his body and we had searched elsewhere. We had sailed to Brvggas. Now that Dorestad had silted up it was where a man could still buy and sell slaves. He was not there but, while in that port, I had talked with Erik Green Eye and Harold Haroldsson. We had used our heads to work out where Rollo if he was still alive, might be. The winds had been from the south. The crews of all the drekar had attested to that. It had made the voyage home hard. We had to look north.

For half a year we had visited as many ports in Denmark as we could. We had been about to give up when we heard of a village sacked by Vikings. We would have ignored it save the word, giant, was spoken. It proved if proof were needed, that my grandson was still alive. Our cover worked and we visited port after port from Svearike to Horderland in Norway. It took more than six months. We traded well and we were in profit but my grandson was as elusive as ever. We gave up that search. I intended to sail to Dyflin and seek information there or perhaps Úlfarrston and the land of the Wolf. There I had friends who would speak the truth.

Then we heard of a band of Vikings who had raided the land of the Cornovi. They had taken many slaves. That was when Harold had come up with an idea, "Jarl we are doing this the wrong way. We are searching for a single fish in a great sea. Let us see if he will come to us. If they have slaves then they need to sell them. We should sail to Dyflin. You will be welcomed by the Vikings there. They are friends of the Dragonheart's family. We can trade."

Erik Green Eye had agreed, "And there we will be more likely to hear of a giant Viking who raids the northern seas. All sailors head to Dyflin. They have the best alehouses and whores in the north."

We had sailed to Dyflin and we had waited. We heard of a clan in Norway. They were a mighty clan and, it was said, the son of one of them was a giant. We dismissed that. Rollo's father lay dead. We thought that the trail had gone cold until ten days since. Word came of a raid on Streanæshalc. It was brought to us by a Saxon who had been there. He had fled across Northumbria with his hoard of jet that he wished to sell. He told us of a giant who had a two-handed sword he used one handed. It was when he spoke of how this giant had defeated horsemen that I knew it was Rollo. It was then that I knew I had stopped searching Norway too soon. We had finished our trading and loaded the knarr. We had set sail for Norway and then we had been followed. A drekar from Man had pounced on us as we headed north. The winds prevented us from heading for the Land of the Wolf and we had tried to outsail them. When we had spied the second drekar we had thought we were doomed. The men of Man had boarded us and I had thought to end my life with my sword in my hand but my son unavenged. I had been laid low by a slingshot and thought I was bound for the otherworld and then Rollo had leapt aboard. Too late to save Erik Green Eyes, he had saved his grandfather. The sword thrust I had taken to my leg would not kill me. I had reason to live.

I saw my wife's face and I saw my son. I realised that I was dreaming. Had I dreamed Rollo? His voice woke me, "Grandfather, open your eyes so that I know you are alive."

I opened them. I saw Harold Haroldsson at the steering board. A bandage covered the side of his head. I saw my grandson. He had grown since I had last seen him and, beneath his beard, I saw a long scar running down his cheek. I reached up and ran my fingers down his scar. "You have had battles."

He nodded and smiled, "I have had battles."

A grizzled warrior standing next to him said, "Göngu-Hrólfr Rognvaldson, will you stay on the knarr? We have two ships to crew."

Rollo turned, "Aye Sven Blue Cheek. It seems we have no need for a second drekar, the gods have sent us one."

The warrior he had called Sven Blue Cheek laughed, "Aye, I wondered how you would manage that trick. It seems you are the chosen one." He looked down at me. "Your grandson says that you met a Norn, Jarl, is it true?"

I nodded, "I am never foresworn; aye it is true."

"Then I have chosen the right warrior to follow. Back aboard the drekar. Boys, we have much to do. Strip those bodies and feed them to the fishes. Bergil, take half the crew and sail the new drekar!"

I looked up at Rollo, "Göngu-Hrólfr Rognvaldson?"

He smiled, "It is the name by which I am known. I am still the same Rollo. I was adopted by the jarl who fished me from the sea. He is dead now." His eyes narrowed, "Does that snake of a brother still live and his murderous crew?"

"He does."

His eyes filled with sadness. I saw that he was close to tears. I felt the same way. We had both thought the other lost and now we had found each other. This was a mighty thread. It was a thread of blood and it bound us tightly. "He killed my father. He slew Magnús the Fish. Arne Breton Slayer tried to kill me. Had not the Danish drekar hit our ship I would be dead. Instead, I fell to the bottom of the sea."

My heart sank. The truth was worse than any story I had concocted to explain the events of the raid on Lundenwic. "A father murderer! There will be no place in Valhalla for your brother. He is jarl now. He and his men rule Benni's Ville. There is bad blood between him and the haugr and the other stad of the Land of the Horse. Your brother has broken the bonds which bound us." I closed my eyes and shook my head. Everything was so clear now. "He has allied himself with a Breton, Lord Wigo. All that we had is now in danger."

My grandson nodded. He looked young but I could see age in his eyes. He reminded me of me when we had lost Raven Wing Island. He was steel and he was determined. "Then when we have traded in Dyflin we will sail north to Norway. I have unfinished business there. I have men to hire and an adopted mother and an aunt to save. When I have them we shall return to the Haugr and I will be the instrument of my brother's death. I will not rest until my father is avenged."

"With the crews of just two drekar?"

Rollo laughed and I realised that he had become a man since I had last seen him, "It is just one drekar crew! Do not worry, we will get more men but I would return with just a handful. I was saved when I fell into the sea. I was dead and I was reborn. I do not fear my brother. There will be blood spilt but it will heal the land. It will take time but I will have my brother's blood. Then I will be happy."

I shook my head, "No, my grandson, Rollo that was, Göngu-Hrólfr Rognvaldson that is, you are the one Skuld prophesied. *'His family will be remembered long after you are dead, Jarl Dragonheart, but they will not know that they would have been nothing without the Viking slave who changed the world.'* You are the one who will be remembered. It will not be my name which echoes through the years. It will be yours. And I will stand at your side as long as the Allfather allows me."

My grandson pulled me to my feet and embraced me, "And may that be for a long time to come, Hrolf the Horseman!"

The End

Norse Calendar
Gormánuður October 14th - November 13th
Ýlir November 14th - December 13th
Mörsugur December 14th - January 12th
Þorri - January 13th - February 11th
Gói - February 12th - March 13th
Einmánuður - March 14th - April 13th
Harpa April 14th - May 13th
Skerpla - May 14th - June 12th
Sólmánuður - June 13th - July 12th
Heyannir - July 13th - August 14th
Tvímánuður - August 15th - September 14th
Haustmánuður September 15th-October 13th

Glossary
Ækre -acre (Norse) The amount of land a pair of oxen could plough in one day
Addelam- Deal (Kent)
Afon Hafron- River Severn in Welsh
Alt Clut- Dumbarton Castle on the Clyde
Andecavis- Angers in Anjou
Angia- Jersey (Channel Islands)
An Oriant- Lorient, Brittany
Áth Truim- Trim, County Meath (Ireland)
Baille - a ward (an enclosed area inside a wall)
Balley Chashtal -Castleton (Isle of Man)
Bárekr's Haven – Barfleur, Normandy
Bebbanburgh- Bamburgh Castle, Northumbria. Also, known as Din Guardi in the ancient tongue
Beck- a stream
Blót – a blood sacrifice made by a jarl
Blue Sea/Middle Sea- The Mediterranean
Bondi- Viking farmers who fight
Bourde- Bordeaux
Bjarnarøy –Great Bernera (Bear Island)
Byrnie- a mail or leather shirt reaching down to the knees
Brvggas -Bruges
Caerlleon- Welsh for Chester
Caestir - Chester (old English)
Cantwareburh- Canterbury
Casnewydd –Newport, Wales
Cent- Kent

Cephas- Greek for Simon Peter (St. Peter)

Cetham -Chatham Kent

Chape- the tip of a scabbard

Charlemagne- Holy Roman Emperor at the end of the 8th and beginning of the 9th centuries

Cherestanc- Garstang (Lancashire)

Ċiriċeburh- Cherbourg

Condado Portucalense- the County of Portugal

Constrasta-Valença (Northern Portugal)

Corn Walum or Om Walum- Cornwall

Cymri- Welsh

Cymru- Wales

Cyninges-tūn – Coniston. It means the estate of the king (Cumbria)

Dùn Èideann –Edinburgh (Gaelic)

Din Guardi- Bamburgh castle

Drekar- a Dragon ship (a Viking warship)

Duboglassio –Douglas, Isle of Man

Dyrøy –Jura (Inner Hebrides)

Dyflin- Old Norse for Dublin

Ein-mánuðr- middle of March to the middle of April

Eopwinesfleot -Ebbsfleet

Eoforwic- Saxon for York

Fáfnir - a dwarf turned into a dragon (Norse mythology)

Faro Bregancio- Corunna (Spain)

Ferneberga -Farnborough (Hampshire)

Fey- having second sight

Firkin- a barrel containing eight gallons (usually beer)

Fret-a sea mist

Frankia- France and part of Germany

Fyrd-the Saxon levy

Gaill- Irish for foreigners

Galdramenn- wizard

Glaesum –amber

Gleawecastre- Gloucester

Gói- the end of February to the middle of March

Greenway- ancient roads- they used turf rather than stone

Grenewic- Greenwich

Gyllingas - Gillingham Kent

Haesta- Hastings

Haestingaceaster -Hastings

Hamwic -Southampton

Hantone- Littlehampton
Haughs/ Haugr - small hills in Norse (As in Tarn Hows) or a hump- normally a mound of earth
Hearth-weru- Jarl's bodyguard/oathsworn
Heels- when a ship leans to one side under the pressure of the wind
Hel - Queen of Niflheim, the Norse underworld.
Herkumbl- a mark on the front of a helmet denoting the clan of a Viking warrior
Here Wic- Harwich
Hetaereiarch – Byzantine general
Hí- Iona (Gaelic)
Hjáp - Shap- Cumbria (Norse for stone circle)
Hoggs or Hogging- when the pressure of the wind causes the stern or the bow to droop
Hrams-a – Ramsey, Isle of Man
Hrofecester-Rochester Kent
Hywel ap Rhodri Molwynog- King of Gwynedd 814-825
Icaunis- a British river god
Ishbiliyya- Seville
Issicauna- Gaulish for the lower Seine
Itouna- River Eden Cumbria
Jarl- Norse earl or lord
Joro-goddess of the earth
Jǫtunn -Norse god or goddess
Kartreidh -Carteret in Normandy
Kjerringa - Old Woman- the solid block in which the mast rested
Knarr- a merchant ship or a coastal vessel
Kyrtle-woven top
Laugardagr-Saturday (Norse for washing day)
Leathes Water- Thirlmere
Ljoðhús- Lewis
Legacaestir- Anglo Saxon for Chester
Liger- Loire
Lochlannach – Irish for Northerners (Vikings)
Lothuwistoft- Lowestoft
Louis the Pious- King of the Franks and son of Charlemagne
Lundenwic - London
Maen hir – standing stone (Menhir)
Maeresea- River Mersey
Mammceaster- Manchester

Manau/Mann – The Isle of Man(n) (Saxon)
Marcia Hispanic- Spanish Marches (the land around Barcelona)
Mast fish- two large racks on a ship for the mast
Melita- Malta
Midden - a place where they dumped human waste
Miklagård - Constantinople
Leudes- Imperial officer (a local leader in the Carolingian Empire. They became Counts a century after this.)
Njoror- God of the sea
Nithing- A man without honour (Saxon)
Odin - The "All Father" God of war, also associated with wisdom, poetry, and magic (The ruler of the gods).
Olissipo- Lisbon
Orkneyjar-Orkney
Portucale- Porto
Portesmūða -Portsmouth
Penrhudd – Penrith Cumbria
Pillars of Hercules- Straits of Gibraltar
Qādis- Cadiz
Ran- Goddess of the sea
Remisgat Ramsgate
Roof rock- slate
Rinaz –The Rhine
Sabrina- Latin and Celtic for the River Severn. Also, the name of a female Celtic deity
Saami- the people who live in what is now Northern Norway/Sweden
Saint Maclou- St Malo (France)
Sandwic- Sandwich (Kent)
Sarnia- Guernsey (Channel Islands)
St. Cybi- Holyhead
Sampiere -samphire (sea asparagus)
Scree- loose rocks in a glacial valley
Seax – short sword
Sheerstrake- the uppermost strake in the hull
Sheet- a rope fastened to the lower corner of a sail
Shroud- a rope from the masthead to the hull amidships
Skeggox – an axe with a shorter beard on one side of the blade
Sondwic-Sandwich
South Folk- Suffolk
Stad- Norse settlement

Stays- ropes running from the mast-head to the bow
Streanæshalc -Whitby
Stirap- stirrup
Strake- the wood on the side of a drekar
Suthriganaworc - Southwark (London)
Svearike -Sweden
Syllingar- Scilly Isles
Syllingar Insula- Scilly Isles
Tarn- small lake (Norse)
Temese- River Thames (also called the Tamese)
The Norns- The three sisters who weave webs of intrigue for men
Thing-Norse for a parliament or a debate (Tynwald)
Thor's day- Thursday
Threttanessa- a drekar with 13 oars on each side.
Thrall- slave
Tinea- Tyne
Trenail- a round wooden peg used to secure strakes
Tude- Tui in Northern Spain
Tynwald- the Parliament on the Isle of Man
Úlfarrberg- Helvellyn
Úlfarrland- Cumbria
Úlfarr- Wolf Warrior
Úlfarrston- Ulverston
Ullr-Norse God of Hunting
Ulfheonar-an elite Norse warrior who wore a wolf skin over his armour
Uuluuich- Dulwich
Valauna- Valognes (Normandy)
Vectis- The Isle of Wight
Veðrafjǫrðr -Waterford (Ireland)
Veisafjǫrðr- Wexford (Ireland)
Volva- a witch or healing woman in Norse culture
Waeclinga Straet- Watling Street (A5)
Windlesore-Windsor
Waite- a Viking word for farm
Werham -Wareham (Dorset)
Wintan-ceastre -Winchester
Withy- the mechanism connecting the steering board to the ship
Woden's day- Wednesday
Wyddfa-Snowdon

Wyrd- Fate
Yard- a timber from which the sail is suspended on a drekar
Ynys Môn-Anglesey

The Norman dynasty

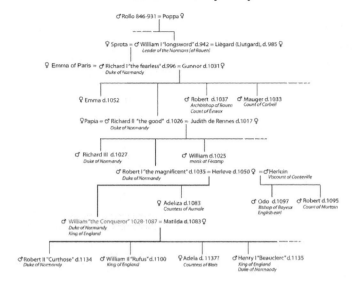

Historical note

My research encompasses not only books and the Internet but also TV. Time Team was a great source of information. I wish they would bring it back! I saw the wooden compass which my sailors use on the Dan Snow programme about the Vikings. Apparently, it was used in modern times to sail from Denmark to Edinburgh and was only a couple of points out. Similarly, the construction of the temporary hall was copied from the settlement of Leif Eriksson in Newfoundland.

Stirrups began to be introduced in Europe during the 7th and 8th Centuries. By Charlemagne's time, they were widely used but only by nobles. It is said this was the true beginning of feudalism. It was the Vikings who introduced them to England. It was only in the time of Canute the Great that they became widespread. The use of stirrups enabled a rider to strike someone on the ground from the back of a horse and facilitated the use of spears and later, lances.

The Vikings may seem cruel to us now. They enslaved women and children. Many of the women became their wives. The DNA of the people of Iceland shows that it was made up of a mixture of Norse and Danish males and Celtic females. These were the people who settled Iceland, Greenland and Vinland. They did the same in England and, as we shall see, Normandy. Their influence was widespread. Genghis Khan and his Mongols did the same in the 13th century. It is said that a high proportion of European males have Mongol blood in them. The Romans did it with the Sabine tribe. They were different times and it would be wrong to judge them with our politically correct twenty-first-century eyes. This sort of behaviour still goes on in the world but with less justification.

The Vikings began to raid the Loire and the Seine from the middle of the 9th century. They were able to raid as far as Tours. Tours, Saumur and the monastery at Marmoutier were all raided and destroyed. As a result of the raids and the destruction, castles were built there during the latter part of the 9th century. There are many islands in the Loire and many tributaries. The Maine, which runs through Anger, is also a wide waterway. The lands seemed made for Viking raiders. They did not settle in Aquitaine but they did in Austrasia. The Vikings began to settle in Normandy and the surrounding islands from the 820s. Many place names in Normandy are Viking in origin. Sometimes, as in

Vinland, the settlements were destroyed by the Franks but some survived. So long as a Viking had a river for his drekar he could raid at will.

The Franks used horses more than most other armies of the time. Their spears were used as long swords, hence the guards. They used saddles and stirrups. They still retained their round shields and wore, largely, an open helmet. Sometimes they wore a plume. They carried a spare spear and a sword.

'KARA'
Griff 2016

One reason for the Normans success was that when they arrived in northern France they integrated quickly with the local populace. They married them and began to use some of their words. They adapted to the horse as a weapon of war. Before then the Vikings had been quite happy to ride to war but they dismounted to fight. The Normans took the best that the Franks had and made it better. This book sees the earliest beginnings of the rise of the Norman knight.

I have used the names by which places were known in the medieval period wherever possible. Sometimes I have had to use the modern name. Cotentin is an example. The Isle of sheep is now called the Isle of Sheppey and lies on the Medway close to the Thames. The land of Kent was known as Cent in the early medieval period. Thanet or, Tanet as it was known in the Viking period was an island at this time. The sea was on two sides and the other two sides had swamps, bogs, mudflats and tidal streams. It protected Canterbury. The coast was different too.

Richborough had been a major Roman port. It is now some way inland. Sandwich was a port. Other ports now lie under the sea. Vikings were not afraid to sail up very narrow rivers and to risk being stranded on mud. They were tough men and were capable of carrying or porting their ships as their Rus brothers did when travelling to Miklagård.

The Norns or the Weird Sisters.

"The Norns (Old Norse: norn, plural: nornir) in Norse mythology are female beings who rule the destiny of gods and men. They roughly correspond to other controllers of humans' destiny, the Fates, elsewhere in European mythology.

In Snorri Sturluson's interpretation of the Völuspá, Urðr (Wyrd), Verðandi and Skuld, the three most important of the Norns, come out from a hall standing at the Well of Urðr or Well of Fate. They draw water from the well and take sand that lies around it, which they pour over Yggdrasill so that its branches will not rot. These three Norns are described as powerful maiden giantesses (Jotuns) whose arrival from Jötunheimr ended the golden age of the gods. They may be the same as the maidens of Mögþrasir who are described in Vafþrúðnismál"

Source: Norns - https://en.wikipedia.org

Viking Raid on the Seine

At some time in the 850s, a huge Viking fleet sailed up the Seine to raid deep into the heart of Frankia. Some writers of the period speak of over a hundred ships. The priests who wrote of the plague that they believe the Vikings to be tended to exaggerate. I have erred on the side of caution.

Greenways

I have used the term greenways in many of my books. We still have them in England. They are the paths trodden before the Romans came. Many of them became bridleways

Coutances and Saint-Lô

Both towns were captured by the Vikings in the late ninth century. Saint-Lô had all of the inhabitants massacred. During the latter half of the ninth century, the Vikings kept moving further up the rivers and further south. The great raid on Paris in 885 was the culmination of these raids and gradual encroachment into what became Normandy.

Rollo

I have used the name Rollo even though that is the Latinisation of Hrolf. I did so for two reasons. We all know the first Duke of Normandy as Rollo and I wanted to avoid confusion with his grandfather. I realise that I have also caused enough of a problem with Ragnvald and Ragnvald the Breton Slayer.

Rollo is generally identified with one Viking in particular – a man of high social status mentioned in Icelandic sagas, which refer to him by the Old Norse name Göngu-Hrólfr, meaning "Hrólfr the Walker". (Göngu-Hrólfr is also widely known by an Old Danish variant, Ganger-Hrolf.) The byname "Walker" is usually understood to suggest that Rollo was so physically imposing that he could not be carried by a horse and was obliged to travel on foot. Norman and other French sources do not use the name Hrólfr, and the identification of Rollo with Göngu-Hrólfr is based upon similarities between circumstances and actions ascribed to both figures.

He had children by at least three women. He abducted Popa or Poppa the daughter of the Count of Rennes. He married Gisla the daughter (probably illegitimate) of King Charles of France. He also had another child. According to the medieval Irish text, '*An Banshenchas*' and Icelandic sources, another daughter, Cadlinar (Kaðlín; Kathleen) was born in Scotland (probably to a Scots mother) and married an Irish prince named Beollán mac Ciarmaic, later King of South Brega (Lagore). I have used the Norse name Kaðlín and made her a Scottish princess.

The beach at Streanæshalc

You can see how narrow the river Esk is at this point, although it is low tide.

Isle of Man

The three legs of Man evolved in the late middle ages. Until then it was four legs; a swastika.

Books used in the research

- British Museum - Vikings- Life and Legends
- Arthur and the Saxon Wars- David Nicolle (Osprey)
- Saxon, Norman and Viking Terence Wise (Osprey)
- The Vikings- Ian Heath (Osprey)
- Byzantine Armies 668-1118 - Ian Heath (Osprey)
- Romano-Byzantine Armies 4th-9th Century - David Nicholle (Osprey)
- The Walls of Constantinople AD 324-1453 - Stephen Turnbull (Osprey)
- Viking Longship - Keith Durham (Osprey)
- The Vikings in England- Anglo-Danish Project
- The Varangian Guard- 988-1453 Raffael D'Amato
- Saxon Viking and Norman- Terence Wise
- The Walls of Constantinople AD 324-1453-Stephen Turnbull
- Byzantine Armies- 886-1118- Ian Heath
- The Age of Charlemagne-David Nicolle
- The Normans- David Nicolle
- Norman Knight AD 950-1204- Christopher Gravett
- The Norman Conquest of the North- William A Kappelle
- The Knight in History- Francis Gies
- The Norman Achievement- Richard F Cassady
- Knights- Constance Brittain Bouchard

Griff Hosker
June 2017

Other books by Griff Hosker

If you enjoyed reading this book, then why not read another
one by the author?

Ancient History

The Sword of Cartimandua Series
(Germania and Britannia 50 A.D. – 128 A.D.)
Ulpius Felix- Roman Warrior (prequel)
The Sword of Cartimandua
The Horse Warriors
Invasion Caledonia
Roman Retreat
Revolt of the Red Witch
Druid's Gold
Trajan's Hunters
The Last Frontier
Hero of Rome
Roman Hawk
Roman Treachery
Roman Wall
Roman Courage

The Wolf Warrior series
(Britain in the late 6th Century)
Saxon Dawn
Saxon Revenge
Saxon England
Saxon Blood
Saxon Slayer
Saxon Slaughter
Saxon Bane
Saxon Fall: Rise of the Warlord
Saxon Throne
Saxon Sword

Medieval History

The Dragon Heart Series
Viking Slave
Viking Warrior
Viking Jarl
Viking Kingdom
Viking Wolf
Viking War
Viking Sword
Viking Wrath
Viking Raid
Viking Legend
Viking Vengeance
Viking Dragon
Viking Treasure
Viking Enemy
Viking Witch
Viking Blood
Viking Weregeld
Viking Storm
Viking Warband
Viking Shadow
Viking Legacy
Viking Clan
Viking Bravery

The Norman Genesis Series
Hrolf the Viking
Horseman
The Battle for a Home
Revenge of the Franks
The Land of the Northmen
Ragnvald Hrolfsson
Brothers in Blood
Lord of Rouen
Drekar in the Seine
Duke of Normandy
The Duke and the King

Brothers in Blood

New World Series
Blood on the Blade
Across the Seas
The Savage Wilderness
The Bear and the Wolf

The Vengeance Trail

The Reconquista Chronicles
Castilian Knight
El Campeador
The Lord of Valencia

The Aelfraed Series
(Britain and Byzantium 1050 A.D. - 1085 A.D.)
Housecarl
Outlaw
Varangian

The Anarchy Series England
1120-1180
English Knight
Knight of the Empress
Northern Knight
Baron of the North
Earl
King Henry's Champion
The King is Dead
Warlord of the North
Enemy at the Gate
The Fallen Crown
Warlord's War
Kingmaker
Henry II
Crusader
The Welsh Marches
Irish War
Poisonous Plots

210

Brothers in Blood

The Princes' Revolt
Earl Marshal

Border Knight
1182-1300
Sword for Hire
Return of the Knight
Baron's War
Magna Carta
Welsh Wars
Henry III
The Bloody Border
Baron's Crusade
Sentinel of the North
War in the West

Sir John Hawkwood Series
France and Italy 1339- 1387
Crécy: The Age of the Archer

Lord Edward's Archer
Lord Edward's Archer
King in Waiting
An Archer's Crusade (November 2020)

Struggle for a Crown
1360- 1485
Blood on the Crown
To Murder A King
The Throne
King Henry IV
The Road to Agincourt
St Crispin's Day

Tales from the Sword

Modern History

The Napoleonic Horseman Series

Brothers in Blood

Chasseur à Cheval
Napoleon's Guard
British Light Dragoon
Soldier Spy
1808: The Road to Coruña
Talavera
The Lines of Torres Vedras
Bloody Badajoz
The Road to France

The Lucky Jack American Civil War series
Rebel Raiders
Confederate Rangers
The Road to Gettysburg

The British Ace Series
1914
1915 Fokker Scourge
1916 Angels over the Somme
1917 Eagles Fall
1918 We will remember them
From Arctic Snow to Desert Sand
Wings over Persia

Combined Operations series
1940-1945
Commando
Raider
Behind Enemy Lines
Dieppe
Toehold in Europe
Sword Beach
Breakout
The Battle for Antwerp
King Tiger
Beyond the Rhine
Korea
Korean Winter

Other Books

Great Granny's Ghost (Aimed at 9-14-year-old young people)

For more information on all of the books then please visit the author's web site at www.griffhosker.com where there is a link to contact him or visit his Facebook page: GriffHosker at Sword Books

Made in the USA
Columbia, SC
11 June 2021